KAT WOLFE
INVESTIGATES

Other books by Lauren St John

KAT WOLFE
INVESTIGATES

A
WOLFE
&
LAMB
MYSTERY

LAUREN ST JOHN

Illustrated by Beidi Guo

MACMILLAN CHILDREN'S BOOKS

For Jean McLean,
one of my favourite armchair adventurers

First published 2018 by Macmillan Children's Books
an imprint of Pan Macmillan
20 New Wharf Road, London N1 9RR
Associated companies throughout the world
www.panmacmillan.com

ISBN 978-1-5098-7122-3

Text copyright © Lauren St John 2018
Illustrations copyright © Beidi Guo 2018

The right of Lauren St John and Beidi Guo to be identified as the
author and illustrator of this work has been asserted by them
in accordance with the Copyright, Designs and Patents Act 1988.

Pan Macmillan does not have any control over, or any responsibility for,
any author or third-party websites referred to in or on this book.

1 3 5 7 9 8 6 4 2

A CIP catalogue record for this book is available from
the British Library.

Printed and bound by CPI Group (UK) Ltd, Croydon CR0 4YY

Contents

1

An Uninvited Guest

Kat Wolfe awoke with a stiff neck and the creeping sensation that she was not alone.

She held her breath. Had she heard something or hadn't she? Then it came again – a faint metallic scraping. Kat relaxed. The latch on the kitchen window was loose. It jiggled with every shift of wind.

Struggling upright, she rearranged the cushions and rescued the duvet from the floor. For the third night running, she'd fallen asleep on the sofa waiting for her mum to come home. Friday evenings were frantic at the city veterinary practice where Dr Ellen Wolfe worked, and her bosses, Edwina Nash and Vince Craw, insisted that their underlings (Kat's mother and two harried nurses) take full advantage of it.

Today was Valentine's Day, which was not as madly busy as Christmas or Halloween but a close second to Easter. Kat could picture her mum bent over the operating table, fighting to save the life of a labradoodle puppy that had swallowed a boxful of chocolate hearts or a diamond ring, or patching up a Maine Coon singed by a thoughtlessly placed candle.

Meanwhile, in a back office, Edwina and Vince would be gleefully totting up the bill. Hunched over a spreadsheet like a couple of Scrooges, they'd be adding up triple-time emergency and admin fees, plus charges for X-rays, IV fluids, vitamin shots, scans, lab tests, antibiotics, catnip, chew toys, flea spray and painkillers. On seeing the total, some pet owners needed hospitalization themselves.

In Dr Wolfe's opinion, a good veterinary surgeon was part psychologist, part animal whisperer. She routinely played peacemaker on behalf of pets caught up in custody battles or family feuds. As for senior citizens, they adored her. Most came to her for the company more than because their pets needed help.

Knowing that their meagre monthly pensions would be swallowed by a single vet's bill, Kat's mum had learned how to magic these and other visits out of existence simply by 'forgetting' to include them in the diary. No appointment; no charge. It's not that Dr Wolfe imagined Nash & Craw Premium Pet Care was a charity. Far from it. But she did believe in fairness.

Somehow Edwina and Vince had got wind of these 'lost' appointments. They'd gone ballistic. For the past three months, they'd deducted every penny they felt sure Dr Wolfe owed them – plus interest – from her wages. Kat and her mum were not quite living on gruel, but beans on toast had become a recurring theme.

The fun had stopped too. For the entirety of Kat's twelve and a quarter years, it had only ever been the two of them against the world. That was fine with Kat. Given a choice between spending her weekends with the selfie-obsessed girls who attended her bleak London school, or hanging out with her mum and the animals at the animal clinic, she'd have chosen her mum and the pets 101 per cent of the time.

But Vince and Edwina had succeeded in snuffing out even that small joy. They'd banned Kat from helping out or watching her mum work on the grounds of Health and Safety. Which meant that every other weekend and three nights a week, when her mum was on call in case of emergencies, Kat was stuck in the house with Naska, the Bulgarian student who lived with them.

Naska was one of the loveliest people Kat had ever

met, but the Bulgarian girl studied every moment she wasn't sleeping, and slept every moment she wasn't studying.

Tonight was an exception. Naska's sister, who worked in North London, had been rushed to A&E with appendicitis. Since Dr Wolfe had already messaged to say she was leaving work shortly, Kat had insisted Naska go to the hospital at once. Her mum would be home any minute, and she'd be fine on her own till then.

As Naska headed out of the door, Kat's phone pinged again. Dr Wolfe was running late. Kat waved Naska goodbye without mentioning it.

That had been nearly three hours ago.

Now it was 1.30 a.m. Kat wasn't worried about being alone. The doors were locked, and she knew her mum would be home as soon as she'd finished dealing with whatever emergency had held her up. But the silent house did make Kat yearn, yet again, for a pet of her own – a dog to guard her and keep her company, or a cat she could snuggle up to.

Ironically, considering her mum spent every waking hour with animals, that wasn't possible. They lived in a rented house, with no outside space, on a busy road in London.

'*If* I can ever find a spare hour to hunt for another job, *if* we can ever afford a place of our own with a garden and *if* we ever have the time to devote to it, I'll get you the cat/dog/pony/hamster of your dreams,' her mum was always saying.

Kat was not a girl much given to scowling, but she scowled now. 'If, if, if.' These days, it was her mother's favourite word.

With Naska gone, she'd lain on the sofa rereading her favourite horse novel. But even that had annoyed her because it had only reminded her how badly she wanted to be around living, breathing horses and not just ones in books.

Reading also made her feel guilty. She'd promised her mum she'd make a further attempt to tackle the overcrowding on the cheap, flimsy bookcase begrudgingly installed by the landlord, but she kept putting it off. To be fair, it was a big job. Where others spent every spare penny they had on clothes, travel and fancy gadgets, the Wolfes were united in preferring novels and cake. In recent months, Dr Wolfe's reduced salary had put an end to both. She'd told Kat that, for once, this might be no bad thing.

'We could turn a negative into a positive by taking the opportunity to do something about your out-of-control book situation.'

Kat was shocked. 'Give some away, you mean?' To her, books were like diaries. She only had to glance at

5

an adventure novel she'd read years earlier and she'd be parachuted right back to that time, with all of its emotions and dreams.

'Just a few,' said her mum. 'Maybe twenty or thirty. Why don't you start with the picture books? It's not as if you're going to read them again.'

'You want me to give away *The Tiger Who Came to Tea*? What kind of monster are you? That's the first book you ever read to me.'

Her mum's face lit up. 'You remember! OK, maybe not that one, but how about recycling some of the mystery novels you've read a dozen times? You've dropped at least half of them in the bath.'

'Only if *you* recycle some of your ancient, dusty textbooks.'

Her mum was scandalized. 'I can't part with those. They're vital, life-saving works.'

'You're telling me you need every volume of *The Merck Veterinary Manual* dating back to 2009? Those things weigh nearly as much as I do. If one fell off a high shelf, it could kill someone.'

The books had mostly stayed, although Kat had taken a sack of picture and fairy ones to a charity shop, and her mum had moved the heavier textbooks to lower shelves. Lack of space had forced Dr Wolfe to leave the current edition of *The Merck Veterinary Manual* on the top shelf, balanced on a spectacularly ugly vase – a gift from a grateful pensioner.

'She can't have been that grateful,' Kat had remarked when the vase first came home. 'It's like the Leaning Tower of Pisa.'

'It's handmade,' her mum had said reprovingly. 'It means more because it comes from Thelma's heart.'

In mid-thought, Kat suddenly became aware of an absence of sound. The first baleful gusts of an incoming storm were slapping at the shutters, but the kitchen-window catch was silent. It was almost as if . . .

An icy finger of dread tiptoed down her spine. It was almost as if someone was holding it, and why would they do that unless . . . ?

A soft thud, a clink of china and a muffled curse confirmed the unimaginable. Someone was in the kitchen.

For one hopeful millisecond, Kat allowed herself to believe it was her mum. Dr Wolfe must have forgotten her keys. Not wanting to wake anyone, and knowing that the window by the sink was easily forced, she'd climbed in.

Any minute now, she'd snap on the kitchen light and make herself a cup of tea. When she discovered that Kat was waiting up for her on the sofa, she'd pretend to be cross while being unable to hide how thrilled she was to

7

see a friendly face. They'd sit up eating crumpets with maple syrup and cashew-nut cream, and Kat would settle in for her favourite part of any day – listening to her mum describe her cases.

But no light came on. No tea was made. Kat lay rigid on the sofa, too terrified to move. Her phone was charging on her bedside table. The stairs that led up to it were in the hallway between the living room and the kitchen. There was no earthly way she could get to them without being seen. Nor were there any nearby cupboards in which she could hide.

The dim glow of the hallway lamp dipped as someone passed it. Kat corkscrewed off the sofa and slipped behind it. Her heart hammered against her ribcage.

Nothing happened for an age. Kat tried not to breathe or cough while desperately wanting to do both. Then a floorboard squeaked.

For as long as she could remember, Kat had been training herself to banish fear. As the daughter of a vet, she spent a great deal of time around animals made angry and/or dangerous by pain or fear. The best way to calm them was to remain calm herself, even if she had to fake it. But it was impossible to stay chilled with a stranger strolling around her dark living room.

A torch beam flared. Like an all-seeing eye, it began to explore the floorboards and crevices. It was only a matter of time before the intruder saw the cast-aside duvet on the sofa and put two and two together. What then? Kat's trembling limbs were about as much use as a broken umbrella in a hurricane. She felt incapable of fighting off a field mouse.

Mid-panic, she became aware of a lump pressing against her thigh. A tennis ball! The previous weekend, she'd helped her mum pet-sit a Jack Russell whose owner was away in Paris. He was a cute dog, but impossibly high energy, and Kat had spent hours retrieving toys from every corner of the house. The tennis ball had gone missing early on.

Now it struck her that if she threw the ball across the hallway, into the kitchen, the intruder might get a fright and think someone was coming. He might fly out of the house, never to be seen again. Or not, but it was worth a try.

The problem was getting the correct trajectory. Too low, and he'd guess where the ball had come from. Too high or too far left or right, and it would hit the doorframe. The burglar would zero in on the source. Kat would be toast.

He was over by the TV now. She could imagine him gawping at their aeons-old set and it dawning on him that he'd chosen the wrong house to rob. Now was her chance. She picked up the ball.

Before she could launch it, there was a grunt of alarm. The torch beam swung crazily. The floor close to Kat flooded with light, suggesting that the burglar had spotted the duvet. Next he'd check behind the sofa.

There was no time to lose. No time to aim. Kat threw the ball as hard and high as she could.

It never made it to the kitchen. It didn't even reach the hallway. It struck the top corner of the door and ricocheted back into the living room.

Kat had always been lamentably bad at tennis. Her first clue that on this occasion she'd scored an ace came when she heard the *thwock* of rubber against ceramic. The intruder heard it too, because the white beam did another zigzag.

It was not enough to save him. The instant the ball hit Thelma's pot, the latest hardback edition of *The Merck Veterinary Manual*, all 3,326 pages of it, soared from its roost like a seabird. The intruder never knew what hit him. It actually dented his forehead.

As he fell, his clawing hands latched on to a shelf. Thanks to the lazy landlord, the bookcase had never been secured. With a sea lion groan, it parted company with the wall, firing books in every direction. Each caused its own mini catastrophe.

The eight-volume *Complete James Herriot* box set demolished the lamp and the remains of Kat's mug of Horlicks, which in turn sprayed glass and malted almond milk all over the rug. The illustrated *Alice in Wonderland* smashed the glass of water holding the pink rose Kat had given her mum for Valentine's Day, drowning Kat's school project in the process. *Black's Veterinary Dictionary* took a picture off the wall, which then crushed the remains of Thelma's lopsided vase to powder.

By now, Kat was peering over the back of the sofa, unable to believe what she was witnessing. As it emptied, the toppling bookcase picked up speed, spewing woodchips, splinters and bits of plaster. The intruder's torch had rolled under the dining-room table. It illuminated his skinny, hooded frame as he attempted to sit up before being flattened by the bookcase. The final crash was deafening. A flying shelf had cracked the TV.

Through a cloud of dust, Kat saw her mum standing open-mouthed in the doorway, keys in hand.

'And I thought that the parties and destruction only started in the teenage years,' Dr Wolfe said faintly. 'Where's Naska?'

Kat shoved back the sofa, rushed to her mother and threw her arms around her. 'Mum, it's not a party. Naska had to go to A&E with her sister, and we've been burgled! Quick, call the police.'

It was only then that her mother switched on the light.

The intruder was stretched out on the living-room floor, framed, like a bad portrait, by the mangled bookcase. Unconscious, his pale, spotty face looked oddly angelic.

Dr Wolfe let out a cry of horror and held Kat's hand tightly while dialling 999.

'Kat, that's it. That's the absolute final straw. If something had happened to you, I'd never have forgiven myself.'

'But it didn't.' Kat grinned. Now that her mum was home and the police were rushing to the rescue, she felt a lot better. 'Long story short, I was saved by Thelma's vase, a chewed tennis ball and *The Merck Veterinary Manual*. What held you up, anyway?'

'Long story short, I quit my job. Or maybe I was fired. There was a bit of a blow-up, and it was hard to tell. Either way, I'm free to go any time or anywhere we choose. I don't know where we're going, Kat, but we're going.'

2

Capuchins and Cockatoos

'How about this one?' said Kat, scrolling through the classifieds on Jobs4Vets.com. '*Exciting opportunity to join our mixed animal practice in Scunthorpe . . .*'

Her mum shook her head. 'Too many earthquakes.'

'*Earthquakes?* In *Scunthorpe?*'

'Maybe it was just the one, back in 2008, but you can't be too careful. At the time, it was the second-largest quake ever recorded in Britain.' Dr Wolfe nudged the ruined bookcase with a foot. 'If this is the damage one tennis ball can do, imagine the scene after an earthquake has finished with the place.'

They were sitting on the sofa amid the wreckage of their living room like sailors marooned on a desert island. Neither had been to bed. By the time the police had finished taking Kat's statement, collecting evidence and drinking tea, the early morning traffic was moving sluggishly through the drizzle.

To add to the mess, there was black fingerprint powder all over the kitchen. A burglar-shaped hollow in the middle of the living-room debris served as a ghostly reminder of the events of the previous night. It made Kat think of the chalk outline that marked the position of murder victims on TV detective shows.

She shuddered. If the intruder hadn't been squashed by a falling library, and her mum hadn't come home when she had, things might have gone dreadfully wrong.

The burglar himself – a youth barely out of his teens – had been handcuffed to a stretcher and carted away. As he went by, blinking stupidly and rubbing his forehead, Kat had noticed a torn scrap of veterinary dictionary stuck to his cheek:

*Amygdala: a distinct almond-shaped part
of the brain's limbic system . . .*

Kat clicked through to the next page of jobs. Dr Wolfe had a tendency to treat all computers as if they were hostile aliens so, even though it was her laptop they were using, it was Kat who was doing the typing.

Kat could see their reflections in the screen. People often remarked how alike they were, which was funny, because they couldn't have looked more different.

14

Where her mum was petite and cuddly, with a blonde bob and bright blue eyes, Kat was tall for her age, with clear green eyes flecked with storm blue, and wavy dark hair that sparked red in the sun. No matter how often she brushed it, it always looked as though she'd been out walking in a wild wind.

Her mum often said that she resembled her 'father'. Whenever Kat thought about the man whose blood ran in her veins, it wasn't as a dad in any shape or form. Dads were supposed to teach you to ride bikes or make catapults, and provide comfort when you had chicken pox or crashed out of school talent shows. They were meant to love and look out for you.

Kat's father had done none of those things. He and her mum had met at university. Rufus had been studying law, but dropped out in his second year to chase big waves across the globe. Surfing had meant more to him than Kat's mum, his own mum or his unborn child. He was last seen in Portugal, being towed by a jet-ski rider up the face of a twenty-metre wave. That was his idea of a good time.

To Kat's mind, going missing because you'd chosen to ride a virtual tsunami was an exceedingly poor excuse for not being around to keep your daughter safe from clumsy burglars.

On the positive side, her mum was her best friend.

When people said they were alike, it made Kat proud, because her mum was kind to the power of ten. She stood up to bullies like Vince and Edwina, was passionate about saving animals and would fight till her last breath against cruelty or injustice.

'Kat, is the screen frozen or are you?' teased her mum. 'You're miles away. What are you thinking about?'

'What a good person you are,' Kat said truthfully. 'We're going to find you the best job in the world. How about this one: *Roving Veterinary Surgeon wanted to travel between six practices*?'

'Too stressful.'

'*Thriving small animal clinic in Edinburgh . . .*?'

'I'd miss the horses and cows.'

'*Busy equine practice in Hampshire . . .*?'

'I'd love the horses, but miss the small animals.'

'*State-of-the-art twelve-vet practice with latest technology seeks VS with can-do attitude*?'

'Too corporate. I'm a vet, not a banker.'

'Oh, wow! Just wow! Mum, you *have* to take this one.'

'Why? What is it? Stop hogging the screen and show me!'

'*Thrilling opportunity in the Outer Hebrides . . .* Oh, Mum – imagine being a vet on an *island*. We'd be like characters out of a book. You'd have puffins and otters for patients, and I could get a Border collie.'

'You might want to get an umbrella too,' her mother said drily. 'It rains at least three hundred days of the year. Anyway, it's too remote.'

Kat didn't have the energy to argue. 'Right, dull jobs in city drought-zones only. *Luton practice seeks VS with GSOH.*'

'You'd need a sense of humour if you lived in Luton.'

And so it went on. If the job had potential, then the town or village was too crowded, too isolated, too crime-ridden, too boring, too full of football hooligans or too cold.

Finally Kat said: 'Is it just me, or are you being a teensy-weensy bit fussy?'

Her mum rubbed a hand over her tired eyes. 'Sorry, hon. I'm wary of leaping from the frying pan into the fire, that's all. For months I've been a terrible mother . . . No, Kat, hear me out. Work has been so nightmarish that I've been grouchy and anxious most of the time. That's not good for you, and it's definitely not good for my patients. So now I don't just want *a* job; I want the right job. I'd like to be part of a practice where I can make a real difference to the lives of animals, and I want us to live in a place where you can thrive and be happy, ideally with a pet of your own.' She smiled. 'That's not too much to ask, is it?'

To see her mum's old spark shining through the dust

and exhaustion lifted Kat's spirits like nothing else. 'Sounds great to me.'

'In that case, let's keep searching for another five minutes.' Dr Wolfe pulled the laptop towards her. 'What's this link here: *ARE YOU READY FOR A CHALLENGE?* I know I am. How about you?'

Kat grinned. 'Always.'

Later, when Kat thought about how one click of the mouse had changed their lives forever, she recalled a giddy feeling bubbling up inside her as the advert unfurled on the screen.

WANTED: CARING, HARD-WORKING VETERINARY SURGEON URGENTLY NEEDED TO RUN SMALL PRACTICE IN IDYLLIC SEASIDE LOCATION. MUST BE WILLING TO TREAT EVERYTHING FROM CAPUCHINS TO COCKATOOS. LETTER & CV TO MR MK MELLS. C/O MELLS SOLICITORS, PO BOX 5089, LONDON W1

'What's a capuchin?' asked Kat.

'A species of monkey originating in Central and South America. If they're in the UK, they've either been stolen from the wild for the pet trade or medical research, or they're in sanctuaries.'

Dr Wolfe squinted at the screen. 'The job sounds so

perfect there's bound to be a catch. Ah, here it is: *T&Cs APPLY*. "Terms and Conditions" usually means you're expected to sign a ten-year contract to work an eight-day week treating boa constrictors and hungry tigers. Still, it might be worth looking into further.'

Kat picked up a pen to jot down the details. 'There's no email address.'

'I like that,' said her mum. 'Snail-mail only. Intriguing. With any luck, it'll reduce the number of applicants. I'll write a letter today. Now, I don't know about you, but after all this excitement I'm starving. Can I interest you in breakfast? We could celebrate my freedom and your tennis-ball-throwing skills with cinnamon buns in Blackheath.'

3

The Way of the Mongoose

The week they spent waiting for a response was pure torture, but it did give Kat time to do some thinking. She'd not forgotten how small and weak she'd felt as she cowered behind the sofa, knowing that at any minute she might be discovered and pounced upon.

Following the break-in, her mum had asked Kat if she'd mind sleeping in the main bedroom for a while. The landlord had belatedly fixed the kitchen window, and the policemen who'd attended the crime scene had reassured them they were safe. Constable Duff was confident that, after being almost crushed to death, then arrested on his first ever attempt at burglary, the spotty young man would be rethinking his career options.

'I'm sure the constable's right, Kat,' said Dr Wolfe, 'but I'm still mildly traumatized. It would help if I knew you were close by in the night.'

Kat saw through the lie, but was grateful. She'd been too proud to ask if she could share her mum's room in case it seemed babyish.

On the fifth evening, she felt fine and returned to her own bed. But in the early hours the nightmares came for her. She awoke sweating and trembling. If she'd been capable of moving, she'd have run screaming to her mum, but she was too afraid that someone was under the bed or in the wardrobe.

It didn't help that the wind was wailing and tugging at the shutters. Then next door's dog began to bark. Before long, Kat believed that whole armies of burglars were on their way up the stairs.

Just when she thought she might faint from fright, she remembered a trick her mother had taught her when she was younger and afraid of the dark. She pretended she had a scared kitten to take care of.

If that was the case, she'd focus on taking deep, slow breaths to bring down her heart rate and that of the kitten. Picturing tranquil, happy scenes usually helped too: sun filtering through the leaves of silent forest glades, lionesses washing their cubs, musical mountain streams. In real life, she'd do that for as long as it took to help the kitten feel safe and secure.

The curious thing was that being brave for a pretend kitten calmed Kat too. She switched on her bedside lamp and checked under the bed and in the cupboard. They could have done with a tidy, but neither hid a burglar.

Still, the episode had got her thinking. She needed to find a way to protect herself. But how? Horse riding aside, she'd never been much of an athlete, though she was strong for her age. The ballet teacher had had her eye on Kat for a time, memorably describing her as a 'fawn with limbs of steel'.

Kat wasn't sure if that was an insult or a compliment and had decided not to ask. It didn't matter. Madame Roux had lost interest as soon as she'd found out that Kat a) had zero interest in ballet, and b) was totally uncoordinated.

Karate was no good either. Kat had given up on the after-school martial-arts club after only four lessons. Sensei Bob had all but evicted her after she'd asked him to teach her the Crane move used in *The Karate Kid.*

'No such thing,' he'd barked. 'They made it up for the film. The Jump Front technique is similar, but if you were attacked on the street it would be a last resort. Too slow to set up, and too easy for someone to take you down while you're mulling it over. Stick to the basics, girl.'

He'd held up a hand, like a warden directing traffic. 'Let me see you throw a punch.'

As her small fist bounced harmlessly off his palm, it

became clear to Kat, and to Sensei Bob, that it would be many moons – possibly a decade or never – before she was able to use karate to defend herself against anyone more threatening than a coma patient.

So the Crane move was not the way forward.

Kat picked up her phone. It was as basic as her karate strikes, but she was able to search for the 'Top Ten Best Martial Arts for Self-defence'. She skimmed past *kick-boxing*, *aikido*, *Brazilian ju-jitsu* and regular *boxing*, and went directly to number one: *Krav Maga*. That was ideal in many ways, but slightly scary. It was not uncommon to rupture organs while training.

Kat suspected that her mum would frown upon a class that caused rupturing, so she continued to scroll down the search results. Most people stopped at the first page. She was five pages deep when she stumbled on *the Way of the Mongoose*. The name caught her attention. It was an obscure martial art, highly rated by its devotees. What interested Kat is that those included not just bodyguards and Special Forces soldiers, but also geeky accountants and scrawny teenagers.

The Way of the Mongoose had been developed by Jun Song, a baker from Shanghai who was a wing chun master. A car accident years before had left his teenage son Jia with a thin, lame leg – but what Jia lacked in strength he made up for in heart. He was the kindest, most lovable boy anyone knew. Jun Song was devoted to him.

Sadly, bullies attacked Jia and left him fighting for his life. His broken-hearted father vowed to create a self-defence system that would enable even the weakest to fight off attackers many times their size in the way a dwarf mongoose can outwit a deadly king cobra. Jun Song did this by taking blocks and other techniques from wing chun, jiu-jitsu and Krav Maga that use an attacker's power against them.

'*NEVER BE A VICTIM AGAIN!*' promised the Way of the Mongoose website. Kat was sceptical. The karate failure was still fresh in her mind.

The Wi-Fi signal was poor, and it took forever to get the demonstration video to play. At last it chugged to life. A weedy boy with arms like matchsticks was being faced down by a tattooed hulk: David vs Goliath. The fight was so mismatched that Kat was sure they were actors, paid to promote Jun Song's ideas.

The brute lunged at the boy and knocked him to the ground with one blow. It looked as if it was all over, but in a flash the boy hooked his left foot round the man's ankle, and used his right foot to shove the back of his attacker's knee. Caught off guard, the man collapsed like a popped balloon. As he crumpled, the boy used him as a launch pad for a forward roll and scampered away.

'*Always exit the scene as soon as possible*,' counselled Jun Song in the video. '*Don't be a hero. Use the element of surprise to get away fast.*'

Kat watched another short clip, but in truth she was already convinced. Any martial art where being light and quick was an advantage, and where you were advised not to be a hero, was one she could get behind. And there was no mention of the Way of the Mongoose causing cauliflower ear, as some martial arts did.

Kat turned off her phone and her bedside light. She'd forgotten about the armies of burglars. For the first time since the break-in, she felt peaceful. In another minute, she was asleep.

4

A Tiny Condition

'Are you sure you're OK, Mum?' said Kat the following Monday. They were on the train, heading for Covent Garden in London's West End.

'Of course,' her mother replied distractedly. 'Why do you keep asking?'

'Because you've shredded the front page of the *Evening Standard*. People are starting to stare. You've ripped the foreign secretary to pieces.'

'Oh.' Dr Wolfe seemed surprised to find herself with a handful of newspaper confetti. 'Well, it's no more than they deserve . . . I'm fine, Kat. Better than fine. I still can't believe that I've been shortlisted for my dream job. I'm trying not to get my hopes up. I've been told that the other job – the one in Milton Keynes – is mine if I want it, but I can't stop thinking about those capuchins and cockatoos.'

'And the idyllic bay,' Kat said dreamily.

'That too. Then I remember the terms and conditions. Even if I do make it through the interview this evening, I might not feel able to agree to those, whatever they may be.'

As she spoke, there was a horrible screech, and the train braked so hard they were almost flung from their seats. They'd arrived at Charing Cross.

'Samuel Johnson famously said that if you're tired of London, you're tired of life.' Dr Wolfe raised her voice as they struggled between packed commuters staring blankly up at the train-departures board like victims of mass hypnosis. 'However, I think even his enthusiasm might have been dampened by rush hour in the twenty-first-century capital. The air is so sooty it's like being down a coal mine.'

But once they'd dodged the red double-decker buses on the Strand and were threading their way through the back streets, Kat could feel the electric energy of the city humming beneath her feet.

She leaned into the twilight and tugged her woolly hat over her ears. The wind was knife-sharp. It teased Kat with hints of wood-fired pizza and other delights. She stared enviously through the window of a restaurant, where a waiter was delivering a Thai curry to a couple at a candlelit table.

The solicitor's office was on Rose Street. Dr Wolfe and Kat were buzzed into a narrow hallway lined with books. Beyond that was a rabbit warren of rooms made miniature by more books. A receptionist greeted them from behind a cherry-wood desk squeezed between two bookcases.

Kat hung back as her mum introduced herself. 'I'm here to see Miles Mells about the veterinary surgeon job.'

The woman's smile slipped, and her chest heaved in a silent sigh. 'Thanks for arriving on time, Dr Wolfe. Wait here, please.'

After she'd gone, Kat nudged her mum. 'Imagine what would happen if I threw a tennis ball in here.'

Dr Wolfe stifled a giggle. 'Don't get any ideas. We have to be on our best behaviour.'

There was a polite clearing of throat. They both jumped. A door had opened in the middle of one of the bookcases. Beyond it was an office crammed with filing cabinets and a desk piled high with files and documents. If there was a man behind them, he wasn't visible.

'Mr Mells will see you now,' said the receptionist,

waving at the mountain of paperwork.

With a wish-me-luck glance at Kat, Dr Wolfe went in and perched on a chair. Kat sank into the reception sofa.

She saw a pair of white eyebrows and the shiny rims of their owner's glasses rise above the files in the other room. 'Come in, come in.'

'I'm here, sir,' said Dr Wolfe, half standing.

'Then who is that young person out there?'

'My daughter, Katarina.'

'But surely this concerns her too?' A hand waved from behind the files. 'Do join us, Katarina, and shut the door behind you.'

Kat went in and sat beside her mum. From this angle, she couldn't see the glasses, only the eyebrows. They reminded her of capuchin eyebrows, only as snowy as Father Christmas's beard. Capuchins, she'd decided, when she'd looked the primates up online, had the best eyebrows on earth.

The eyebrows stood to attention. 'Miles Mells. Pleasure to meet you both. Thanks for your letter and CV, Dr Wolfe. Most impressive. I think you'll do admirably. You're hired. Now, would you like to know a little more about the job?'

Dr Wolfe was taken aback. She'd anticipated a long, gruelling interview, followed, if all went well, by a second interview at a later date. She hadn't expected to be handed the job – a job she knew next to nothing about – in the first minute.

'Uh, u-mm, thank you,' she stammered. 'Yes, it would be helpful to know more about the role. Perhaps you could start by telling us where the practice is based?'

'Bluebell Bay in Dorset. You'll have heard of it, no doubt. In my opinion, it's the prettiest cove on the Jurassic Coast.'

Kat leaned forward. 'The Jurassic Coast?'

'That's right. Dinosaur country. You'll be walking in the footsteps of sea monsters. Recently they discovered one that makes *T. rex* look like a kitten. In just ninety-five miles of coastline, there are one hundred and eighty-five million years of history. On some beaches, you can pick up ammonites – they're related to modern octopuses, squid and cuttlefish – as easily as you can build sandcastles.'

'So the practice is located in the cove itself?' asked Dr Wolfe, keen to keep the interview on track.

'Indeed it is. Bluebell Bay Animal Clinic was owned by my late client Lionel Baker. Tragically, he had a heart attack, aged just forty-eight, while out jogging. He was a health nut. A vegan. As you know, they're frequently the first to go.'

Kat and her mum exchanged glances. '*We're* vegan.'

'What, both of you? Well, I read that in the *Daily*

Maelstrom, so it may have been fake news. These days, it's hard to tell the difference. Now, where were we?'

'You were saying that Lionel Baker passed away,' said Dr Wolfe. 'I'm so sorry to hear that. When did it happen?'

'Three and a half months ago. I'm acting on behalf of his relatives, who live abroad. It took some time to wind up his business affairs, and even longer to pack up his home, for reasons I've yet to get to the bottom of. Did I mention that the job comes with a cottage? It's beside the practice, with far-reaching views over the bay. It has a wonderful garden too, although that may be in need of attention.'

With each fresh detail, Kat's excitement grew. Dr Wolfe was doing her best to be professional, but she was quivering.

'You didn't mention the cottage, but that's fantastic news. I can get started more quickly if we don't have to hunt for somewhere to live. Your advert did say something about capuchins. Are there a couple in the area?'

'Seventy-nine, to be exact. They were rescued from a medical laboratory and are now in Monkey World, a local ape sanctuary. I daresay they have their own vets, but I know that Dr Baker helped out from time to time. As well as the usual cats, dogs, sheep and horses, you'll be dealing with the pets of tourists and other folk who visit the area. Geologists and the like. And soldiers. Their pets, I mean. There's an army base nearby.

'And, of course, you'll be travelling out to farms. Lionel Baker had a four-wheel-drive vehicle. If you're interested, his family have agreed that it can be included in your salary package.'

'Sounds too good to be true,' said Dr Wolfe.

There was a chuckle behind the files. 'I can assure you it's not, but I think it'll be a happy match – you, Katarina and Bluebell Bay Animal Clinic. Are you agreeable to the terms I offered in my letter, Dr Wolfe?'

'Yes, but—'

'And you can start by mid-March or before?'

'Yes, but—'

'Excellent, excellent. Then, if you don't mind stopping at reception on the way out, Radhika will give you your contract. Please sign it before you leave. Any questions?'

Dr Wolfe took a deep breath. 'Mr Mells, the terms and conditions in the contract. What are they exactly?'

'Eh?' The eyebrows dipped out of sight. 'Ah, the terms and conditions! Nothing to worry about. There's just the one.'

'And what is it?' prompted Dr Wolfe.

The eyebrows crept above the files. 'You want to know what it is? Yes, naturally, you do. Like I said, it's just the one condition. A tiny one, in a manner of speaking.'

'How so?'

There was a pause.

'I'll be honest with you, Dr Wolfe. Lionel Baker was obsessed with his cat – a rescue. His mother has made it a condition of the job that whoever takes it must take the cat too. She won't countenance anyone running the practice and living in Lionel's former home unless they promise also to cherish and look after the cat.'

Inside, Kat was turning ecstatic cartwheels. A cat! The world's most perfect job came with a cat!

Dr Wolfe couldn't disguise her relief. 'That's it? That's the condition?'

'It's trickier than you might suppose. A staggering number of vets don't like or appreciate cats. Or they have allergies.'

Kat thought about Edwina Nash and Vince Craw, who seemed to loathe all animals equally.

'We've had one or two hurdles trying to find the right candidate for the job,' Mr Mells went on. 'I'll admit that until I received your letter I was beginning to despair.'

'Well, we love cats,' Dr Wolfe said firmly. 'My daughter, especially, adores them – don't you, Kat?'

Kat nodded. 'I promise you, Dr Baker's cat will get all the cherishing it could possibly want. What's its name?'

The eyebrows pivoted in her direction. 'His name is Tiny. A tabby, I'm told.'

'Who's been taking care of Tiny?'

'Margo Truesdale, a local shopkeeper. I hired her to take care of the place until I found a replacement for Dr Baker. I gather it's been a bit of a strain trying to manage everything, so she'll be glad we've found you. As am I.'

A hand came over the top of the files. 'Now, if you'll excuse me, I have another client to see. The very best of luck to you, Dr Wolfe and Katarina.'

As they made their way back out to the wintry lights of Covent Garden Piazza, where a juggler on a unicycle was wobbling around the cobbles, Kat couldn't stop pinching herself.

For years she'd dreamed of living in the country or by the sea and having a pet of her own. Now she'd have all three at once. Within weeks, she and her mum would be living in the Jurassic Coast's prettiest bay, surrounded by rolling fields. Best of all, she'd have a little tabby cat – she'd already decided that Tiny was *her* cat – to play with during the day and cuddle up to at night. If he'd only had part-time care for the past three months, he'd need a lot of love and attention.

Kat bent to pick up a yellow gerbera daisy left behind by the market flower sellers. She presented it to her mother.

'Congrats, Mum. I'm soooo proud of you.'

'Thanks, honey. That means the world. It'll be a new chapter for both of us – that's what I'm most thrilled about. Happy to be moving to the seaside, Kat?'

'I cannot wait. Most of all, I can't wait to meet Tiny.'

'Neither can I,' said her mum. 'Neither can I.'

5

Dark Lord

'I could *walk* to the Jurassic Coast quicker than this,' despaired Kat as pulsing brake lights once again made a scarlet sea of the motorway. Rain played percussion on the roof of the Ford Fiesta. It didn't help that the car was laden down with books and possessions that hadn't fitted into the moving van.

Her mum reached for the flask of coffee, thought better of it, and replaced the lid. 'It's another one hundred and fifty-four kilometres to Bluebell Bay. If you get there before me, send a postcard. I'll stay in the car where it's warm and dry.'

Kat slumped in her seat. 'When you put it like that . . .'

She sat up again as sirens drowned out the music in the car. Three police cars and an ambulance screamed past on the hard shoulder.

Her mum turned off the radio. 'Must be a major

incident up ahead. I do hope no one's badly hurt.'

'There are more police cars than ambulances,' Kat pointed out. 'Maybe there's an escaped convict in the crash.'

'Could be. Or someone famous is involved.'

The cars in front grumbled to life. Dr Wolfe started the engine, and they crawled forward. The wiper blades beat back silvery tadpoles of rain. Kat squinted through the gloom as they neared the accident. She knew it was none of her business, but she wanted to see who or what had caused it.

A white van had rear-ended a black limousine. The van had come off worst, spinning out across two lanes. It had a crumpled wing and a blown front tyre. A woman in a Honda Civic had also been caught up in the crash. The van driver and the Honda woman were arguing in the drizzle while a traffic officer refereed.

A short distance away, a smart chauffeur held an umbrella over the limo passenger. It was immediately obvious that his boss was the Very Important Person. A thicket of police surrounded the pair. As Dr Wolfe steered past, Kat couldn't resist trying to catch a glimpse of the passenger. A celebrity maybe? But he had his back to the road and was on his phone.

The traffic picked up speed. Just when she thought that the identity of the VIP would forever remain a mystery, the ambulance moved to make way for a tow truck, revealing the limousine's custom plate: DRK LORD.

Kat bit back a gasp. Her gaze shot to the VIP as he ducked out from beneath the umbrella, lip curled, jaw clenched. His silver hair was as thick and well groomed as ever, his suit taut across broad shoulders. Only the slightest stoop betrayed his age.

An anxious officer escorted him to a police car and opened the passenger door for him. Before getting in, he turned and stared hard in Kat's direction. Her window was blurry with rain, and there was no way he could see her, but she scooted down in her seat anyway.

A moment later, the jam cleared. Her mum, who'd been focused on the road, put her foot down flat, and they whirled away from the scene.

'Thank goodness for that,' said Dr Wolfe. 'I was beginning to think we were going to be stuck in traffic forever.' She gave a joyous whoop. 'New life, here we come!'

And Kat did not have the heart to say that she'd just seen Lord Dirk Hamilton-Crosse, a man so rich, powerful and arrogant that he had a custom-made number plate to confirm it.

No doubt he found it amusing.

To Dr Wolfe, there was nothing funny about the 'Dark Lord', as the tabloids called him. She hadn't laughed eleven and a half years ago when he'd turned up at the hospital, the day after she'd given birth to Kat, accusing her of being a gold-digger. He'd refused to accept that his son Rufus was Kat's father and had told Ellen Wolfe that if she ever tried to claim a penny from the billion-pound Hamilton-Crosse estate, he'd wipe her and her daughter off the face of the earth.

To protect Kat, Dr Wolfe had kept this to herself for over a decade. Kat's first inkling that there might be more to her dad's background than surfing had come a year ago when a limousine had pulled up beside her as she walked home from school. A blackout window slid down, and a man who seemed more falcon or cyborg than human leaned out.

'Hello, Katarina,' he'd said. 'I'm your grandfather.'

Kat, who'd been told her grandparents were dead, had got such a shock that she'd cleared a picket fence in a single bound and escaped through two gardens and a council estate. She'd arrived home looking as though she'd been crawling through hedges, which she had. When she relayed what happened, her mum had gone nuclear.

Shortly afterwards, Dr Wolfe had left Kat in the capable hands of Naska and gone out. When she returned three hours later, she'd seemed lighter. She'd sat Kat down and told her everything. Well, nearly everything. She'd refused to reveal what she'd said to Dirk Hamilton-Crosse. All Kat knew was that the gleaming limousine never again prowled the streets of their scruffy London suburb.

She'd seen the Dark Lord several times since, but only on the news. As Minister of Defence, he was hard to avoid.

That their paths should cross today of all days seemed a freakish coincidence. Kat couldn't help wondering where Lord Hamilton-Crosse had been going and what he'd been doing when the accident happened. She shivered when she recalled how he'd turned his hard, brilliant gaze on their rusty Ford Fiesta. She'd never forgiven him for being so hateful to her mum all those years ago.

So, when Dr Wolfe cried, 'New life, here we come!' Kat cheered with her. She couldn't, and wouldn't, say a word about the VIP in the bulletproof limo. Not for anything would she wipe the smile off her mum's lovely face.

Determined to shrug off the encounter, Kat concentrated on counting down the kilometres to Bluebell Bay. She wanted to remember every detail of their journey to Dorset, from the flat, urban outskirts of London, to the New Forest's dainty spotted deer. She wondered if Tiny would sleep on her bed in her new room that night. Probably not. It might take him a couple of days to get comfortable with her.

A lot of people had the notion that cats did not want or

need affection the way dogs did, but in Kat's experience the opposite was true. Cats craved love. It's just that they were picky about who they wanted it from, and they did it on their terms.

Her phone vibrated in her pocket. She knew without checking that it was her daily reminder from the Way of the Mongoose website. She'd made it her mission to learn two new WOM moves a week and to practise those she already knew in between.

Unfortunately, it was proving tricky to learn them on a small screen. It would be ages before her mum could afford to buy her a laptop of her own, so Kat planned to save up for one herself. As soon as they were settled in Bluebell Bay, she was going to figure out a way to earn pocket money. Dog-grooming was at the top of her list.

The sun came out as they crossed the Dorset border. The colours changed with the landscape. Gone were the greys and dirty browns of the suburbs. The sky was cobalt silk. Fluffy cream lambs wobbled through meadows as green as a brilliant bird's wing. Red campion and yellow gorse lit the hedgerows.

A sign flashed by: BLUEBELL BAY 2 KM.

Kat nearly bounced out of her seat with excitement.

Another sign: WARNING! SUDDEN GUNFIRE!

She twisted round. 'What was that?'

'What was what?' asked her mum. 'Oh, honey, look!

Just look! It's the Jurassic Coast.'

Kat faced forward as they ramped over a rise. Below them was an aquamarine bay so sparkling it looked as if a galaxy had taken up residence in the ocean. Caramel cliffs hugged the cove. From a distance, it could have been California.

'That's our new home?' she said in wonder. 'That's Bluebell Bay?'

From there, the road dropped steeply. High hedges shut out the view. When the sea reappeared, they were on a narrow lane, winding past twisted hawthorn trees and thatched cottages, their gardens bright with daffodils and bluebells.

A snarling iron dinosaur skeleton bared its fangs on a front lawn. Kat smiled at it as they went by.

The town was arranged in a half-moon around the cove, with the higher houses clinging to the slopes. Her eye was caught by the sleek, ultra-modern one nearest the cliff edge. It had a glass front and a wooden deck.

'Left turn in a hundred metres,' intoned the sat nav. 'Summer Street.'

'This is it,' said Dr Wolfe as they rounded the corner. 'Fingers crossed that it's all that Miles Mells promised.'

At the far end of the cul-de-sac, set against the slopes of the hills that curved around the town, was a low, white building. A friendly blue sign announced it as

43

BLUEBELL BAY ANIMAL CLINIC. A small crowd was gathered in front of it.

As they approached, their faithful Ford Fiesta backfired, did a series of bunny hops and began coughing up smoke. With its last gasp, Dr Wolfe managed to steer it into a parking spot. Under normal circumstances, Kat would have died too – of embarrassment – but she didn't get a chance.

Before she could open the door, it was yanked open for her. Smiling faces crowded around. A banner billowed: BLUEBELL BAY WELCOMES DR ELLEN WOLFE! Everyone spoke at once.

'So nice to meet you, Dr Wolfe . . .'

'Dr Wolfe, my schnauzer puppy . . .'

'Our son's guinea pig . . . a red swollen eye . . .'

'. . . lambing emergency . . .'

'Chloe, she's called . . . can't stop scratching . . .'

'Listless, not eating . . .'

With everyone focused on her mum, Kat had time to take a gulp of sharp, salty sea air and look around. There were five thatched cottages on Summer Street, each trimmed in a different shade of pastel and facing the cove. Number 5 was next door to the animal clinic. It was built of golden stone and had blue window frames and a matching door. A dormer window was cut into weathered thatch. As Kat looked up, a shadow streaked across it.

The front door burst open, and a young woman fled across the lawn, discarding an apron and a feather duster as she went. Something electrical had happened to her blue-black hair. She looked as though she was wearing a fright wig.

A stout woman with cheeks the colour of an overripe nectarine raced to head her off. It was hard to hear above the clamour of competing pet ailments, but Kat distinctly made out the words 'rabid tiger'.

She wondered if she should draw her mum's attention to the unfolding drama. No one else seemed interested in it.

She edged nearer. The stout woman pleaded, 'Just this once, and I'll pay you double . . .' but in vain. The cleaner wrenched herself from the woman's grasp with a volley of reproaches and vanished between the cottages.

The other woman rearranged her features from dismayed to delighted before hurrying over. 'Heather! Bernie! Mrs Percy! What did I tell you about letting Dr Wolfe have a cup of tea before you bombarded her with problems?'

The crowd parted. She wrung the hands of Kat and her mum. 'Such a thrill to meet you, Dr Wolfe. And this is your daughter, I presume. I'm Margo Truesdale, owner and proprietor of the Jurassic Fantastic Deli. I've been caretaking Dr Baker's cottage. As you can tell, he's sorely missed. We're in dire need of a vet in Bluebell Bay. There's no other practice for miles.'

She turned to the agitated group. 'I'm sure there's nothing so urgent it can't wait until tomorrow.'

Dr Wolfe interrupted: 'Thank you, Mrs Truesdale . . .'

'Margo.'

'Margo, I'm afraid there are two things too urgent to wait. Mrs Percy, from what you're describing, Lucky might be unlucky enough to have meningitis. Give me two minutes to freshen up, then let's go to him as quickly as we can. Bernie, I'm guessing that the muddy Land Rover is yours. If you'll give us a ride, we can go straight from Ruth Percy's house to your lambing shed.'

She raised her voice above the chorus of protests. 'The rest of you will have to wait until Monday, I'm afraid. Our moving van will be here within the hour, and if I leave it up to my daughter the only thing that'll get unpacked is the books. However, Kat is going to be helping out at the animal clinic until I can hire a veterinary nurse. If you call in the morning, she'll make you an appointment.'

She turned to Kat. 'Hon, I'm so sorry. This is not quite what I had planned for our first day. Would you mind waiting with Margo till the removal men arrive?'

'Course not, Mum! Go and do what you do best. You can tell me all about it over dinner.'

6

A Leopard in the Attic

Walking up the path to the cottage, Kat had the curious feeling she was being watched – and not just by the neighbours. Inside, the sense that all was not as it seemed was even stronger. She could see nothing to explain it, particularly since Margo Truesdale had gone to huge lengths to make the place welcoming.

The fiery-orange Aga and cream-painted kitchen cupboards were spotless. The flagstones shone. There was a loaf of bread, a Dorset apple cake and some farm vegetables in a basket on the counter. A vase of daffodils brightened the worn table. Pots of coconut cream and homemade strawberry jam sat beside a plate piled with fat scones. When Kat bit into one, it was still warm.

'Is Tiny around?' she asked as Margo Truesdale took a sip of tea. 'I'm longing to meet him. I—'

The deli owner's mug smashed to the ground,

splattering them with hot Darjeeling. She threw up her hands. 'Oh, I'm such a clumsy goose! Excuse me a moment while I sweep this up. Don't want you cutting yourself on your first day.'

Kat rushed to help, but Mrs Truesdale waved her away. Only when order was restored did she say, 'Tiny is a great wanderer. Don't be disappointed if you don't see too much of him. He's not a cuddly cat.'

If Kat had a pound for every time she'd been told a cat was aloof, mean or 'not cuddly', only to have that same cat become a soppy, floppy purr factory as soon as Kat laid a hand on it, she'd have been a millionaire. Kat spoke cat. But she smiled politely and followed Margo Truesdale on a tour of the cottage.

The living room was cosy and modern, with a real fireplace, oak floorboards and glimpses over the rooftops of the bay and biscuit-coloured beach. There was space for the Wolfes' sofa and coffee table when they arrived.

Upstairs was a bathroom with an immense claw-footed tub that Kat decided she would fill with bubbles later. The master bedroom with the sea view would be her mum's.

'And this is yours,' Mrs Truesdale announced grandly, ushering her into a room decorated with floral wallpaper.

But Kat had spotted the spiral staircase leading up to the attic. 'What's up there?'

The storekeeper stiffened. 'Nothing.'

'Nothing?' Kat thought of the shadow she'd seen from the road.

'A grimy storeroom is what I mean. Not worth the effort. Besides, it's dangerous. Loose floorboards and choking dust. Hideous. Unfortunately, Maria quit before she could tackle it. Can't get the staff these days. Come away downstairs.'

Kat didn't budge. 'Why did Maria quit? She seemed upset. I heard something about a rabid tiger.'

Margo Truesdale's turkey neck wobbled in agitation. 'Rabid tiger . . . ? How hilarious. No, no – she was fretting about rapid *spiders*. Attic's full of them. There's talk of a ghost too – not that I want to scare you. All round, it's a bad idea going up there. Come downstairs. I'll—'

Her phone burst into song. 'My daughter,' she huffed when she clicked it off. 'Forgotten her keys again. I'll pop out to the street with them to save her time. Why don't you wait in the kitchen? Help yourself to another scone.'

Kat followed dutifully, but as soon as the door shut, she ran upstairs. She didn't believe a single one of Mrs Truesdale's garbled excuses about the attic. Mountains of grime. Battalions of spiders. Poltergeists. The deli owner was hiding something – Kat was sure of it.

The spiral staircase was steep and narrow. Kat wasn't nervous about who or what might be lurking in the attic. She'd learned only three Way of the Mongoose moves, but they'd boosted her confidence.

At the top of the steps, she paused and knocked. No answer. Pushing the door open, she found herself in a bedroom. Odd that Margo Truesdale had insisted the space was only used for storage. A Japanese futon was pushed against one pale blue wall, a duvet and fresh sheets folded at its foot. A wooden trunk served as a bedside table. On it sat a lamp decorated with sailing boats, gulls and waves.

Best of all were the floor-to-ceiling bookshelves. There was space enough for every novel Kat owned and hundreds more.

She perched on the window-seat and looked out to sea. The intense blue of the English Channel filled her vision. Framing the cove was the pastel-painted town.

Among the homes that clung to the higher slopes was the glass, wood and steel one she'd noticed as they drove in. A man stood on the deck, his eye pressed to a telescope.

A chilly gust gave Kat goosebumps. She was about to close the window when a paw print caught her eye. It was pressed into the dust on the sill. She stared at it, uncomprehending. It was lynx-sized.

A low growl made her jump. It came from the wardrobe. Kat straightened in a hurry, nerves jangling. Any sane person would have run first and asked questions later, but Kat was curious. The last time she'd heard a snarl like that was when her mum was treating a serval, a strikingly beautiful African wildcat. The sad creature had been brought to Britain by a breeder.

Cautiously she crept towards the wardrobe. The growl became an enraged hiss.

'Tiny, if that's you, my name is Kat. I've wanted to meet you for ages. Don't be afraid. I know you've had a hard time with Dr Baker dying and lots of strangers coming and going, but I'm here now and I'll take good care of you. We'll be best friends, you'll see.'

The wardrobe door was ajar. Leaning on it, she peered into the gloom. A split-second snapshot of vivid green eyes was all she got before a paw snaked out and claws raked her forearm, raising three bloody lines.

As she reeled back, the biggest cat she'd ever seen – a monster patterned like a leopard – flew past her and out of the high window. Kat recognized it instantly as a Savannah. Judging by its size and markings, it was an F1 or F2 hybrid, only a generation or two removed from its wild ancestor.

'Kat!' called Margo from the floor below. 'What was that crash? Kat, are you up there?' She clanked and panted up the iron steps. 'Are you hurt?'

In the nick of time, Kat pressed shut the cupboard door and tugged her jumper sleeve over the bloody scratches on her arm. When the deli owner came in, she was over by the window, gazing serenely at the view. From what she could tell, Tiny had used the oak tree that overhung the thatched roof as an escape route down to the garden.

Margo Truesdale stared around suspiciously. 'Is everything all right? I thought I heard . . . Oh, never mind. Why are you in here, anyway? I told you it wasn't safe.'

'Thanks, Mrs Truesdale, but you really don't have to worry. I've never been afraid of spiders or ghosts, and the floorboards seem solid enough to me. This is the bedroom I want. It's completely perfect.'

And it was. To share a room in the eaves with a small, sweet tabby would have made Kat extremely happy. To share it with a Savannah cat almost as large and wild as its serval parent or grandparent was more than she could have dreamed of.

The scratches on Kat's arm stung horribly. Still, as she followed Margo Truesdale down the stairs, she couldn't stop smiling.

All her life she'd been told she had a way with animals. Cat whispering, though, was her special gift. It might take a little longer than she'd hoped, but – Kat was confident – some day soon, she'd win Tiny over.

7

Charming Outlaw

The man on the telephone was desperate and made no attempt to hide it.

'Please, ma'am, I'm counting on you to help. You're my last, best hope.'

Kat had never been called 'ma'am' before, nor had she ever been anyone's last, best hope and, though the waiting room at the Bluebell Bay Animal Clinic was crammed, she was intrigued.

She loosened her scarf. It was making her itch. The temperature had risen with the press of bodies and poorly pets, but she didn't dare take it off. Her mum would have a stroke if she saw how close Tiny's claws had come to Kat's jugular vein that morning. He'd ambushed her from the top of the kitchen cabinet.

Kat didn't blame him. It wasn't his fault. He had kittenhood issues. According to Sheila, their purple-haired neighbour, he'd been abandoned in a cardboard box on Dr Baker's doorstep at only a few weeks old.

'He was a wee, drenched scrap. Skin and bones. Wild as anything, even then. It was touch and go whether he'd survive. Who knew he'd grow into a giant –' she searched for the right word – 'menace. My King Charles spaniel is afraid to leave the house.'

Kat felt for the spaniel, but not because of Tiny. More often than not, timid animals were made more fearful because their owners projected fearful vibes. Sheila's anxiety about Tiny had probably caused the situation in the first place.

It wasn't Kat's place to say so, and she didn't. The best thing she could do was keep trying to bond with her cat in the hope of persuading him to be kinder to small dogs and neighbours in the future.

It wouldn't be a picnic. The previous evening, her mum had opened a kitchen drawer and discovered the wild-animal licence Lionel Baker had needed in order to keep an F1 Savannah. Dr Wolfe had raised an eyebrow. So far, all she'd seen of Tiny was a blur of spots and stripes moving between the bushes in the garden.

'So we've inherited an almost-serval? That could be a challenge. Many Savannahs have wonderful dog-like natures and are affectionate and loyal. Then there are those that are feral and kind of terrifying. Give Tiny time and space, Kat. Be patient and, most of all, be *careful*.'

Her gaze went to a new scratch on Kat's hand. 'Any problems, let me know.'

'Absolutely.' Kat crossed her fingers behind her back, relieved that the gouges on her arm were hidden by her clothing.

'I mean it, hon. Don't suffer in silence.'

'What about Dr Baker?' Kat had asked Sheila the next day. 'Did Tiny love him?'

'That feline horror? Wouldn't know the meaning of the word. Tolerated him, is all. Yet Lionel doted on him. Wouldn't hear a bad word.' Sheila frowned. 'Oh, Kat, I hope you and Dr Wolfe won't leave like all the others. Margo's sure you will.'

'What others?'

'The other vets. One barely lasted an hour. He came screeching out of number five with Tiny stuck to his head like a barnacle. Thought I'd be calling the fire brigade to prise the spotted devil off. Luckily my garden hose did the trick. The poor wee man ended up half drowned on top of looking as if he'd been set upon by lions. Probably still in therapy.'

Kat hoped Sheila wouldn't feel the need to share that particular story with Dr Wolfe. 'Mum and me are here to stay, I promise. We're not bothered by a couple of scratches. All Tiny needs is some TLC and he'll be a new cat. Anyway, we like Bluebell Bay. We feel at home already.'

It was true. With the aid of a local handyman, the Wolfes had spent much of the previous weekend painting the animal-clinic waiting room and fixing up the kennels and aviary for overnight emergencies. One week after opening, their noticeboard was plastered with cards from well-wishers such as Farmer Bernie, whose ewe had given birth to healthy twins.

The vast bunch of tulips was from Ruth Percy, whose schnauzer Lucky had been saved from meningitis. The flowers made seeing over the reception desk tricky for Kat. She was helping out after the third agency nurse in a row had let her mum down – this one with car trouble.

She stood as she took the call from the desperate American who considered her his last, best hope.

'How can I help you, Mr, uh . . . ?'

'Professor. Professor Theo Lamb. Let me ask you this. What kind of dad puts his own daughter in the hospital? If there's a trophy for Worst Father of the Year, my name's on it.'

Kat was startled. She wondered if she'd misheard. A mongrel was yapping at a spitting Persian and a yowling Siamese. The decibels in the waiting room were shooting up, along with the temperature.

'I'll tell you what kind,' the American was saying. 'A father so obsessed with Predator X that he forgets he's living in the real world. If I hadn't been preoccupied with finding my own Predator X here on the Jurassic Coast, Harper would have been spared a trip to the operating theatre.'

He paused for breath, and Kat jumped in. 'Professor, I think you have the wrong number. We're a veterinary practice.'

'Why do you suppose I called? Who better to give me advice on the Pocket Rocket?'

'The Pocket Rocket?'

'You must have heard of him. Everyone around here has. His reputation stretches far and wide. Just not across the Atlantic, sadly. Not to Connecticut.'

'Connecticut?'

'Yes, ma'am. That's why our landlady advertised in *Academics Abroad*. She was cunning enough to realize that if the advert went out in Dorset there'd be no takers. So she put it in a magazine that landed on my desk on a dull day in the Geology and Geophysics Department at Yale. You can see it now, can't you?'

'See what?' Kat strained to catch his words above the din.

'A photo of a redbrick country house in a sunlit English garden, with yellow roses round the door and Charming Outlaw—'

'Charming Outlaw?'

'Why do you keep repeating everything I say? That's the beast's poetic *nom de guerre*. In the picture, he's charm personified. A chestnut thoroughbred leaning over a paddock fence, ears pricked, blaze as white as fresh-fallen snow, lipping at a rosy apple. For Harper, it was love at first sight. She adores horses.'

'So do I,' Kat said warmly. 'Is Harper the daughter you put in hospital?'

'You don't pull any punches, do you? Yeah, Harper is my just-turned-thirteen-year-old . . . although, to be accurate, it was Charming Outlaw who sent her to the emergency room.'

'I'm confused. You said Predator X had something to do with it. Is that a video game?'

'Hardly. *Pliosaurus funkei* has been extinct for a hundred and forty-seven million years.'

Mr Newbolt leaned across the reception desk, pushing the tulips out of the way. Scrunched up in disapproval, his broad, flat, lilac-tinged face bore a strong resemblance to that of the lilac point Persian glowering at Kat from the cat basket beneath his arm. If it weren't for his trilby hat and tartan blazer, they could have been related.

'How much longer does Dr Wolfe intend to keep us waiting? Empress Swan Moon is not amused. She's accustomed to tranquillity. Her nerves—'

'Excuse me a moment, Professor Lamb.'

Kat put the call on hold. 'I'm sorry for the wait, Mr Newbolt. Dr Wolfe will be with you as soon as possible.'

'She's been in with that old biddy and her obese retriever for the last fifteen minutes. How much time can one geriatric need?'

Kat had an overpowering urge to tip the tulips over his head, but she'd been well schooled by her mum to combat rudeness with courtesy. 'Empress Swan Moon must be very special to you, Mr Newbolt. I'm sure you treat her like royalty.'

'That I do. Empress is my whole world.'

She beamed at him. 'Then you'll appreciate it when my mum makes her feel special too and doesn't pay any attention if people try to get her to hurry.'

He scowled. 'S'pose I will.'

'Why don't you sit over there, Mr Newbolt, away from the dogs? It'll be more tranquil for Empress.'

He moved off, muttering something about 'amateur hour'. Empress Swan Moon gave Kat the evil eye through the basket's metal grille. If looks could kill, she'd have been incinerated. Kat wondered if she was losing her touch with cats. So far, Tiny had proved immune to her usual methods.

'Hello? Hello?'

Kat lifted the phone to her ear. 'Apologies, Professor. I'm back.'

'Look, can you help me out or not? I'm desperate to make amends. It's not Harper's fault her dad's a muppet. What they don't teach you at Yale is that a PhD is no insurance against idiocy. I've tried contacting the landlady who took a year's rent in advance for the horse and house, but she's gone to ground in Kyrgyzstan.'

'I'm sorry you've had so much trouble, but I'm not sure what Dr Wolfe can do about it,' said Kat. 'She's a vet, not a lawyer.'

'I was hoping that someone there – a nurse or whoever – might offer a pet-minding service that would stretch to horses. Our housekeeper's been attempting to groom him, but it's taken its toll. I tried the local stables, but they hung up when I mentioned the Pocket Rocket. That's another thing our esteemed landlady "forgot" to tell me: Charming Outlaw is an ex-racehorse. He's small but, by gosh, he's quick.'

At long last the penny dropped. Kat felt a flutter of excitement. 'Are you saying you're looking for someone to exercise him?'

She had a sudden, delicious vision of herself galloping along the beach on a chestnut racehorse, spray flying up around them.

The professor sounded peeved. 'Haven't I made that clear? Harper's going to be out of action for months and she's worried sick about the horse. As am I. It's barely been ten days and he's so restless and depressed – it's sad to see. He's a sweetie, really – just . . . keen.'

The consulting-room door opened, and a golden retriever waddled out. Dr Wolfe followed, shepherding an elderly woman, bent and frail, through the door.

Kat made a split-second decision. 'I'll do it, Professor! I'll ride Harper's horse! I mean, I'll need to check with my, uh, with Dr Wolfe, but I'm sure it'll be fine. We'll let you know by this evening at the latest.'

She ended the call before he could ask any awkward questions.

Her mum leaned on the desk. 'Kat, Edith here has been battling to give Toby the exercise he needs. How would you feel about walking him a few times a week?'

'This is outrageous,' interrupted Mr Newbolt. 'How can you justify twenty-five minutes on a single appointment? Anyone can tell there's nothing wrong with that blob of a dog that a diet wouldn't fix.'

The hurt on Edith's face was awful to see.

Dr Wolfe stepped between them, her eyes darting to

the appointment book. 'Mr Newbolt, is it? A pleasure to make your acquaintance, although I must say it looks suspiciously as if your own precious angel has been at the cream puffs. We might need to have a little chat about that. It's not good for her health, sir. Puts pressure on her heart.'

Mr Newbolt clutched at his trilby. 'How dare you. I, umm . . . It's only the occasional scoop of clotted cream. Empress has a weakness for it.'

Turning away, Dr Wolfe winked at Edith, who glowed.

Kat kept a straight face, but inwardly high-fived her mum. As Mr Newbolt followed Dr Wolfe into the consulting room, grumbling all the way, Kat introduced herself to Edith's golden retriever and made a big fuss of him. He washed her face in return.

'I'd be happy to walk your gorgeous dog, Edith. He can show me around Bluebell Bay. We could do some fossil-hunting together, if that's all right with you.'

Edith nodded shyly. Leaning on Toby, she shuffled across the waiting room, her patient retriever wagging his tail beside her. Kat rushed to get the door for them.

Edith's son was waiting outside in a BMW with the radio turned up too loud. He didn't get out of the car. As Edith struggled into the passenger seat, Kat heard him snarl: 'You call this five minutes? Next time, you're taking a taxi.'

The morning appointments ended at 11 a.m. By then, Dr Wolfe had worked her usual magic on both animals and owners. Even Mr Newbolt and Empress Sour Puss left smiling, albeit through gritted teeth. When her last patient had gone, Dr Wolfe came over to give Kat a hug.

'Thanks, hon. I couldn't have managed without you. I'll make it up to you, I promise. You've barely sat down since we arrived in Bluebell Bay. Some school holiday this is turning out to be.'

'I've had fun, Mum, honestly. It's good to see you smiling. Don't worry – we'll find you a great nurse soon.'

Dr Wolfe grimaced. 'Hope so. Boy, do I miss Tina,' she said, referring to the veterinary nurse who'd been her friend and ally at Nash & Craw Premium Pet Care.

'Mu-u-u-m,' said Kat.

'Ka-a-at,' mimicked her mum. 'Go on – ask me whatever it is you're dying to ask me.'

Kat laughed. 'This American professor called. His daughter's around the same age as me. She's been in hospital and is going to be laid up for a while. They're struggling to find someone to exercise her horse.'

'Horse or pony? I'm not having you riding some towering eventer.'

'It's a small horse,' said Kat. 'Pocket-sized, apparently.'

'Then I don't see why not. You'd love that, wouldn't you, darling? Give me the professor's number. I'll call him once I've tidied up. Provided it's above board, I'd have no problem with you helping out. If his daughter's your age, you might even make a new friend.'

8

The Case of the Missing Pumpkin

'A *pet-sitting* agency?'

Dr Wolfe stopped so suddenly that the tourists behind her had to take rapid evasive action. She and Kat were on their way to the deli for lunch. It was only their second visit to Bluebell Bay High Street, and Kat had hoped that her mum would be so distracted by the shops that she'd agree to her daughter's request without a murmur.

Instead, anyone would have thought Kat had demanded a nose ring and a tiger tattoo.

'Only for the holidays,' Kat said hastily. 'I already have two clients on my books. All I—'

'Your "books"? What are you launching, a pet-minding corporation? Floating it on the stock market? Seriously, hon, why do you want to do this?'

'Because,' Kat said, 'I need my own laptop. It'll be a while before we – *you* – can afford one. That's fine, and I understand,' she went on as her mum opened her mouth to protest, 'but I'd like to try saving for it myself. You told me that the professor wants to pay me something for looking after Harper's horse. If Edith—'

'You can't charge the professor for giving you free use of his daughter's horse, or Edith for walking Toby,' her mum cut in, striding on briskly. 'You know that.'

Kat didn't know, but wasn't surprised. Nor would she be surprised if Bluebell Bay Animal Clinic went bankrupt by the end of the month. They'd barely been open a week and already Dr Wolfe had stamped 'NC' (No Charge) on the invoices of four pensioners, a student and an unemployed mum.

Without missing a beat, Kat said, 'That's why it would be good if my agency had a few more *paying* clients.'

'Darling, it's one thing doing a bit of dog-walking for a senior citizen. It's quite another for you to be venturing into the homes of strangers. We're new to the area. For all I know, Bluebell Bay could be like one of those quaint English villages in an Agatha Christie mystery: a hotbed of kidnappers, poisoners and art thieves. I thought it was a safe place, but after last night I'm not so sure. It was like being on the front line of a war zone.'

Kat laughed. Another detail Miles Mells had failed to mention was that number 5 Summer Street backed on to an army firing range. Every Tuesday evening, soldiers fought raging tank and machine-gun battles from 6 p.m. to midnight.

As a result, Dr Wolfe was owl-eyed from lack of sleep. So was Kat, but for happier reasons. When the firing was at its noisiest, Tiny had come flying into his lair – AKA her bedroom. He hadn't growled, spat or tried to attack her. He'd hidden in the depths of the wardrobe.

To Kat, that was progress. Afraid, he'd chosen to run *to* her, not away from her. Well, he'd dived under her T-shirts and jumpers, which was practically the same thing.

Her mum halted outside the deli. 'Here?'

Kat nodded and swung an arm as a smiling family went by, nearly lopping the tops off their ice-cream cones. Despite the blustery weather, the cobbled street was packed with tourists enjoying the pastel-painted shops. Poppies and daffodils waved from every window box.

As if to prove her mum's point, an open-topped army vehicle roared round the corner, shattering the peace. It pulled up outside the pub and two athletic-looking young men in jeans and crisply pressed shirts hopped out.

'Thanks for the ride, Chef Roley,' said one to the driver, an older, thickset man in uniform.

'Any time, Lieutenant Winterman. Enjoy your day off. Best of luck today. Hope she says yes.'

'Thanks, sir. If she does, you'll get an invite to our wedding.'

'Wouldn't miss it for the world, son.'

As the driver pulled away, Margo Truesdale came out of the deli. She waved to the departing army vehicle and clapped a hand on Kat's shoulder.

'I know that face! My niece wears the same expression when she's hungry. Come in, come in. Let's get you fuelled up. Dr Wolfe, put your wallet away. Lunch is on the house. Specials are on the board. I'll be back to take your order in a jiffy.'

Before they knew it, they were tucking into wild mushroom soup with crusty bread at a table spread with a blue gingham cloth. Behind a counter stuffed with local cheeses and cakes was a brightly painted mural. Pterodactyls wheeled over choppy seas while dinosaurs gnashed their teeth on the cliff tops.

Kat was disappointed that her mum couldn't see that her pet agency was the greatest idea since bubblegum, but she wasn't about to give up on the laptop.

'How about dog-grooming, then, Mum? I could do it in the kennels behind the practice. That way—'

'If you're looking for a first-class dog groomer, look no further than Alicia who runs Fluffy Friends,' cut in Margo, putting a raspberry smoothie and a coffee on the table. 'I'd have her do my own hair if she'd let me.'

Kat's face fell.

Dr Wolfe sighed. 'Margo, Kat was thinking of doing some pet-sitting over the holidays. I wasn't sure it was a good idea.'

'It's an excellent idea. What are your concerns?'

'Crime.'

'What about it?'

'Do you get much around here?'

Mrs Truesdale laughed so hard she had to grip Kat's chair to stop herself falling over.

A woman at the next table answered for her. 'Bluebell Bay's been voted the UK's safest seaside town for nine of the past ten years, and it's all down to one man . . .'

The shop bell tinkled, and a policeman walked in.

'Well, how about that!' the woman crowed. 'I've conjured him up.'

Kat did a double take. Repeated exposure to TV detectives and the bobbies who patrolled her suburb in London had led her to believe that all policemen were doughnut-shaped. This one was as sinewy as a marathon runner. His collarbones jutted like wishbones from the neck of his white shirt. In a stiff breeze, all that would tether him to the ground would be his helmet.

He removed the helmet now and tucked it under one arm.

'We were just talking about you, Sergeant Singh,' said Margo. 'Josie here was telling our new vet, Dr Wolfe, that, as our town's only policeman, it's thanks to you that Bluebell Bay is a crime-free zone.'

Sergeant Singh regarded her gravely. 'I am most gratified, Mrs Truesdale, but a police officer cannot afford to be complacent. Anything can happen anywhere at any time. Constant vigilance is required. If one drops one's guard for a second, criminals are waiting to strike.'

Kat smothered a snigger. She made no sound, but his eyes flicked to her as if he'd read her mind.

'Yes, yes, but on the whole Bluebell Bay is as safe as houses,' Margo added impatiently.

'That's a relief,' said Dr Wolfe. She smiled at the policeman. 'Great to meet you, Sergeant Singh, but I'm curious. What happened in the other year?'

'Begging your pardon, madam?'

'The year that Bluebell Bay didn't make it on to the list of the UK's safest seaside towns. What knocked it off the top spot?'

A hush fell over the deli.

Sergeant Singh shifted in his shoes. 'That was an unfortunate incident, no doubt about it.'

His radio crackled and he muted it before continuing. 'Two years ago, on the night of May twenty-first, a pumpkin was stolen.'

Kat put down her smoothie. 'That's the worst ever crime in Bluebell Bay – a stolen pumpkin?'

'It wasn't just any pumpkin,' Margo said defensively. 'It was a County Fair prize-winning, record-breaking pumpkin grown by Edith Chalmers's son, Reg. It was so massive that a forklift was required to move it. He was devastated when it was snatched. The insurance company paid out, but he never got over it. Says money can't mend a broken heart.'

'Especially when you never had one to begin with,' muttered a nearby diner.

'Ghastly business,' Josie told the Wolfes. 'Divided the community. Friends turned on neighbours. Wives accused husbands. Bosses threatened to fire workers. Sergeant Singh left no stone unturned in hunting down the culprit, but no one was ever brought to justice.'

Sergeant Singh gripped his truncheon. 'But they will be. I'll solve this mystery if it's the last thing I do. Criminals who believe they've got away with their crimes become vain and arrogant. That is their undoing. When the pumpkin thief boasts of what he has done, sooner or later it will reach my ears. It's then that I'll pounce. He or she can expect no mercy.'

Walking back to the practice, Dr Wolfe put an arm round Kat. 'If the most dire incident ever to befall Bluebell Bay is the Case of the Missing Pumpkin, you can start your pet-sitting agency with my blessing. What are you going to call it?'

'Paws and Claws.'

'Paws and Claws? What a cute name. That'll keep you entertained for the holidays.'

9

The Honesty of Parrots

There were no appointments until mid–afternoon because Dr Wolfe was out on a farm visit. At Bluebell Bay Animal Clinic, Kat spent a happy hour designing and drawing business cards. She also made a sign for the reception desk:

Paws & Claws Pet-Sitting Agency
Holiday Blues? Business High-Flyer?
Leave Your Furry Pals in Safe Hands
Kat Cares! Phone: 07782 016923

When she was done, she went out to the kennels to check on a stray cat that had been brought in. The calico had been found in a barn scheduled for demolition. She was scrawny and her coat was mangy, but she was surprisingly friendly for an animal that had only ever lived outdoors.

Kat had named her Hero. She'd been fighting to survive since she was born. Somehow, she'd kept her spirit and her sweetness. That made her a hero in Kat's book.

Unfortunately, finding Hero a home would be difficult. Few people wanted ageing cats, and those who did wanted pets, not feral mousers.

'I wish we could keep her,' Kat had said longingly to her mum, though she knew Tiny would never tolerate another cat in the house. He barely tolerated her.

Strolling back to reception, Kat heard a peculiar sound. Speeding up, she flung open the door.

'FREEZE!' barked an unseen man. 'KEEP YOUR HANDS WHERE I CAN SEE 'EM, OR YOUR NEXT MOVE WILL BE YOUR LAST. I'LL PUT A BULLET BETWEEN YOUR EYES! DON'T THINK I WON'T RID THE WORLD OF ONE MORE COCKROACH.'

The metallic double-click of a revolver being cocked chilled Kat to the marrow.

Instinct took over. She threw herself into Move 5 – a Way of the Mongoose front break-fall – followed by a forward-roll that carried her behind the reception desk.

A high-pitched cackle greeted her efforts.

So much for Bluebell Bay being as safe as houses, Kat thought grimly as she crouched low and awaited further demands. No doubt the armed robber would want her to open the till. He'd get a shock when he saw how empty it was.

A shadow loomed over her.

'What a catastrophe!' cried Mr Newbolt, who'd acquired a dark tan and a foreign accent in under two hours. 'Now I'll never get a pet-sitter.'

Kat blinked. It wasn't Mr Newbolt at all, but a bronzed man in a similar blue-grey trilby. He extended a hand and helped her up.

'Ramon Corazón, at your service. On behalf of my naughty bird, please accept my sincere apologies.'

'Your bird?'

Kat's heart was pounding. She'd thought for a second she might die.

'Si. A yellow-crowned Amazon.' He went over to a pet carrier and took out a small parrot with exquisite green, yellow and scarlet plumage. It sidled up his arm and nibbled his ear affectionately.

'May I introduce Bailey, named in honour of Florence Augusta Merriam Bailey. Like myself, Florence was an ornithologist – although, unlike me, she was a legend. I'm only a humble bird artist.'

'You draw birds?'

'Paint them. Apologies again if Bailey frightened you, miss. Hold me responsible, not him. Parrots can become stressed if they're left alone. For years I was in the habit of putting DVDs on for him if I was out birdwatching. Ever since, he's had a habit of reciting scenes from action movies when he's anxious. It's got us into trouble more than once, but I've been unable to train him out of it.'

Now that she'd recovered, Kat thought an action-film-loving parrot the funniest thing ever. 'You made a comment about a pet-sitter. Do you need one?'

He clapped his forehead. 'I almost forgot. That's why I'm here. I have urgent business in my home country, Paraguay. I'm due to fly tomorrow, but disaster has struck. My cleaner has a family emergency and is unable to take care of Bailey. I've asked practically everyone in the village, but no luck. Then Mrs Truesdale told me that the new vet's daughter is a pet-sitter. Where can I find this Kat?'

'I'm Kat. Katarina really, but most people call me Kat.'

'*You?* That will not do at all. With respect, you are a mere girl.'

He looked sadly at his parrot. 'After everything, to fall at this final hurdle.'

'I am not a mere girl,' Kat said crossly. 'I'm twelve, and I can do anything—'

She got no further because Bailey suddenly launched himself into the air and flew across reception. He came swooping in, green wings spread wide, and landed on her shoulder.

'*Te quiero*,' he cooed, caressing her cheek with his beak.

Ramon was astounded. 'In all our years together, I've never once seen him do such a thing. Bailey is mostly a one-man bird. I rescued him from a cruel trader, and he has always distrusted strangers. Not only has he now chosen to fly to you, he is telling you he loves you in Spanish. It is something he says rarely, and it's revealing.'

Kat decided that Bailey was a bird of impeccable taste and judgement. 'Why is it revealing?'

'Because, unlike humans, parrots never pretend to like someone when they don't. They're honest to the bone. The main difference between a parrot and a person is that a parrot is incapable of lying.'

'Animals are the world's greatest truth-tellers,' agreed Kat. 'They might not all be able to talk, but if you look closely, their eyes and body language always give away their real thoughts and feelings.'

'Interesting, interesting,' murmured Ramon. 'Perhaps all is not lost.'

Kat rubbed the parrot's head. It crooned with pleasure. 'How long are you away for, Mr – er, Corazón?'

'Ramon, please. Thirteen days.'

'And you live in Bluebell Bay?'

'*Si*. I'm renting Avalon Heights.'

'The eagle's-nest house on the cliff? So *you're* the telescope man,' she said with a smile.

The change in him was dramatic. 'What are you talking about? Have you been spying on me?'

'Spying? No! We only moved here last week. I was looking out of the attic window and I saw someone with a telescope on your deck. I suppose you were birdwatching.'

Ramon ran a hand through his hair. 'Sorry, Kat. My nerves are not what they should be. I've been out of my mind about Bailey and what would happen to my business if I couldn't find the right person to take care of him. He's my best friend, you see. Yes, it was me with the telescope. Birdwatching, as you say.'

Under the guise of fussing over the parrot and returning him to his master, Kat studied the Paraguayan. He had a strong, decent face, but it was haunted, perhaps with worries about his business trip. Despite the cool weather, he was sweating too. When he'd lifted the parrot from its carrier, his shirt had clung to his back.

'Forgive the question, but something puzzles me,' he said. 'Faced with what you believed was an armed robber, your reaction was an unusual one. Are you a student of Brazilian jiu-jitsu?'

Kat shook her head. 'I'm a student of a martial art

invented by a baker from Shanghai. You won't have heard of it.'

'Try me.'

'It has a funny name: the Way of the Mongoose.'

Ramon slapped his thigh. 'Unbelievable! When destiny calls, she doesn't take no for an answer.'

'Excuse me?'

'You may be the perfect pet-sitter after all. I myself have been a Mongoose practitioner for over a decade. How about you?'

Kat was overjoyed to meet a fellow WOM enthusiast. 'I'm only a beginner and I'm struggling to learn it on my useless mobile phone. That's why I'm pet-sitting – to save up for a laptop.'

The reception door swung open, and in came her mum, medical bag in hand. She greeted Ramon warmly. 'Hello! I'm Ellen Wolfe.'

The Paraguayan whipped off his hat. 'Ramon Corazón. I've heard many good things about Bluebell Bay's new vet, and now I've met the director of Paws and Claws. I was about to ask if she'd care for my parrot for a couple of weeks.'

'If Kat's happy to do it, I'm happy to let her,' Dr Wolfe assured him.

Her phone rang and she excused herself to answer it. Ramon zipped the parrot into his carrier. After putting his contact details in Kat's phone, he pressed his hands to his heart.

'There's no way for me to express my gratitude. Thanks is quite inadequate. I'll call you later with instructions for getting into the house.'

Kat smiled. 'Don't fret about Bailey when you're gone. I'll give him lots of treats and love. Hope your business trip goes well.'

He picked up the parrot carrier, hesitated, then put it down again.

'Kat, if it would help you learn the Way of the Mongoose, you're welcome to borrow my spare Surface Book while I'm away. It's a small but powerful notebook computer. I'll leave it in the bread bin, under the rye. I'd recommend Move 58. All are excellent, but in a life-or-death situation Mongoose masters consider that to be the most effective. They call it the "Get Out of Jail Free Card".'

Before Kat could respond, he was gone.

10

Private and Confidential

The path to Avalon Heights was steeper than Kat had expected and wound unnervingly close to the cliff edge. She was grateful for the guard-rail. Though ice cold and slippery, it felt solid, which counted for something on a day when mist made a mystery of most of Bluebell Bay.

Halfway up, a scarlet sign reared out of the gloom: DANGER! SLIP HAZARDS! SUDDEN DROPS! TRIP HAZARDS! FALLING ROCKS! CRUMBLING CLIFFS! Beside each warning was a yellow triangle in which stick figures slipped or tripped to their doom, or were simply crushed to death by boulders.

Kat was nervous, and the

sign didn't help. She was thankful when the path brought her, at last, to the steps of Avalon Heights. Up close, its steel, glass and sharp angles gave it the air of a futuristic fortress. Kat fought the urge to run away. She'd begged to be allowed to pet-sit, and now she had to see it through.

Her main concern was that she wouldn't be able to get in. The door had a sophisticated locking system. Ramon's instructions had been complicated. For added security, the fourth number of the six-digit code moved forward by one digit every day. Seven became eight, and so on. Kat had visions of locking herself out. Bailey would slowly starve. Ramon would arrive home to find his beloved parrot with his toes in the air.

As it turned out, no code was needed. Kat was reaching up to tap it in when the door slid open.

Her first thought was that Ramon's trip had been delayed or cancelled. She hoped it was the former. That way, she'd get the best of both worlds. He'd show her where everything was, and she'd still get her parrot-sitting cash. With luck, he'd have time to teach her another Mongoose move before he left.

She rang the bell, then knocked for good measure. 'Ramon? Anyone home?'

Only the wind answered.

The unlocked door made Kat uneasy. Ramon had

been obsessive about his fancy security system. He'd even asked her to memorize the numbers.

'Tell no one,' he'd said in a hushed tone, as if imparting nuclear codes. 'Write nothing down.'

She was about to knock again when she noticed a pebble trapped in the sill, preventing the door from closing. Ramon must have left in such a hurry that he hadn't noticed. She flicked it away. Before her feet could take over and carry her back down the hill, she stepped boldly into the hallway.

Freed, the door hissed shut. Bolts shot into place.

'Hello?' called Kat. 'It's the pet-sitter.'

Silence.

In Kat's favourite mystery novels, these scenes often ended with the hero – i.e. her – finding a dead body on a Persian rug.

There was a rug on the stripped wood floor, but it was fluffy and white. Pleasingly, it was also corpse-free.

At that point, she forgot to be scared because she was too busy gaping at the house. The living area was straight out of a Hollywood film. The furniture was wall-to-wall designer luxury in matching shades of charcoal, white and smoky blue. A vast flat-screen TV was suspended from cables. Wildly expensive gadgets blinked on every surface.

The ceiling was two storeys high, and the entire front wall was glass. Beyond it was a deck with a hot tub and

Ramon's telescope. In clear weather, the bay would be a sparkling wonder of blue. Today it was more like whipped cream. Far below, the waves whispered.

A faint crunch made Kat snap round.

What she'd thought was an oversized black lampshade was actually a covered cage. In her excitement, she'd forgotten the reason she was there.

When she lifted the drape, she was distressed to see the parrot huddled against the bars. His water and food had spilled. When she reached for him, he shrank away.

'Bailey, angel, don't be sad,' said Kat. 'Are you pining for Ramon? He'll be back before you know it. Meantime, you and me are going to have lots of fun. Let's start by getting you out of this horrid prison.'

On the sofa, she rocked him like a baby. Bailey's downy green feathers trembled beneath her hand. She fretted that he might be ill.

She was on the verge of calling her mum when he perked up. He waddled up her arm. 'Tell Kat,' he squawked. '*Tell Kat!* TELL KAT!'

Kat wondered if Ramon had taught Bailey a few phrases to amuse her. 'What do you want to tell me?'

'September Nile!' shrieked the parrot. 'Poor Bailey. Otto quarter. Otto quarter!'

'Yes, poor Bailey. I think you might be hungry.

You're not making sense.' Kat took a packet of almonds from the pocket of her jeans. 'Here, have a nut.'

After cleaning his cage with the dustpan and cloth Ramon had left in a bag beside the table, she carried his water dish through to the kitchen. A white breakfast bar with sky-blue stools separated it from the living room.

For reasons known only to himself, Ramon had left instructions for Bailey's care in a book: *As Kingfishers Catch Fire*. It was squeezed between his recipes. As with the secrecy around the door code, it all seemed a bit cloak and dagger.

Fortunately, his note was normal enough.

Welcome, Kat! Mi casa es su casa. *My home is your home, as we say in Spain. I trust you will take care of it, but please also enjoy it. See the framed photo of* Tyto alba? *That's ornithologist for 'white owl', though some call it the ghost, silver or death owl. I've spent half my life in pursuit of this silent hunter. Wrapped up in this one picture is my whole history. Ha! But I must keep to the point or I will miss my flight.*

Behind the owl is what I call my box of tricks. You'll figure them out, I'm sure.

On the wall above the toaster was a photo of a snowy barn owl in flight. Kat had to stand on a chair to reach it. The frame was heavier than she expected and she almost dropped it.

An iPad-type panel was secured to a metal plate. It had thirteen functions. The first made drinks. Kat selected vegan hot chocolate. There was even a choice of milks, including Kat's favourite, almond. A puff of cocoa tipped into a mug and was whisked to a froth.

Kat was impressed. Next time, she'd order a mango smoothie.

Tapping option 2 set the Jacuzzi bubbling on the outside deck. Option 3 switched on the stereo. Kat selected a few tracks. As music filled the room, Bailey bobbed and danced on her shoulder, making her laugh. Option 4 unfurled a home cinema screen and offered up hundreds of films. Option 5 controlled the lights. Option 6 heated up ready meals in the microwave. Option 7 turned an armchair into a massage therapist. Option 8 fired up the barbecue on the deck. Option 9 turned on the air conditioning. Option 10 watered the living wall of herbs, tomatoes and lettuces in the kitchen.

Kat was in her element as she worked her way down the list, sipping hot chocolate, flicking between tunes, and considering a black-bean enchilada for lunch. Her earlier anxiety had gone. She didn't mind being alone in Ramon's empty house – not with so many toys at her fingertips. Until he returned, she was Queen of a Highly Entertaining Castle.

Option 11 powered up the state-of-the-art equipment in the small gym next to the living room. Option 12 was for the CCTV. She clicked on 'Living Room' and rewound a few frames. There she was in black and white, cuddling Bailey on the sofa.

Option 13 was the only button not labelled. When she pressed it, a password request popped up. She entered the door code, but it was rejected.

The doorbell rang. With a screech of alarm, Bailey fluttered on to the breakfast bar. 'Tell Kat!' he shrieked over the music of Sia. 'TELL KAT! TELL KAT!'

Whoever was outside leaned on the bell. Kat killed the music. In the hallway, she peered through the spyhole. An eyeball filled it. She sprang away. 'Uh, who is it?'

'Delivery for Raymond Curzon,' said a muffled voice.

'Thanks. Just put it through the letter box or leave it on the step.'

'Needs to be signed for. 'S'urgent.'

Kat put the chain in its slot, unbolted the door and opened it a crack. 'I'll sign for it.'

A courier in a baseball cap grimaced on the misty steps. He scratched his sweaty forehead. 'No can do.

'S'private and complimentary.'

'Confidential, you mean?'

''S'what I said. My orders were to give it to Raymond Curzon poisonally. Nobody said nothin' about a daughter.'

Kat didn't bother correcting him. 'Ramon's not here. You can come back another time or leave it with me. I'll make sure he gets it.'

His buggy eyes veered to the cliff path. She could almost hear the gears clanking beneath his cap. 'I could lose my job.'

'I won't tell if you don't.'

He wrestled with his conscience for all of two seconds before shoving a grubby tracking device through the slot. 'Mind you sign yer dad's name.'

Kat used the attached plastic pen to do an elaborate scrawl on the screen. It could as easily have said 'My Dad Lost a Fight with a Twenty-metre Wave' as 'Ramon Corazón'.

In exchange, she received a padded brown envelope marked 'PRIVATE AND CONFIDENTIAL' and 'URGENT' in black ink.

After he'd gone, she studied the package. There was no postmark and nothing to indicate who'd sent it. Nor could she feel anything inside it. Sherlock Holmes might have been able to tell what sort of person had written out the name and address, but Kat couldn't. They'd used a

Sharpie like half a trillion other people.

The house was worryingly quiet. Leaving the parcel on the hall table, she hurried into the kitchen. The parrot was gone.

She did a quick search of the living room and gym, even checking behind the sofa and cross-trainer. No Bailey.

Butterflies did a fly-by in Kat's stomach. What if he'd escaped while she was signing for the parcel and was now free in Bluebell Bay? Her pet-sitting career would be over before it had begun. Ramon would kill her. Forever more she'd be known as the girl who'd lost a parrot in her first hour on the job.

Then she remembered the CCTV. If Bailey was in the house, the camera would find him.

Her fingers were clumsy on the control panel as she navigated from room to room. The parrot wasn't in any of the three bathrooms, nor was he in Ramon's messy study or the spare bedroom. Finally she spotted him. He was strutting along the headboard in the main bedroom.

Kat took the curving wood stairs at a sprint. The first door she tried was a marble bathroom. The next was Ramon's study. Unlike the rest of the house – which, despite the luxury, had a hotel feel to it – this was homely. Books on birds and flowers, and artist's supplies were piled on every surface. An easel with a half-finished painting of a sparrowhawk stood in one corner.

His desk was cluttered and dusty.

Seeing it, she recalled Ramon's promise to leave his laptop in the bread bin.

The main bedroom was at the far end of the passage. Bailey looked pleased with himself when she walked in. He lifted a foot in greeting. 'September-Nile-Otto-Quarter. Deuce Testy It.'

'What are you on about, you naughty bird?' scolded Kat, holding out a hand. He skipped up to her shoulder. 'Are you speaking Spanish?'

She stopped. Stared.

On the other side of the bed was an open suitcase, half packed. Clothes spilt from it. Socks, toothpaste and a can of shaving cream were strewn across the carpet.

A cold feeling went through Kat. Something was wrong. She'd known it from the minute she saw the unlocked front door.

'Tell Kat,' Bailey crooned as she backed out of the room. 'Tell Kat, tell Kat,' he repeated as she rushed down the stairs.

'Tell me what?' she asked him. 'Where's Ramon? You know something, don't you?'

Her mind was a whirl of dark possibilities. If Ramon had decided to postpone or cancel his trip, he'd have called her. Why hadn't he?

Could he have nipped out with the rubbish and fallen

over the cliff in the fog? Or, worse, had someone broken in? Was someone in the house right now?

Kat wanted nothing more than to flee and never return, but for Bailey's sake she forced herself to keep a cool head.

She was being silly. There had to be an explanation. Ramon might have been taken ill. He could be lying in a hospital bed, unable to call.

Or perhaps it was a sliding-doors situation. As she'd been puffing up the hill to Avalon Heights, he'd been on his way to the Bluebell Bay Animal Clinic to tell her that he wouldn't be going to Paraguay after all.

It was easy enough to find out. She rang the practice. The agency nurse answered.

'Hi, it's Kat . . . Dr Wolfe's daughter. Has anyone been in asking for me?'

'Like who?'

'Ramon Corazón. I'm pet-sitting his parrot. He's from Paraguay.'

'From *where*?'

'Never mind,' said Kat. 'Thanks.'

She hung up and dialled Ramon's number. If he was in the country, he'd answer and reassure her. If he was in mid-air, he'd at least pick up her message when he reached Paraguay. Either way, she had a good excuse for calling – the 'Private and Confidential' parcel.

71

His number rang only once before a recorded message intoned: '*This number is no longer in service. This number is no longer in service. This number . . .*'

Kat switched off her phone, as if shutting it down would make whatever was happening stop happening. She was desperate to leave Avalon Heights, but she didn't want to abandon Bailey.

Earlier, she'd seen his carrier in the corner of the gym. She fetched it and bundled him in. Before leaving, she returned the ghost owl picture to its hook above Ramon's 'box of tricks'.

The computer was in the bread bin, beneath a dish towel and two loaves of rye. She stuffed it into her backpack, along with Ramon's note. The blinking gadgets watched her go.

At the last second, she grabbed the brown package off the hall table. She'd promised to take care of it, and that's what she intended to do.

Outside, it was drizzling. Mist floated like a wraith above the cliff path. Kat took hold of the wet, cold guard-rail with one hand and hoisted the carrier on to her shoulder with the other. She and the parrot stepped blindly into the unknown.

11

The Trust Technique

Kat knew she'd found the right place before she saw the sign on the gate, half hidden by a shaggy hedge and fragrant strands of jasmine: Paradise House.

She was surprised that the name in itself hadn't been a warning to Professor Lamb. In her London suburb, the Paradise Fish Bar had been exactly where you'd buy fish fingers if you had a hankering to spend a week in intensive care. The nearby Paradise Motel was a soulless carbuncle overlooking a flyover shrouded in toxic fumes. And the Paradise Pet Shop traded in tragic farmed puppies, kittens and goldfish, all looking as if they hoped

that the end – *any* end – was nigh.

But this Paradise House did look heavenly. Exuberant roses climbed the redbrick walls. The garden was a riot of apple and cherry trees. Kat inhaled. The air carried a delightful hint of horse.

She propped her muddy bike against the trellis, took off her riding hat and untied a large blue gym ball from the carrier. Inside the house, someone pecked listlessly at a piano.

As she reached for the door knocker, a raised young voice with an American lilt carried clearly through an open window. 'Oh, Nettie, I'm so bored I might have to hack into the Pentagon, if only to stop myself going stark staring crazy.'

'*Tch*, Harper Lamb, one of these days you're going to get yourself into hot water, and I, for one, will not shed a tear.' This was an older woman with a Welsh accent. 'MI5 will be paying you a visit.'

'Huh, if only. When is the pet-sitter getting here anyway? That'll kill five minutes. Only another nine million and fifty-five to go while I'm stuck indoors, missing out on life, on fun. Without adventure, what's the point of even breathing?'

She stabbed a piano key in frustration.

'Let's play a game, Nettie. I'll have a try at guessing what she's like, and you can do the same, then we can compare and contrast when she gets here. She'll be nuts, of course. All pet-sitters are. You should see them in Central Park in New York. They're like human merry-go-rounds, with leads going in every direction, and eight dogs winding themselves around lamp posts, getting into fights and going to the bathroom in flowerbeds.

'Bet you two pieces of fudge that this pet-sitter's hair will be like wire wool and sticking out from under a rainbow beanie she's knitted herself. She'll be squeezed into jodhpurs and have a loud, commanding PE-teacher voice. Charming Outlaw will whimper at the sight of her. He won't dream of bolting and leaping over a five-barred gate the way he did with me . . . Nettie, where've you gone now?'

The door opened so suddenly that Kat had no time to pretend that she'd only just arrived. A long, lean woman, her hair hanging like basset-hound ears on either side of her face, smiled down at her. The Welsh housekeeper, Kat presumed. She must have spotted Kat coming up the path.

Nettie pressed a finger to her lips. 'I disagree,' she said over her shoulder. 'If I were to consult my crystal ball, I'd say our new pet-sitter is going to be wearing breeches that err on the baggy side . . .'

'That's Amazon's fault,' whispered Kat. 'They sent the wrong ones.'

' . . . muddy long boots, a khaki-green jacket with lots of useful pockets, and a red "THIS GIRL CAN" T-shirt. You might be right about the hair, though. Not the wire-wool bit. My crystal ball tells me that it's wildfire hair, in serious need of a brush.'

She beckoned Kat in. Kat left her boots on the doorstep and followed Nettie into the living room in her socks.

A girl of around her own age lolled in an armchair between the window and the piano. She was staring down at a laptop. Her legs were up on a footstool: the right one in a blue plaster cast that reached her knee, the left in a bright pink ankle cast. She also had a bandaged wrist and a scratch on one cheek.

She was hemmed in by heaps of books and audiobooks with titles such as *Learn Mandarin Chinese*, *A Latin Primer* and *The Coder's Lexicon*.

'So what's your best guess, Nettie?' she said, without looking up from her computer. 'Are you right, or am I?'

Some instinct made her glance round. A beetroot flush spread from the neck of her cream jumper to the roots of her glossy dark hair.

'Oh. *Ohhhh*.'

She shut her laptop with a snap. 'How much did you overhear?'

'Everything from the part where you were wanting to

hack into the Pentagon,' Kat answered truthfully. 'What does the Pentagon do anyway?'

'It's the United States Department of Defense in Arlington, Virginia.'

Kat was shocked. 'And you could really hack into it?'

''Course she couldn't,' snorted Nettie. 'She likes to torment me, is all. Drawn to mischief the way a bee is to honey, that one.'

Her twinkling eyes belied her stern tone. 'Would you like some tea and cake, miss, er . . .'

'Kat. Yes, please – but, if it's OK with Harper, I'll take care of Charming Outlaw first.'

Left alone, the girls sized each other up. Despite their awkward start, Kat warmed to Harper at once. Her round face was open and likeable, and comma-shaped dimples appeared in her cheeks when she smiled. Behind her glasses, her gaze was smart and unwavering.

'Sorry about earlier,' Harper said. 'Dad didn't tell us the new pet-sitter was a local kid. He can be vague like that. Shame it's not going to work out. As you can tell, I could use a friend.'

'You're *firing* me?'

'Good gosh, no. It's only that I wouldn't want you to get hurt. Charming Outlaw is an ex-racehorse. On the track, his nickname was the Pocket Rocket. I thought it was a laugh until a rabbit popped out from behind a bush, and he bolted. I've always fancied myself a good rider, but it was like being strapped to a comet. We found out later that that's why his owner sold him for a song, and why our landlady, who tried to train him for polo, gave up on him. When he gets the bit between his teeth, even pro jockeys struggle to stop him. You wouldn't have a chance. You don't wanna end up like this, do you?'

She lifted the pink ankle cast and winced.

'For starters,' Kat said, 'I'm not planning to ride him today. Charming Outlaw and I need to get to know each other first. I thought we might play some football.'

The pink cast thudded on to the chair. 'Oh dear. You *are* a crazy pet-sitter after all.'

'Why don't we let Charming Outlaw decide? One hour is all I need. Your father told me the Pocket Rocket's depressed because he's cooped up. I can fix that. Trust me, horse football will help.'

Harper was unimpressed. 'Why should I trust you? I don't even know you.'

Kat could feel her longed-for dream of galloping along the beach on Charming Outlaw slipping from her grasp. 'Oh, give me a chance, Harper! I couldn't bear it if another job went wrong – not after what happened with my first client.'

'And you want me to let you play games with my

horse?' cried the American girl. 'What became of the other pet? What was it – cat, dog or a more exotic creature?'

'A yellow-crowned Amazon parrot. Bailey's fine. It's his owner I'm worried about. I'm convinced something dreadful has happened to him.'

Harper's brown eyes widened. 'Are you talking illness or masked robbers? Did you see something suspicious? Tell me everything.'

'Why should I trust you?' demanded Kat. 'I don't even know you.'

Harper grinned. '*Touché*. That's French for "you've got me there", in case you were wondering.'

Kat smiled back. 'I wasn't.'

'There's an easy way to settle this,' said Harper. 'Do you believe that animals are good judges of character?'

'The best,' answered Kat, recalling Ramon's comment on the honesty of parrots.

'Then let's allow Charming Outlaw to decide, like you suggested. You can see if he trusts me, and I can see if he trusts you. Deal?'

'Deal.'

'If you help me into my wheelchair, I'll come with you. Ohmigod, I can't believe I'm saying that. It's like I'm ninety.'

'Special Olympians don't think that way,' Kat

pointed out. 'They use their wheelchairs as chariots for superhuman feats.'

Harper brightened. 'That's true! My chariot only has to get me to the yard.'

12

Wolfe & Lamb, Inc.

'When I got out of bed today, Paradise House was draped in apocalyptic fog,' said Harper as Kat pushed her wheelchair through the cherry blossoms. 'It was as if there'd been a nuclear disaster, and me, Dad, Nettie and Charming Outlaw were the only survivors.'

Kat had a flashback to her own perilous journey to visit the parrot. 'That's how I felt when I was climbing the cliff path to Avalon Heights this morning,' she said, momentarily forgetting their bargain. 'In places, the sea mist was so thick it was hard to know which way was up and which was down.'

The wheelchair braked sharply. 'Avalon Heights? The house that looks as if it's owned by a movie star or a Bond villain? What happened? Tell me, tell me.'

Kat refused to be drawn. 'Later.'

She was tense about meeting the Pocket Rocket, but trying not to be. Few animals were as sensitive to emotional turmoil as horses. It wasn't Charming Outlaw's reputation that scared her. Mainly, she was afraid that Harper would send her away before she'd been able to spend time with him.

For Kat, horses had always been as necessary as breathing. Between the ages of five and nine, she and her mum had lived on London's Isle of Dogs, close to a riding school. Riding came so naturally to Kat that the woman who ran the local Pony Club had asked Kat to join the team. But after winning a couple of showjumping rosettes, Kat had quit. She had no interest in competing. She wanted to be with horses and to understand them, nothing more.

Moving to the other side of London had put an end to all but the occasional ride. However, she had done an online natural horsemanship course with her mum. Now that she had a chance to test it out on an actual horse, she didn't want to blow it.

They'd reached a neat stableyard with two stalls. One was filled with hay. The other just barely contained a chestnut thoroughbred with a white blaze. When he saw Harper, he whickered with pleasure. But, after a quick hello, he let out a full-throated whinny and resumed pacing his stable, stamping and snorting.

'See what I mean?' Harper said anxiously. 'He's so explosive that I doubt you'd even manage to groom him. Nettie's been doing it since my accident, and she's frazzled. You can quit now if you like. I won't hold it against you.'

But Kat was already walking up to the stable. Inside, the horse rushed in circles, coat flashing like a fire-juggler's torch. He barged the door, ears pinned to his head.

Kat dipped her right shoulder and half turned away, but she stood her ground. Curiosity got the better of Charming Outlaw. He remembered his charming side. His ears pricked and he stretched over the stable door, breathing her in. When at last she laid her hand on his cheek, he shut his eyes and gave a great sigh.

For Harper, watching, it was like intruding on a private moment. There was an exchange between Kat and the horse. They spoke the same language.

However, as soon as Kat let him out of the stable, Charming Outlaw forgot his manners. He tore around the yard and down to the field with Kat clinging to his lead rope as if she were the tail of his racehorse kite. To Harper's astonishment, Kat was unfazed. She was endlessly patient, firm and sure of herself.

Over the next hour, Harper watched as Kat transformed Charming Outlaw from a frantic, sweating barrel of frustration to a happy, shiny horse. He was full of beans and far from perfect, but it was a good beginning. They left him in the field, rugged-up and playing with his new ball.

'What are you – an animal psychic?' asked Harper over a cup of tea and a slice of home-baked chocolate and raspberry sponge.

Kat found it hard to take her eyes off a model of a dinosaur that took up the whole of the dining room table. She supposed that the professor and Harper ate on their laps. 'I listen to animals, that's all. Anyone can do it.'

'No,' Harper said. 'They couldn't. If you still want to be our pet-sitter after I insulted you and nearly fired you, I'd love you to do it. Charming Outlaw trusts you, and that's good enough for me.'

'Yes, please!' Kat grinned. 'By the way, you've passed the Charming Outlaw trust test too.'

'Ooh, goody. *Now* will you tell me the secret of Avalon Heights?'

A hard knot balled in Kat's stomach. She knew she'd

never forget her flight from the house – the cold, slippery guard rail beneath her fingers, and the wind trying to suck her off the cliff into oblivion.

It was a relief to talk to someone about it. When she'd returned, shaken, to Bluebell Bay Animal Clinic, her mum had been operating and couldn't be disturbed. Kat had installed Bailey in the aviary for sick birds, petted Hero and gone home for a sandwich.

Oddly, it was Tiny who'd comforted her. He'd been perched on top of the kitchen cabinet, tail swishing. His fierce green gaze made her feel safe again. She knew that nothing and no one would get past him. She'd told him about the strange events at Avalon Heights, but had decided not to tell her mum until she knew for certain Ramon was gone. It might all be in her mind. Talking to Harper made everything vividly, scarily real again.

'You're awfully courageous,' the American girl said admiringly. 'I'd have been so creeped out after finding the suitcase I'd have run away and left behind the parrot and the parcel. Five stars for being quick-thinking enough to take both.'

Unused to praise from her peers, Kat speared a raspberry to hide a sudden attack of shyness.

'So what's your opinion, Harper? Is something criminal going on, or is it a misunderstanding? Maybe I got the date wrong. Ramon could be on the phone to the police at this very minute, telling them his pet-sitter's stolen his parrot.'

Harper took a yellow-lined pad and a black pen from a basket beside her armchair. 'I think we both know that Ramon is not at Avalon Heights. Something – or someone – interrupted him last night or first thing this morning as he packed his bags. We need to find him. His life could be at stake.'

She wrote 'MISSING PERSONS REPORT' at the top of the pad and underlined it three times. 'Let's start with what we know.'

NAME: Ramon Corazón
AGE: 50-ish
ADDRESS: Avalon Heights, Bluebell Bay, Dorset
JOB: Bird artist
LAST CONTACT: Called Kat at 8.16 p.m. on Wednesday from unlisted number
PLANS: Said he was leaving at the 'crack of dawn' on Thursday on urgent business trip to Paraguay
REASON FOR TRIP: ???
SUSPECTS: 0
SUSPICIOUS THINGS:
1) door open when Kat arrived at about

10.45 a.m. on Thursday
2) half-packed suitcase
3) phone number not working
4) suspicious package

'Lots of parcels have "Private and Confidential" written on them, especially business ones,' said Kat. 'Doesn't mean they're suspicious.'

'Yes, but they're not all addressed to people who've vanished, leaving their special security door unlocked and their luggage scattered across their bedroom floor,' said Harper. 'I'd also like to know why Ramon password-protected Option Thirteen on his high-tech kitchen iPad. He wouldn't have bothered securing it if there was nothing to hide.'

'There's something else,' said Kat. 'When I got there, Bailey was cowering in his cage. I thought he was pining for Ramon, but now I'm not so sure. He kept gabbling, "Tell Kat! Tell Kat!" and some other words I didn't understand. Ramon speaks Spanish, so it could have been that.'

'If he says it again, try recording him on your phone. I'm half Cuban, so I can translate. In case you were wondering, my mom was an archaeologist who got pneumonia on a dig and passed away when I was knee-high to a gnat. All I have of her is pictures. She was born in Miami, but her parents were doctors from Havana. Granddad's gone, but Grandma's still around, living in the Florida Keys. She and Dad made sure I grew up speaking Spanish.'

Harper's tone was breezy when she spoke about her mother, but Kat knew from experience that just because painful things became easier to say with time it didn't mean they didn't hurt.

'I'm sorry about your mum. My father's gone too. He was lost at sea before I was even born.'

'That's tough. Was your dad a sailor?'

'A surfer. But I don't call him Dad, because he kind of wasn't one, if you know what I mean.'

'I know exactly.'

For a minute, they ate their cake in silence.

Harper took the cap off her pen. 'Let's get back to work. We have a missing man to find. What are the chances that Señor Corazón fell off the cliff in the fog?'

'It's possible, but I'm hoping there's another explanation. Suppose Ramon was in debt, and the bailiffs came calling? He might have spotted them on his CCTV, escaped to the airport with only his passport and the clothes he was wearing, and flown away to Paraguay.'

Harper jotted down some notes on the yellow pad.

'Excellent theory. We'll add it to our list of possibilities. If Ramon hasn't turned up or called by tomorrow morning, I'd say we're looking at three options. One: he's sick or had an accident leaning out over a precipice in pursuit of a rare bird. Two: he's on the run because he's done something wicked. Or three: foul play.'

'But why would anyone want to harm a twitcher?' asked Kat. 'It doesn't make sense.'

'What in the world is a twitcher?'

'A bird watcher. That's what they call themselves.'

'That figures, I've always thought at least sixty-five per cent of twitchers are completely bonkers and this proves it.'

'You said pet-sitters were mad too,' Kat reminded her. 'And here I am.'

Harper had the grace to look ashamed. 'Fair point.'

'Ramon adored Bailey, which is usually a good sign. He told me that the difference between a person and a parrot is that a parrot never lies.'

'He said that?' Harper noted it down. 'Curiouser and curiouser.'

'Plus he's a Way of the Mongoose student like me.'

'Way of the what?'

'Mongoose. It's a martial art that takes the best bits from wing chun, Krav Maga and Brazilian jiu-jitsu. I've only been doing it for a few weeks. Ramon told me to learn Move 58. He said it's handy for life-and-death situations.'

Harper chewed her pen thoughtfully. 'Why would a bird artist need to be an expert on life-and-death situations? Come to think of it, what urgent business could a bird artist have in Paraguay? This whole situation stinks.'

'We should call the police,' said Kat.

'The cops won't lift a finger until an adult's been gone for at least twenty-four hours.'

'So what's our plan?'

The word 'our' fell so easily from Kat's lips that she had to remind herself that she and Harper had only just met. Everything was happening so fast. A couple of hours earlier, they'd been strangers. Now they were a team: Wolfe & Lamb, Incorporated.

Harper brimmed with energy and ideas. 'There's only one thing for it: we need to return to Avalon Heights.'

'You have two broken legs!'

'When I say *we*, I mean you,' Harper clarified. '*You* have to go back. If Ramon's been kidnapped, or worse, there'll be evidence. Footprints, a threatening letter, bloodstains . . .'

Kat stared at her. 'You're joking?'

'About which part?'

'Why do *I* have to do it? Earlier, you told me that you'd have been scared out of your wits if you'd seen what I saw at Avalon Heights. You said you'd have run away.'

'Yes, but I'm not a black belt in Mongoose kung fu or whatever it is you do. You're brave.'

'Not that brave!' cried Kat. 'And I'm only a Mongoose apprentice.'

Harper considered. 'OK, how about this: if Ramon hasn't texted you or shown up by morning, ask Sergeant Singh to go with you to Avalon Heights. He'll be over the moon to have a missing-person mystery in Bluebell Bay. Beats hunting for stolen pumpkins. Nettie says that's the only crime they've ever had around here. Just don't give away our best clues. And, whatever you do, don't tell him about the parcel. That's *our* secret.'

'What will you be doing?' Kat asked. 'You know, while I'm crawling around Ramon's carpet looking for bloodstains.' She paled. 'Oh Lord, I hope there are none. He's such a nice man.'

Harper softened. 'There won't be. My guess is he's taken a tumble in the mist and has amnesia. He'll be wandering around a nearby village like a zombie, unable to remember his own name. I'll check the local papers for news.'

She patted her laptop. 'While you're at Avalon Heights, I'll be searching for other leads online. If Señor Corazón is a well-known artist, he'll have a website. Or the galleries that show his work might have some info. A biography would help us fill in the blanks. There could be old articles or blog posts about him too.'

Kat put on her jacket. She needed to get home for dinner. 'I'll report back tomorrow. Same time, same place?'

Harper's dimples deepened. 'Same time, same place. Thanks for what you did for Charming Outlaw too . . . Wait up, Kat. Which courier company delivered the package to Avalon Heights?'

'The delivery guy wore a navy blue hat and black jacket. I didn't see any badge.'

'Pity. I could have hacked into their system to see who sent it.'

'Not hacking again!' scolded Nettie, coming in to take the tray. 'You're playing with matches, Harper Lamb. Any day now, MI5 will be dragging you off in handcuffs. I might call them myself. It would be a treat to have some peace and quiet around here.'

'Yes, but who will help you remove spiders from the bath?' retorted Harper.

The banter between the pair did nothing to conceal the deep affection between them. Though originally from Cardiff, Nettie had spent the past three years working for Professor Lamb in Connecticut. She and Harper seemed to have a strong bond.

Kat liked it. It made her feel at home.

'Thanks for the cake, Nettie. It was delish. Like eating

chocolate air.'

'You're welcome, honey. See you tomorrow.'

After she'd left the room, Kat said, 'Nettie's right, Harper. You should be careful online.'

'The FBI and MI5 don't bother with small fry like me,' Harper replied airily. 'And I'd never touch any government websites – not unless the Pentagon or the UK Houses of Parliament were under siege by a hostile foreign power. Just so you know, I am on the side of the angels.'

13

The Oxford Street Phantom

'Whatever you're selling, we don't want it,' snapped Reg Chalmers, Edith's BMW-driving son. 'Not unless you have cupcakes, in which case you can leave some free samples. I'll get back to you if they're edible. What are you – a Brownie?'

His nose twitched as if had been assailed by a foul odour. A less kind person than Kat might have suggested that he use less cologne. His outfit was loud too – gangster pinstripes and a big-collared white shirt that reminded Kat of Elvis.

'I'm not a Brownie, and I don't have cupcakes,' she began.

He cut her off. 'Collecting for charity, are you? Bit early, isn't it? It's barely 9 a.m. If you think you can weasel cash out of my ma with some weepy tale about starving orphans or endangered polar bears, you can forget it. I'm wise to those tricks.'

'Reg?' called a tremulous voice from inside the cottage. 'Reg, is that the dog-walker?'

A barrel of gold fur shoved past Reg, nearly knocking Kat off the front step. She hugged Toby, and he showered her with licks and joy.

Reg grunted. '*You're* from Paws and Claws? I was expecting someone older. Same still applies. If you're here to squeeze pocket money out of my ma, you'll have me to answer to.'

Kat stood up. 'There's no charge. Edith's doing me a favour. I love dogs and hardly ever get a chance to walk them.'

His smile advertised his expensive dental work. 'Why didn't you just say so? Come on in and bring the hound. Ma's expecting you.'

Kat followed the retriever into Kittiwake Cottage. It was postcard-pretty and set at the opposite end of the cove to Avalon Heights, beyond the harbour. Through the bay window, colourful boats bobbed on an inky sea.

'Kat, you came!' Edith started up from her chair. 'I wasn't sure if you'd find the time, but Toby sensed you would. He's been whining and scratching at the door since daybreak.'

Reg rolled his eyes. 'Tell me about it.'

He glanced at his Rolex. 'Gotta run to the office. Think

about what I said, Ma. I'll take care of the paperwork. Easy-peasy lemon squeezy. The whole process will be smooth as silk. You'll be free as a bird then. No more stressing about bills or keeping on top of the weeds. At Glebe Gardens, life will be one long holiday.'

He swept past Kat.

Standing beside Toby, Kat felt rather than heard the retriever growl.

Reg smirked. 'Good luck getting that tub of lard to waddle to the end of the street, though I applaud you for trying.'

He left in a blast of cold air, shouting over his shoulder, 'Love you, Ma. Have a great day.'

Edith flinched as the door slammed. 'He's a good son, my Reg,' she said. 'Always taking care of me.'

Then why, Kat wondered, *do you look so unhappy?* She made it her mission to make Edith smile at least once that day.

It took twenty seconds – about as long as it took Kat to spot the library in the next room.

'Wow! Look at those books! Edith, are they yours? I thought Mum and I had a lot, but you must have thousands.'

It was like turning on a lamp. Edith shone with pride. 'Two thousand, four hundred and twelve, last time I checked. In alphabetical order too. That's what half a lifetime in a school library does for you.'

'You were a librarian?' Kat looked at her client as if she was a superhero in a cardigan.

'Lived and breathed it,' smiled Edith. 'The best part was reading to children, especially those stories that got their pulse – and mine – racing: *Emil and the Detectives*, Nancy Drew, *Stormbreaker*, that sort of thing. But sixty-five came around faster than a bullet train, and that was the end of it. Forced retirement. There's a saying: "Old librarians never retire. They just get re-shelved." I suppose that's what I am these days – on the shelf.'

She stopped, embarrassed. 'I mustn't hold you up. I expect you want to get out with Toby.'

On the one hand, Kat was eager to find Sergeant Singh. On the other, she wanted to delay visiting Avalon Heights for as long as possible. Overnight, there'd been a deafening silence from Ramon Corazón. His phone number remained out of service.

Harper had texted her at 6 a.m. *Any news??????*

Not a word, Kat had messaged back.

No way!

Yes way.

I checked the local papers online. No reports of men falling off cliffs or wandering around with amnesia either. Don't go to AH without SS.

OK.

118

Promise?!!

Kat had sent a smiley face for an answer. It gave her a warm feeling to know that Harper had her back. She couldn't get over how their names fitted: Wolfe & Lamb. It was almost as if everything they'd ever done in their lives – every twist, Predator X and unwanted burglar – had been leading them to the point where they'd team up to solve this mystery.

If there was a mystery.

'Do you still read those books that get your pulse racing?' she asked Edith as she took Toby's lead off the coat rack.

'Would if I could. They made me feel alive, as if I was a spy or adventurer myself. Unfortunately, my eyes are failing, along with my back. These days, I lead a quiet life. Soon it will be even quieter.'

She turned away quickly, but not before Kat saw a tear splash on the arm of the sofa. Sensing his mistress's distress, the retriever was at Edith's side in an instant.

Kat pretended to be busy untangling his lead. She felt terrible for making Edith cry.

Or had she? Reg had asked his mother to think about signing some papers that would make her life one long holiday. *Easy-peasy lemon squeezy*. Rather than being happy, Edith had seemed to shrink in her shoes.

Kat doubted that Reg had meant the Caribbean. And,

from what Edith was saying, sitting slumped in front of a TV or staring out of a window was not her idea of being as free as a bird.

'My friend Harper has two broken legs and a sprained wrist, but she refuses to let that stop her from having adventures.'

Without looking round, she could tell she had Edith's attention.

'Was it the adventures that put her in traction in the first place?'

Kat turned. 'Oh, no. It was the Pocket Rocket.'

Edith was aghast. 'The notorious racehorse?'

'It wasn't his fault. He only wants to do what's natural – gallop and be free.'

'Don't we all?' Edith said drily. 'How does Harper manage these adventures if she's trussed up like a mummy in plaster?'

'She's a sort of online investigator,' Kat began, before deciding she'd said too much already. 'If you miss reading, Edith, why don't you try audiobooks?'

Edith looked dejected. 'I wouldn't know where to start. I don't have a CD player, and Reg says a smartphone would be beyond me.'

Comments rose like bees in Kat's throat, but she swallowed them down. 'I have a thought.'

She fetched her rucksack, took out the Surface Book

and sat beside Edith on the sofa. 'One of my clients lent this to me. Maybe I could find a good novel for you, and you could listen to it while I'm out walking Toby. I'm sure my client won't mind.'

Not if he's strawberry jam at the bottom of the cliff, added a voice in her head. She squashed that thought down too.

Edith twisted her hands. 'It's kind of you to offer, Kat, but I can't be trusted with a computer. I'd only get in a muddle.'

'Sorting out muddles is what librarians are best at,' Kat reminded her, hoping it was true.

She'd expected Ramon to leave her one of his old, out-of-date tablets. In fact, it was slim, shiny and expensive-looking.

He'd told her the Surface Book was a spare and that he'd deleted every file on it but, as it powered up, an owl icon flapped twice in the top right-hand corner of the screen. When Kat clicked on it, a password box appeared.

'What a beautiful barn owl,' said Edith. 'I've never understood why some people call them ghost owls or, worse, death owls. Whose computer did you say this was?'

'It belongs to Mr Corazón. Do you know him?'

'A true gentleman,' Edith said with feeling. 'Two years ago, I suffered a dreadful fall near the harbour. Ramon was new in town, but he came rushing out of nowhere, carried me home, made me sweet tea and took care of me. Wouldn't leave, even after Reg arrived. Said he wanted to be sure I didn't have concussion. Next morning, the biggest bunch of flowers I've ever seen was left on the doorstep.'

'So he's a kind man?' Kat prompted.

'Very. Reserved, but so polite and thoughtful. Popular with everyone. Well, everyone except Maria, my cleaner.'

Kat had a vivid memory of the wild-haired maid tearing across the lawn of number 5 Summer Street on the day the Wolfes arrived in Bluebell Bay. 'Doesn't she like him?'

'I wouldn't put it that way. Maria's from Spain, but she spent her gap year volunteering on a Pantanal swamp turtle project in Paraguay. When she heard there was a fellow animal enthusiast from Paraguay living in Bluebell Bay, she couldn't wait to chat to him. She was so disappointed when it didn't happen. He made excuse after excuse for not meeting her for a coffee. Eventually, she gave up. She's convinced he was avoiding her. I can't think why. She's a wonderful person.'

Not in Tiny's opinion, Kat wanted to say, but didn't.

She turned her attention to the computer. 'What are you in the mood to listen to, Edith? I can find you a podcast or a radio play.'

Kat logged on to her own local Wi-Fi service and brought up the BBC's website. Her fingers froze on the keypad. The arrogant face of the Dark Lord stared back at her from the Live TV news link.

'Lord Hamilton-Crosse is devilishly handsome, but he does remind me of the *Mona Lisa*,' Edith said unexpectedly.

Kat hooted with surprised laughter. It was like hearing the Dark Lord compared to a skipping spring lamb. 'What do you mean?'

'Whenever I see him on TV, his eyes seem to follow me around the room in the way of the Mona Lisa, that famous Leonardo da Vinci painting. However, Dirk Hamilton-Crosse is rather more sinister. Let's hear what he has to say.'

The interview was wrapping up. Watching her grandfather talk about the unveiling of the latest model of smart tank for the British Army made Kat feel the way Edith did, as if his laser gaze could see her through the screen.

'*These digitized armoured fighting vehicles are vital to the future of our military,*' he was saying. '*By 2020, we'll need video gamers to operate them, not regular soldiers. When I visited the Royal Tank Regiment last week . . .*' Kat now realized why she and her mum had passed the Dark Lord's limousine on their way to Bluebell Bay. He'd been at the military base on the outskirts of town on the exact same day. It was a spooky coincidence.

If one believed in coincidences.

Mostly, Kat did not.

A new headline popped up: '*HAVE YOU SEEN THE OXFORD STREET PHANTOM?*'

'Ooh, a real-life mystery,' Edith said with relish.

The TV studio cut away to a roving reporter with candyfloss hair. People with bulging shopping bags flowed around her like a river around a log.

'*Oxford Street is Britain's best-loved outdoor mall,*' she gushed into a fluffy microphone. '*A paradise of designer clothes, perfume, coffee shops and bling.*'

Edith spluttered. 'Paradise? On my one and only visit, it was hell. Wall-to-wall bad-tempered shoppers and glittery things nobody needs.'

'*But today London's premier tourist destination is buzzing with conspiracy theories. It all started at nine thirty-nine yesterday morning when a man collapsed with a suspected heart attack outside John Lewis department store.*'

Grainy grey CCTV footage showed a confused scene in Oxford Street. It was just about possible to make out a figure crumpling to the pavement. Four people ran to help. An ambulance skidded up minutes later.

'*Eyewitnesses say that paramedics were quickly on the scene. They whisked him away in an ambulance. It was only*' *when police, journalists and eyewitnesses tried to discover the identity of the man that the questions started. No London hospital had any record of admitting him. Every enquiry drew a blank. Appeals on social media have drawn a huge response, but no answers.'*

The reporter paused for effect.

'Now, in breaking news, a police spokesman has confirmed that the ambulance number plate was false.'

'That's strange,' said Kat. She and Edith bent over the screen, their heads almost touching.

'Could be a mob boss from the criminal underworld being snatched by a rival Mafia gang,' suggested Edith.

'Or a celebrity being kidnapped and held to ransom,' suggested Kat.

'Or a political assassination.'

Kat grinned. 'Or a spy.'

Edith was breathless and glowing. 'Do you really think so? At *rush hour*? In *broad daylight*?'

The reporter ended by asking anyone with information on the Oxford Street Phantom to call the police as soon as possible.

Toby put his nose on Kat's knee and gazed up at her beseechingly. She ruffled his golden fur. 'Sorry, boy, we got distracted. Let's get you out and about.'

After putting on a Radio 4 play about an SAS mission for Edith, Kat and the retriever headed for the door.

A letter addressed to Reg lay on the mat. There was a Glebe Gardens logo on it.

As she set off along the harbour, with Toby ambling amiably at her side, Kat did a search for 'Glebe Gardens' on her phone. It was one of those soulless 'homes' where families put their ageing loved ones when they grow tired of them or can no longer cope.

On the surface, it seemed pleasant enough. The gardens were full of well-behaved hydrangeas, and Pilates was on offer. But the residents' smiles didn't reach their eyes. Loneliness leaked from them.

She wondered if Reg's enthusiasm for Glebe Gardens had anything to do with his hopes of getting a slice of the sale of his mother's cottage. As one of the prettiest and largest cottages on the seafront in Bluebell Bay, Edith's home had to be worth a fortune.

Kat's heart clenched painfully. If her kind, gentle client had to move, what would become of the dog she adored and her 2,412 books?

More importantly, what would become of Edith?

14

Body Snatchers

Kat didn't have to search far for Sergeant Singh. He found her.

She was staring through the window of the Fossil Museum when he loomed up behind her. Their reflections merged, and for a second Kat had two heads, one of which wore a police helmet. She let out a guilty squeak.

'May I ask what you're doing with Edith's retriever, Ms Wolfe? I must caution you that dog theft is a serious offence.'

'I'm a dog-walker,' she said indignantly. 'I have permission. Call Edith if you don't believe me.'

He smiled his grave smile. 'I do. I've already checked.'

'Then why . . . ?'

She stopped, realizing he was teasing her.

He cleared his throat, as if light-heartedness was a liberty he seldom allowed himself. 'A little bird told me you were asking for me, Kat Wolfe. You're concerned about Mr Corazón?'

Kat wondered which little bird in the deli had told Sergeant Singh she was looking for him when she'd dropped in after leaving Edith's cottage. There'd been quite a few. Margo Truesdale; a gossipy guinea pig-owner Kat knew from the animal clinic; three soldiers; and Roley George, the man she'd seen with the lieutenant who was planning to propose to his girlfriend. Turned out Roley George was head chef at the army base.

And then there was the colonel, who'd blown into the deli like an extreme weather event, brooding and heavy-booted. Kat had taken the first opportunity to flee, but not before he, too, knew that she had business with Sergeant Singh.

'Did Margo tell you that Mr Corazón is out of the country on business?' the policeman asked now.

Kat explained about pet-sitting Bailey and gave Sergeant Singh the edited lowlights of the previous day: the unlocked door, the forlorn parrot, the half-packed suitcase.

She didn't say a word about the 'Private and Confidential' package.

With every sentence, Sergeant Singh seemed to grow taller and stricter. 'You're telling me that you suspected Ramon could have met with an accident or been the victim of foul play at noon yesterday, and you have waited until now to raise the alarm?'

'Harper says that when adults go missing the police don't lift a finger until they've been gone for at least twenty-four hours. So here I am, twenty-four hours later.'

His brow scrunched. 'The American professor's daughter? What does she have to do with anything?'

'I'm taking care of her horse.'

'The infamous Charming Outlaw?' Sergeant Singh's fingers strayed to his handcuffs as if the racehorse was an actual outlaw, not just in name. 'I hope you're insured.'

'Why is everyone so mean about him?' demanded Kat. 'Don't you know that if you tell animals they're bad all the time, they begin to believe it?'

Sergeant Singh examined her thoughtfully. 'The same is true of humans. All right, young lady, I'll accompany you to Avalon Heights. Doubtless there's an innocent explanation, but it'll do no harm to put both of our minds at ease.'

*

'Wait for me,' puffed Kat as Sergeant Singh's long strides ate up the cliff path to Avalon Heights. He wore black trainers rather than polished police boots.

'The better to catch criminals,' he'd told her. 'A policeman's most effective weapon is his fitness, not his truncheon. If he can't run after burglars or run away from knife-wielding maniacs, what use is he?'

One day ago, Kat would have laughed out loud at the notion of Sergeant Singh sprinting after the non-existent burglars and knife-wielding maniacs of Bluebell Bay. Now anything seemed possible.

She was glad he was with her. She wasn't sure she'd have had the courage to walk into Avalon Heights again alone. The cliff path was also made easier by fine weather. The icy wind kept pulling her off balance, but the view was worth it, and Toby insisted on walking between her and the crumbling edge.

At last, the trio reached Avalon Heights. The retriever flopped down on the doorstep, panting and drooling. Sergeant Singh held out his hand for the keys.

'There aren't any,' Kat told him. 'Ramon gave me the security code. If you turn your back, I'll enter it.'

He was incredulous. 'I'm a policeman.'

'I gave Ramon my word I wouldn't tell a soul. A promise is a promise.'

A smile tweaked his mouth. 'It is indeed.'

When his back was turned, Kat entered the code, remembering to move the fourth number one digit forward. It didn't work. She tried again, this time changing the fourth digit from a six to an eight. There was a beep as the alarm was deactivated.

'Let me take a look around – make sure it's safe,' said Sergeant Singh. 'Was this the door you found unlocked?'

Kat nodded, and he disappeared inside.

He was back in moments. 'As far as I can see, all is in order on this level. If you notice anything unusual, tell me at once.'

It was strange going into the house she'd departed from in a state of near-terror just yesterday, especially in sunny weather. Light flooded in, making a nonsense of her fears. The bay was bluebell blue. Dahlias swayed in their pots on the deck.

'What made you think that something was amiss?' asked Sergeant Singh. He grimaced at his watch as if he'd already decided that the entire expedition was a monumental waste of time.

If she were him, Kat would have felt the same way. Back in Ramon's luxurious living room, she struggled to recall what had sent her stumbling from Avalon Heights as if the hounds of hell were after her. She literally had to dredge the memory of the half-packed suitcase from the pondweed at the bottom of her brain.

'It's in the main bedroom at the end of the passage,' she told Sergeant Singh. 'On the other side of the bed.'

'I'll check the others first. Stay down here until I give the all-clear.' He was at the top of the stairs in three bounds, truncheon in hand.

In the kitchen, Kat filled a bowl with water for Toby. She could hear the policeman opening and closing cupboards. Suddenly she could think of 101 innocent reasons why a suitcase – perhaps a spare, or one belonging to a friend – had been on the floor of Ramon's bedroom.

Was it even his room? She'd just assumed . . .

And yet there was something about the air in the house that felt different. She was sure she'd returned *As Kingfishers Catch Fire* to its slot among the recipe books. Now it was on the breakfast bar.

If Ramon's been kidnapped or worse, there'll be evidence. Footprints, a threatening letter, bloodstains . . .

The CCTV! If something had happened to Ramon, it might have been caught on camera.

The floor upstairs creaked as Sergeant Singh moved along the passage. Kat scrambled on to the kitchen counter, took down the ghost owl picture, and tapped Option 12 on the control pad. The 'Living Room' CCTV was a square of fizzing grey. The 'Front of House' camera was the same.

She navigated from room to room with growing

unease. Every camera in the house was down. There was nothing but grey static until 11.01 a.m. on Thursday, when she saw herself staring up at the camera with Bailey on her shoulder.

She rewound the video further, looking for Ramon or any visitors. At twelve minutes past midnight, about eleven hours before she'd arrived to find the unlocked door, the outside camera had picked up a partial view of a person on the deck. He or she was holding something sharp and triangular. A weapon?

Fog blurred the jerky movements of the silhouette, making it impossible to identify whether it was Ramon or a stranger.

She snapped a couple of shots with her phone before returning to the home page. Option 13 still gnawed at her. What was it hiding?

She couldn't resist trying it again. When the password box came up, she entered Ramon's birthdate, which she'd found in Bailey's notes at the veterinary practice. It was rejected. 'One more try remaining' scrolled across the screen.

'Miss Wolfe, would you come up here, please?' Sergeant Singh's voice boomed down the stairs.

Kat wrestled the owl picture back on to its hook. It was crooked, and she hoped the policeman wouldn't notice it before she had time to straighten it.

He was leaning against the banister on the second floor. His expression reminded her of the time she'd tried to convince a teacher that a dog really had eaten her homework.

'Be kind enough to show me where you found the suitcase, Miss Wolfe. I can't see it anywhere.'

'Sure.' She led him to the room at the end of the passage. 'It's over . . .'

The words died on her lips. The carpet was bare.

She rushed into the room and peered under the bed. 'It was here! Look, there's even a smear of toothpaste on the carpet.'

Sergeant Singh folded his arms across his chest.

'I think I can guess what's happened. When you came to feed the parrot yesterday, Ramon hadn't left yet. He'd probably nipped down to the shops for a last-minute item, or spotted some rare bird he wanted to draw. That explains why the door was open. Bluebell Bay is so safe that many residents don't lock up. After you'd gone, he returned, finished packing and caught a train to London.'

Kat ran a hand over the carpet. 'No. I don't believe it. Somebody's been here. That's why the door code had to be moved on by an extra number. They've cleaned up and taken the suitcase. For all we know, they've snatched Ramon's dead or bleeding body too.'

The policeman groaned. 'You've read a few too many

mystery novels, Kat Wolfe. You were right to notify me of your concerns, so I'm not going to tell you off, but I do have to get back to some real work.'

Kat rushed after him. 'Sergeant Singh, you have to investigate this. Ramon's in danger – I can feel it in my bones.'

'Unfortunately, or fortunately, police officers can't rely on feelings in people's bones. We need concrete evidence.'

His radio chirruped, and he paused to answer it. 'Give me a moment. I need to make a call. This won't take long.'

Kat thought quickly. If there was any evidence of where Ramon had gone or what he'd been up to before he went missing, it would be on his desk or in a filing cabinet.

Sergeant Singh had his phone between his ear and shoulder and was scribbling in his notebook. 'You say a fight has broken out over a parking space? At the harbour?'

Kat darted into Ramon's study. She was about to open a drawer when she noticed a light gleaming through a glass vase holding an orchid. Behind the vase was a landline and answering machine. A blue number one shone in the display.

Kat pressed play, noting the date and time:

11.26 p.m., the night before Ramon was due to leave.

The line was distorted, but there was no mistaking the menace in the caller's voice: '*Breathe a single word about what you* think *you saw, Mr Corazón, and I'll hunt you to the ends of the earth . . . Take my advice: go to darkest Peru and stay there . . . If I see you again, you're chopped liver.*'

'Sergeant Singh!' yelled Kat. 'Sergeant Singh!'

He burst into the room, brandishing his truncheon. 'What's going on? What are you doing in here?'

'There's a threatening message on Ramon's answering machine. Listen.'

Kat jabbed at the play button. Nothing happened. A blue zero now showed in the little window.

'I must have deleted it by mistake. Don't worry, I remember it. The man who rang was a complete psycho. He threatened to hunt Ramon to the ends of the earth if he told anyone what he thought he saw. He said that if Ramon ever returned from darkest Peru – I suppose he meant Paraguay – he'd be chopped liver.'

'Enough!'

Sergeant Singh radiated disapproval. 'I don't like fibs, and I like fibbers even less. I expected more from a girl who claims to believe that a promise is a promise.'

He steered her from the study and down the stairs, ignoring her protests.

'I'm not lying and I can prove it. Whoever made

the call was near a railway or maybe a factory. In the background, there was this stamping sound with pings in between. *Stamp, stamp, stamp, ping. Stamp, stamp—*'

'Are you aware that wasting police time is a criminal offence?'

Kat knew she was testing his patience but was too frustrated to care. 'I don't understand. You spend years sweating over a stupid stolen pumpkin, then when a real mystery lands on your lap you can't be bothered.'

Sergeant Singh had the look of a man with many unprintable words boiling in his brain, but he managed not to say any of them.

'Miss Wolfe, the reason police officers investigate petty crimes is that the pumpkin thieves, bullies or shoplifters who commit them often aspire to more-wicked deeds. If we can root out the seeds of crime, we can sometimes stop them growing into evil empires, with branches and roots spreading in all . . . Uh, where's the dog?'

He was staring past Kat, into the kitchen.

'The dog!' Kat's hand flew to her mouth.

She and Sergeant Singh dashed into the hallway. The door was open and chewed papers were scattered across the floor.

Outside, there was no sign of Toby. The pair gazed with horror at the cliff edge. Kat had visions of the retriever laid out like a bearskin rug on the rocks below. What would she say to Edith?

'I'm the world's worst pet-sitter,' she despaired, wondering what else could possibly go wrong.

'Maybe not *the* worst . . .' mused Sergeant Singh unhelpfully.

The clang and crash of falling bins had them racing round the back of the house. Toby crawled out from beneath a colourful sea of rubbish, shedding old pizza crusts, soda bottles, carrot tops and potato peelings along the way. Something grey was clamped between his jaws.

Kat wrestled it away from him and gave a strangled cry. It was a torn T-shirt, sticky with dried blood. She thrust it at Sergeant Singh. '*Now* will you believe me that something awful has happened?'

But rather than leaping into action and calling for back-up and a forensic team, as detectives did in books, Sergeant Singh treated this revelation with a disturbing nonchalance. He sniffed the T-shirt – unscientifically. Then he sniffed it again.

Kat almost gagged. 'Ewww!'

'Tomato sauce,' he said, tossing the soiled garment on to the heap of rubbish. 'Heinz, if I'm not mistaken. *Now* will you believe that nothing awful has happened?'

15

Death Owl

'Ketchup?'

Harper was unable to keep the disappointment from her tone. 'And he's absolutely sure?'

'A thousand per cent,' said Kat, who'd cycled directly to Paradise House after dropping off the retriever at Edith's cottage. 'On top of that, when we tidied up the papers Toby had chewed, we found Ramon's itinerary. He was only due to fly to Asunción, the capital of Paraguay, on Thursday night. That means that Sergeant Singh's theory about him still being in Bluebell Bay when I went to feed Bailey in the fog yesterday morning is most likely correct.'

Kat tried not to sound deflated. Of course she wanted Ramon to be safe and sound, but for nineteen hours she'd also enjoyed the adrenalin rush of being part of a team working to solve a mystery and, perhaps, to save a life.

If their missing man wasn't really missing, she was nothing but a pet-sitter with an overactive imagination.

Harper put down her yellow pad. 'So there's no mystery?'

'Not according to Sergeant Singh.'

'What does *he* know!' cried Harper in annoyance. 'Policemen are trained to be cynical. It's in their job description.'

She took a consoling sip of her ginger-beer float – a froth of soda and coconut ice cream whipped up by Nettie. The resulting milk moustache gave her a strangely learned air.

'Yesterday was the best day I've had in ages,' she said despondently. 'In between searching for clues online, I even designed us a logo on my laptop, using the Chinese symbols for wolf and lamb. Want to see it?'

Kat sat beside her as Harper opened her laptop. Her martial-arts-style design included a mongoose and a 228-million-year-old fossil.

'The ichthyosaur symbolizes the Jurassic Coast. It was a kind of prehistoric dolphin known for its speed – something we'd need if we were going to be real detectives. Nettie's a whizz at crafts. I told her we were starting a book club, and she promised to use this to embroider us a couple of badges that we'll be able to stitch to our jackets. Only you and I will know their true meaning.'

Glumly she closed her laptop. 'But there's no point in badges now. We can't be detectives if there's no mystery to solve.'

Kat felt downcast too. No cool badge and no Wolfe & Lamb Detective Agency.

Then she remembered the bare carpet with its smear of toothpaste. Something flamed inside her. Her mum fought injustice every day. Kat wanted to do the same.

'Yes, we can,' she declared. 'What if our gut instinct is right, and Sergeant Singh's is wrong? Ramon could be in hiding. He's clearly witnessed something he shouldn't have. Why else would anyone want to hunt him down and turn him into chopped liver? We owe it to Ramon to find out the truth.'

Harper rallied. 'I agree. What harm can it do? If Ramon returns fit and well from his business trip in a couple of weeks, we'll simply close our case and start work on the Mystery of the Missing Pumpkin.'

Kat laughed. 'Meanwhile, we should investigate why the security cameras have crashed at Avalon Heights. It's a bit convenient that there's no record of the suitcase being spirited away. Oh, I nearly forgot – I have these.'

She took out her phone and showed Harper the CCTV snaps of the man on the deck.

'Ping them over to me. I'll blow them up on my laptop.'

Enlarged, the images were grainy and distorted. A grizzly bear could have been prowling around the deck for all they could see.

'What's that triangle-shaped object the visitor is holding?' Harper asked. 'Either Ramon is doing some midnight gardening, or it's a murderer clutching a weapon.'

Kat leaned closer. 'Can you make it any clearer?'

'No, but my friend Jasper in Connecticut might be able to boost it. He's a Photoshop genius. I'll ask him to try to get more detail on this.'

She pointed to a mottled patch – perhaps a logo or pattern – on the person's shirt. The shape of it reminded Kat of something, but she couldn't think what.

'How did your online investigation go, Harper? Find anything?'

'Not a lot.'

Harper logged on to Ramon's website. 'Our man in Paraguay seems nice but dull. No skeletons anywhere.'

Kat watched as the pictures loaded. Ramon's bird paintings were never going to make it into the National Gallery, but they were perfect for the cards, calendars and magazine articles he showcased on his website.

The 'About Me' page showed him smiling on a beach

with his easel, painting a puffin. Harper gave Kat a summary of his biography.

'Born in Asunción, Paraguay. Only child of a single mum. Obsessed with birds and painting from an early age. Moved to North Carolina, USA, in his teens. Joined the army after school. Left after five years because he wanted to make the planet a better place. Spent eighteen months volunteering on a Pantanel swamp turtle project in Paraguay. It was there that he rediscovered his love of painting birds.'

'That's weird,' said Kat.

Harper looked up. 'What's weird?'

'Edith told me that Maria, her cleaner, spent a year before going to university in Paraguay helping the swamp turtle. When she arrived in Bluebell Bay and found out that Ramon was from Paraguay, she was dying to chat to him. He made so many excuses she gave up. Why would he do that unless . . . ?'

'Unless it wasn't true,' Harper finished.

Kat looked again at the photo of Ramon's likeable, if sad, face. 'What kind of person lies about working for a charity?'

'Someone who wants to seem caring so that more people buy his paintings? Or someone who's spent time doing something he doesn't want anyone to know about. Sitting in prison, say.'

'Prison?'

Harper shrugged. 'It happens. What you said about Maria ties in with something I noticed. See how "Pantanal" is misspelled on Ramon's biography? *Pantanel*. It should have three As. It happens twice more – once in his blog, and another time in an interview with a local paper. Chances are, the reporter was in a hurry and asked him to spell it. Either Ramon can't spell for toffee, or he's never been anywhere near the Pantanal swamp turtles.'

Harper scanned her notes. 'I also listened to an interview with Ramon. The blogger asked about his family in the US. Ramon didn't really answer. He just said, "Some ties go deeper than blood."'

Kat stared at the words scrawled on Harper's yellow pad. 'What did he mean?'

'I'm not sure, because the next moment he was talking about Bluebell Bay. He said he came here because he liked the thought of living in a place where dinosaurs once walked and barn owls still fly.'

'Ghost owls again,' murmured Kat.

'What about them?'

'There's a picture of a white barn owl in Ramon's kitchen. Some people call them ghost or death owls. There's also an owl icon on the laptop he lent me.'

Harper cupped an ear. 'I'm sorry – I thought

you just said you had his laptop.'

'I did.'

'And you were planning to tell me this when exactly?'

'I didn't think it was important,' protested Kat. 'He only lent it to me so I could learn Move 58. That's the Way of the Mongoose technique I was telling you about. There's nothing else on the computer. Ramon erased all the files.'

'You said there's an owl icon,' Harper reminded her. 'Icons are shortcuts to files or programs.'

'Maybe, but it's password-protected.'

Harper gave her a cheeky smile. 'We'll see about that.'

Kat bounced off the chair. 'Forget it. You're not touching it. I'm going out to exercise Charming Outlaw. I have a new game for him.'

Harper said slyly, 'Does the new game have whiskers and a tail?'

Kat went red. 'How did you know?'

'Because a white-and-ginger paw keeps poking out of the holdall on the back of your bike. I can see it through the window, parked against that cherry tree.'

'She's a stray,' admitted Kat. 'Her name's Hero, and she's a gorgeous calico colour. But she has one chewed ear and a kink at the end of her tail where it's been broken, and she's an older cat, and nobody wants those, even when they're perfect, and—'

'Are you trying to break my heart into a million pieces?' Harper said unhappily. 'I'm sure she's lovely, but Dad is allergic.'

'But she's an outdoor cat. If Charming Outlaw takes to her, I think she'd help him as much as he'd help her. Most of his problems stem from him being lonely. If he had a stable companion, he'd be so much happier.'

'Sorry, Kat. Dad would have a fit.'

Kat pretended to be looking for something in her rucksack so Harper wouldn't see her blink away tears. 'I understand. I shouldn't have brought her without checking with you first.'

But Harper hadn't finished.

'Course, if Nettie finds a feral cat hanging around the stable yard when she goes out to feed Charming Outlaw tomorrow morning, what can we do? We'd have to look after the cat then. Nettie would never let a stray go hungry on her watch. Nor would Dad. And if Charming Outlaw likes her she'll have to stay.'

There were footsteps in the hallway. Kat whispered, 'Thanks, Harper. You won't regret it.'

She left her rucksack within reach of Harper's chair. 'For the next hour, I'll be busy with Charming Outlaw. If someone sneaked a peak at Ramon's computer, I'd never know.'

Nettie came in as Kat was strapping on her riding hat. 'Rather you than me, girl. Mind that rascal doesn't kick your head off. The Pocket Rocket's in a right old mood today.'

'Maybe it's because he's lonely?' mused the American girl as if the thought had only just occurred to her.

Pulling on her boots in the hall, Kat smiled to herself when Harper added, 'One of these days, Nettie, we really should think about finding darling Charming Outlaw a friend.'

16

Trojan Horse

Harper fired up Ramon's computer and double-clicked on the death owl icon. When the password box appeared, she ran through the most obvious options: birthdate, pet's name, football teams, Password and 123456. She wasn't expecting a hit, but it was worth a try.

She didn't feel guilty about trying to hack into a private account. If she could use what she knew to help Ramon, she was going to try everything in her coding toolbox.

Thanks to Jasper, one of her father's students at Yale, that was safer than it sounded. Professor Lamb's head was mostly in the Triassic period and he could barely send an email, but he was also a father – a fiercely protective one.

As soon as he'd learned that Harper had a passion for coding, he'd asked Jasper to teach her how to keep secure online. Jasper was a painfully shy teenage prodigy with glasses as thick as a snorkel mask, but he worshipped Professor Lamb. He took this responsibility seriously.

As a result, Harper could whizz around cyberspace as if she wore an invisibility cloak. Among friends, she kidded about hacking, but Jasper had taught her that it was no laughing matter.

Online, she followed a strict code of conduct. She never, ever engaged with real people, and she didn't believe in 'breaking and entering'. She only moved through 'open doors'.

Harper's dream was to become a cyber-security expert or environmental lawyer when she grew up. She figured that if, while she was young, she practised slipping undetected in and out of the websites of companies who were mean to their employees or dumped toxic waste in the Antarctic, it could be an important weapon in her future fight to help innocents trampled on by the cruel, greedy and powerful.

She'd never expected to be using her untested skills a month after her thirteenth birthday.

At the same time, she wasn't surprised. Harper loved quaint, sparkly Bluebell Bay, but it fairly bubbled with intrigue.

'If we're going to solve this mystery while I'm stuck on the sofa in a cast, you'll need to be my eyes and ears around town,' she'd told Kat earlier.

So Kat had described Edith and her ghastly son, Reg, and a peculiar scene in the deli, where she'd gone in search of Sergeant Singh.

According to Kat, three young soldiers had been trying to cheer up Roley George, head chef at the army base.

'He was down in the dumps because he'd been to his aunt's funeral in Newcastle, and it had rained so much he'd caught a cold,' Kat explained. 'They said he was devoted to her and visited her every chance he got. The soldiers were trying to convince Margo to brighten his day by giving him her famous lasagne recipe for the Royal Tank Regiment's anniversary dinner next weekend.'

Harper scoffed. 'What kind of chef can't cook lasagne?'

'It isn't just any lasagne. It's a family secret, passed down for generations.'

'Did she give it to him?'

'Eventually. You could tell she didn't want to. She only felt sorry for him because of his aunt and his cold. What clinched it was when he told her that a super-famous VIP will be attending the dinner. It's rumoured to be Prince William.'

'I love Prince William!' said Harper. 'Although Harry is much more fun.'

'Margo loves Prince William too. Chef Roley told her that if her recipe's a success he'll give her all the credit, and it'll put the Jurassic Fantastic Deli on the map. She gave him the recipe then and there. Everyone cheered, and Chef Roley gave her a hug. It was sweet. Then, suddenly, the laughter stopped and the deli went quiet.'

Harper was agog. 'What happened?'

The way Kat had described it, the deli door had swung open and in stomped Colonel Axel Cunningham, the base commander, like a gunfighter sweeping into a saloon in a western.

'All he did was growl, "Good morning," and the place cleared as if he'd lit a stick of dynamite,' Kat reported. 'The only people left were Margo, the waitress, the guinea-pig lady, Chef Roley, Colonel Cunningham and me. The colonel isn't big, but he made the deli feel small. He's like a walking, talking granite statue. The waitress trembled so much that she spilled his coffee and had to get him another. Before I could escape, Margo told everyone I was the vet's daughter and about Paws and Claws. She even said I was taking care of your horse, Edith's retriever and Ramon's parrot. She was trying to be kind, but it was embarrassing. I was desperate to get away, so I just blurted out that I was looking for Sergeant Singh. Then they all clamoured to know why.'

Harper felt for her. 'What did you say?'

'It was hard to get a word in because Margo and the guinea-pig lady freaked out as soon as I mentioned the police. They were sure I'd lost Ramon's parrot or set fire to Avalon Heights. I had to invent a lame excuse about wanting to ask Sergeant Singh a homework question. The whole time the colonel was glaring at me as if he eats children alive with a side order of nails. Then he barked, "Isn't it school holidays now? Why are you doing homework?"'

'Poor you,' sympathized Harper. 'What a beast.'

'Chef Roley came to my rescue and told them that these days homework happens all year round. While they were distracted, I shot out of the door. Five minutes later, Sergeant Singh found me.'

Harper had taken an intense dislike to Colonel Axel Cunningham without even meeting him. How dare he terrorize Kat? When she got a minute, she was going to do some digging on him.

Now, she turned her attention to Ramon's computer, beginning with the browsing history. In the past twenty-four hours, Kat had searched for Way of the Mongoose videos, the BBC news and a radio play on an

SAS mission. No surprises there.

The earlier search history had been erased, but there was a year-old bookmark for a pest-control company. A red-eyed rat with vampire teeth loomed out of the page, accompanied by shivery type.

ANXIOUS? CALL VANQUISH!

Had Avalon Heights been overrun by vampire rats? If so, Harper supposed they'd been vanquished.

After checking for cookies, she signed into her own email account and downloaded a Trojan horse virus on to Ramon's Surface Book. It wouldn't do it any harm, and it would give her route access to it, allowing her to see if anyone other than Kat was using it remotely. The owl icon bothered her. She couldn't shake the feeling it was watching her.

For added security, she stuck a privacy sticker over the webcam.

Her phone pinged. She had an app set up to alert her to any activity spotted by the Trojan horse. Harper was startled to see that in the two minutes since she'd installed the virus, her Trojan horse had already picked up movement – from another Trojan horse.

Had Ramon put it on the Surface Book to protect Kat, or had someone been tracking him before his disappearance? Who was that someone? A fraudster? A rival bird watcher? British or US Intelligence?

Kat's riding hat bobbed past the window. Harper gulped. If she was caught red-handed installing a virus on Ramon's computer, it could put a strain on their brand-new friendship.

Fortunately, Nettie called out and Kat was diverted to the kitchen.

Harper was torn. If she told Kat about the second Trojan, she'd have to admit how she'd found out about it. If, however, she left her own stalking horse on Ramon's computer, she'd have access to it. She could try to find out who was tracking it – a stranger or Ramon himself. She'd be keeping Kat safe.

When Kat came in with a warm apple pie wrapped in foil, Harper was practising Mandarin characters with a fountain pen. She looked up with a smile.

'How did it go with Charming Outlaw and Hero?'

Kat grinned. 'There was a lot of hissing and snorting, but I think it'll work out.'

Harper put down her pen. 'I've been thinking. How about giving our opponent – whoever we're up against in our quest to find Ramon – a code name? We could call him or her Arch Villain Number One.'

Kat looked at her. 'We're really doing this, aren't

we? We're really going to investigate what's going on at Avalon Heights.'

It was only then that it hit Harper that their mystery train was about to leave the station. If she didn't leap off now, it would be too late.

'We're really doing this,' she heard herself say.

'I'll report back tomorrow,' said Kat. 'Same time, same place.'

That evening, Kat was dead to the world by 9 p.m. She slept the dreamless sleep of the good, blissfully unaware that she'd attracted the notice of one of the UK's most deadly men.

Shortly after midnight, Arch Villain Number One turned into Summer Street. He chain-smoked in the shadows as he stared up at the dark windows of number 5.

No human noticed him come and go. He was as stealthy as a death owl.

But Tiny saw him. Growling softly, the Savannah cat watched from the dormer window until the assassin crushed out his cigarette and melted into the night. Tiny glanced at the sleeping girl. Springing on to the futon, he snuggled up as close as he dared.

Kat slumbered on. Tiny kept one eye open.

17

Hat Trick

'You'll never guess what's happened!' Edith called from the sofa when Kat returned from a beach walk with Toby on Saturday morning.

Kat hung the lead on the coat rack. 'I think I might. Bluebell Bay is buzzing with the news about Prince William being guest of honour at the Tank Regiment's dinner next weekend. It's supposed to be a secret, but Mum says it's all anyone can talk about. The woman who runs the sailing club told her that Will – and Kate, if she joins him – will bring tourists flocking to Bluebell Bay!'

'Really?' Edith pursed her lips. 'I can't abide the royals. Except for the Queen. I do have time for the Queen.' She added hopefully, 'Kat, help yourself to a lemonade if you have a minute to spare. I wasn't referring to Prince William. There's been a new development in our case.'

Kat was confused. Had Edith somehow found out about the Wolfe & Lamb investigation? Did she want to join them?

'Our case?'

'The Oxford Street Phantom Mystery, of course.'

'Oh, that one.' Kat was relieved. 'Yes, I do have time, and I'd love a lemonade. Thanks, Edith.'

The sharp, cold fizz was exactly what she needed. Her fossil-hunting expedition with Toby had been fun but tiring. While sipping her drink, she studied a photo on the fridge of Reg and his giant pumpkin. There was, Kat thought uncharitably, a similarity between the two. They were both orange, for one thing.

'What's the startling development?' she asked Edith as she flopped down on the sofa.

Edith handed over Ramon's computer. Kat had left an audiobook playing for her while she was out walking Toby. She'd convinced herself that Ramon wouldn't mind. He and Edith were friends, after all. Added to which, Edith was proving a quick learner on the laptop. She'd spent most of the past hour surfing the net.

'Breaking news on the BBC,' Edith announced. 'They've found a hat on Oxford Street.'

'Isn't that like saying they've found a bee in a hive, or a fish in the sea?' Kat said lightly. 'Aren't there trillions of hats on Oxford Street?'

She was finding it hard to be serious. She'd been on cloud nine ever since she'd woken to discover a Tiny-shaped hollow in her duvet. By then, the Savannah had gone AWOL, but there was no doubt he'd slept there.

Kat was elated. It was the first sign that she might one day get through to him. She'd left some chicken treats on the window ledge to say thanks.

There were other reasons to be cheerful too. Harper had messaged to say that Nettie's reaction to finding a stray curled up in the Pocket Rocket's stable had been positive.

N told Dad that Charming Outlaw's taken a shine to the cat. Long as she keeps away from my father and his allergies, she can stay. I've named her Hero! Ha ha! xx

After breakfast, Kat had gone over to the animal clinic to play with Bailey. He'd objected so noisily to staying in the aviary that Dr Wolfe had allowed him to sit on the reception desk during the day. He loved greeting each new client. They were less sure about him.

'By the way, is there anyone on board who knows how to fly a plane?' he'd demanded as Kat walked in.

'Please can he be my new assistant?' asked a woman perched on a large suitcase. 'Any bird that can quote from *Airplane!* is a star in my eyes.'

'Tina!' cried Kat, rushing forward to hug the veterinary nurse she'd last seen in London. 'What are you doing here? If you promise to come and work with my mum in Bluebell Bay, I'll ask Bailey if he'll assist you on reception – at least until his owner comes home.'

No sooner had she wished it than it happened. When Dr Wolfe found that Tina Chung had quit her miserable job at Nash & Craw Premium Pet Care, she hired her on the spot.

Better still, Tina was going to move into their spare room until she found a place of her own. Kat hoped that took forever. Her mum was a first-class vet, but a hopeless cook. Tina, on the other hand, could rustle up Malaysian laksa and black-bean stir-fries with the best of them.

At Kittiwake Cottage, Edith broke into Kat's happy reverie. 'You don't seem very interested in the Phantom. I suppose it's daft of me to get caught up in these things. It's not as if they're any of my business.'

Something in the sag of her shoulders tore at Kat. She thought of the Glebe Gardens website, the residents smiling thinly over their poached eggs.

'I'm extremely interested,' she assured Edith. 'And getting caught up in mysteries is not daft in the least. Me and Harper do it all the time.'

She tapped the screen and it came to life.

'There's the link,' said Edith a little impatiently as Kat hesitated.

Her grandfather was on the front page again, being interviewed about cyber security. The prime minister, sour as last month's milk, stood beside the Dark Lord.

Kat dragged her gaze away. She pressed play on a video headlined 'TRILBY HAT CLUE IN OXFORD STREET PHANTOM MYSTERY'.

A cocky reporter recapped on the story so far. He revealed the latest twist with the ghoulish enthusiasm of a conjuror showing off an assistant he's sawn in half.

'*The clue that might hold the key to the identity of the so-called Oxford Street Phantom was discovered this morning in the lost-property box at John Lewis.*'

He thrust the microphone at the store spokeswoman. '*Why did it take twenty-four hours for your management to report the hat to the police?*'

'*The trilby was handed in to a junior assistant shortly after the man collapsed outside our store,*' she explained. '*With all the drama, nobody understood its significance. We stand ready to assist detectives in any way we can. Our thoughts and prayers are with the unknown victim of this concerning event.*'

The reporter faced the camera with a sombre stare. '*If any member of the public has information that could lead to the arrest of what detectives now believe was an audacious abduction, or if you recognize this hat, contact this number . . .'*

A blue-grey trilby flashed up on the screen.

Kat and Edith gripped hands.

'That could be Eric Newbolt's trilby!' gasped Edith. 'I mean, it's not, but it could be. It's the same blue-grey tweed. A Dorset milliner makes them.'

'That looks like Ramon Corazón's hat!' cried Kat. 'It's the exact same shape and size!'

'It can't be Ramon's,' said Edith. 'He's in Paraguay. You told me that yourself. Aren't you pet-sitting his parrot?'

'Well, it's definitely not Mr Newbolt's hat,' Kat told her. 'I saw him going into the newsagent while I was out walking Toby.'

Edith gave her a curious glance. 'It's interesting that you made the leap from the Phantom to Ramon. Do you have any reason to believe that he's not in South America?'

Kat jumped to her feet and grabbed her rucksack. 'Sorry, Edith, I have to fly. There's something I need to do.'

Edith was taken by surprise. 'What's going on? Is Ramon in some kind of trouble? You can tell me – I won't breathe a word.'

Kat could hardly take in what Edith was saying. The dark possibilities were crowding her mind again. All she could think about was getting to Paradise House to talk to Harper.

'I have a hunch. It's probably nothing. Have a good day.'

She was halfway across town on her bike before she remembered she'd forgotten Ramon's laptop. Now she wouldn't be able to get it until Monday. She debated whether to go back for it, but what she had to tell Harper was too important. Edith would take care of it, she was sure.

Kat put it out of her mind and pedalled faster.

18

Bullseye

The parcel lay on the only corner of the dining table not occupied by the model dinosaur.

'It's Private and Confidential,' said Kat.

'It's evidence,' insisted Harper.

'We don't know that. I was sure the trilby on the news was Ramon's because it was frayed on the brim, as if a mouse had nibbled it, but now I'm having doubts. Maybe we should wait a few days before we open the package. There are a hundred reasons why Ramon might not have called. He could have had his phone stolen.'

'Then he'd have borrowed another one or emailed,' Harper told her. 'What if you're right and Ramon *is* the Oxford Street Phantom? We know from our timeline that it's possible. The last person to see him alive—'

'That we know of,' interjected Kat.

'. . . was Margo. She told Sergeant Singh that Ramon

popped into the deli just as she was closing on Wednesday night and bought some OJ—'

'OJ?'

'Orange juice, and his favourite protein bars for the train journey. After that, this is what we have.' Harper took out her notepad.

> **Wed: 11.26 p.m. – Ramon gets threatening phone call.**
> **Just after midnight on Weds – CCTV shows person on deck at AH.**
> **Thurs: 9.39 a.m. – Man collapses on Oxford St, London.**
> **Thurs: 10.45 a.m. approx – Kat finds unlocked door and suitcase at AH.**

'We should call Sergeant Singh,' said Kat.

'And say what? That you saw a hat that looks like ten thousand other hats on the news and now you're certain that Mr Corazón has been kidnapped on Oxford Street by fake paramedics?'

Kat slumped in her chair. 'Do you have a better plan?'

'We open the package. If there's something illegal in it, we'll take it to the police.'

'What sort of illegal?' Kat asked warily.

'Anthrax?' suggested Harper.

Kat was even less keen on looking inside the parcel then. She had no desire to be infected by deadly bacteria, and anyway it seemed wrong to open Ramon's private post. Yet what choice did they have? They needed answers.

Harper took some scissors out of a nearby drawer and sliced open the parcel with the precision of a surgeon. She pushed it towards Kat. 'You look first.'

'No, you look first!'

'You're the one Ramon trusted with his house and his parrot. I think it should be you.'

Still thinking about the anthrax, Kat used the tongs from the ice bucket to withdraw the contents of the parcel. There were only two items: an old black-and-white photograph and a copy of an official document.

A pink Post-it note was stuck to the photo. Two words were scrawled across it:

REMEMBER THIS?

Both girls spoke at once.

'What does it mean?'

'Is it a threat, or a question from a friend?'

'Who do you think wrote it?'

'Do you suppose it's from the man who left the threatening message?'

When they ran out of steam, they studied the yellowing photo. It showed six athletic young men, beers in hand, laughing on a boat. A couple had fishing rods. All had close-shaven military haircuts, and two wore US Army baseball caps.

Though they were turned towards the photographer, some leaned across others or wore sunglasses or had their caps pulled down low. Only three faces were clearly visible and another was partially visible. That one belonged to a youthful Ramon.

In the picture, he wore a white T-shirt. Someone – possibly the author of the pink Post-it note – had taken a red Sharpie and drawn a bullseye on the photo.

Over Ramon's heart.

'That's creepy,' said Kat.

Harper picked up the blue document. 'So is this. It's a US death certificate for someone called Vaughan Carter. Issued in Austin, Texas, three years ago. Cause of death: cardiac arrest. I wonder if he's one of the men in the photo, though they don't really look like the heart-attack kind.'

She pulled her laptop towards her with her right hand. The left was still bandaged. 'I'll do a quick search. See what comes up on him.'

A minute later, she had it. There were a few brief messages of condolence in the classified section of an Austin paper, dated 5th March, ten days after the date on the death certificate. The first was from Vaughan's family:

> Taken from us far too soon. Our hearts are
> broken. We'll miss and love you always,
> Annie, Jack and Justin xxx

The second was from a rowing club. And the third was anonymous:

> All 4 One, One 4 All. RIP, brother.

Something about it reminded Kat of Ramon's comment to the blogger: *Some ties go deeper than blood.*

She turned over the photo. 'There's a date on the back – 1985 – and a name: Evan Ross. Do you think that means he was the photographer? Maybe he sent Ramon the parcel to remind him of the good old days.'

'Possibly,' said Harper, 'although they can't have been that good if he's the one who drew a target on Ramon's heart. Also, you said the courier was a local guy. If Evan or his buddies mailed the photo from the US, they'd likely have used FedEx, DHL or UPS. Can you make out anything else?'

'There's a faded stamp: *Crisp Photographic* . . . *San . . . onio, TX.*'

'San Antonio, Texas,' finished Harper, typing as she spoke.

A San Antonio newspaper article dated 25th February, two years ago, filled the screen. A man with a determined chin grinned from the inset photo.

LOCAL HERO HONOURED
AFTER SUDDEN DEATH

The Texas Tigers yesterday paid tribute to their Little League soccer coach when they unveiled the Evan Ross Player of the Year trophy.

The Tigers are still in mourning after losing Coach Ross to a suspected stroke last month. Ross, 54, who received a Medal of Honor for heroism in combat in Afghanistan in the mid-eighties, had struggled after his best friend and fellow Green Beret, Tony Baranello, suffered a cardiac arrest six weeks ago.

'When Tony passed, it ripped the life out of Evan,' said his widow, Nancy. 'They'd already been through so much with losing Tony's twin, Mario, in Afghanistan in '86. Evan never talked about it, but what happened over there, what went wrong, haunted him.

'Coaching Little League soccer and hiking our country's great trails with Tony was Evan's salvation. He'd be proud to have a trophy with his name on it.'

Kat picked up the photo of the men in the boat. 'These two are almost identical, so they must be Tony and Mario. And the guy with the square chin is Coach Evan Ross. I wonder what went wrong on the mission in Afghanistan.'

'I wonder what went wrong *afterwards*,' responded Harper. 'Maybe that's the link between everyone in the picture: they were in the army together. Maybe even in Afghanistan. We know that Ramon was in the military, and this tall guy with broad shoulders in the US Army baseball cap could be Vaughan Carter. He looks like a rower.'

'It's weird that Vaughan, Evan and Tony had cardiac arrests and strokes in their early fifties,' said Kat. 'They look so fit in this picture. Maybe Mario being killed and whatever happened in Afghanistan put too much strain on their bodies as they got older.'

Harper peered at the photo. 'Probably did, but they'd still have been healthier than a lot of people. Vaughan was in a rowing club, and Evan and Tony hiked the great trails.'

'Evan also coached football,' added Kat.

'We call it soccer,' Harper said with a smile. 'American football is football.' She tapped the photo with a pen. 'It's the math here that bothers me.'

'You mean the maths?'

'You say tomarto, I say tomayto,' quipped Harper, and they giggled.

Harper sobered. 'Say we're right, and this photo shows Ramon and his friends when they were young and in the army. And say Ramon does turn out to be the Oxford Street Phantom, who supposedly also had a heart attack.'

Kat saw where she was going. 'That means that five out of six friends – Ramon, Mario, Tony, Evan and Vaughan – are either dead or missing. How spooky is that!'

'Don't forget the person behind the camera,' Harper reminded her. 'There were seven on the boat. It's odd that Evan's name is written on the back of the picture if he didn't take it, but I suppose that back in those days digital photography didn't exist. It's possible that the photographer had the photo shop make copies for each of his mates.'

'They look so happy,' said Kat. 'Ramon must have been in pieces if he lost four friends. Maybe he moved to Bluebell Bay to start a new life.'

Harper frowned. 'Judging by the target over his heart, his old life followed him here. I wonder if someone had a grudge against him.'

She put the photo on the coffee table. 'I'll make a hi-res scan of this and send it to Jasper. He might be able to use face-mapping software to identify the men we're not sure about, or track down the boat's owner. It would also help if we could find out how and why Mario was killed in Afghanistan.'

Her phone pinged. 'How's that for timing? Jasper just emailed.'

Kat looked up. 'Can we trust him?'

'I'd trust him with my life. The FBI has Jasper on speed dial. That's what a genius he is. Mostly he ignores them, but if it's a mission he believes in he'll lend a hand. Let's see what he's got.'

Hey, Ace,

Had to get funky with the pixels on this beauty. Fun project. First off, Ramon's guest at Avalon Heights was human! Wearing British Army camo and carrying a garden trowel or a weapon with a triangular blade.

Tread carefully on this one, Ace. Don't run before you can walk – especially now you're injured!

May the Force Be with You!

J

'*British* Army camo?' said Kat.

Not for the first time, she had the sense that they were blindly poking at a hornet's nest.

'Even if it does turn out to be Ramon on the deck, star-gazing, surely he'd be in one of his old US Army outfits, not British camouflage?' said Harper.

'What if it's not him?' asked Kat. 'What if the intruder is a British soldier? He could even be the soldier who left the threatening message. When Ramon didn't pick up the phone, he might have decided to threaten him face to face.'

Harper opened the attachment sent by Jasper. 'Let's take a look at the new, improved CCTV images.'

Her mentor was highly skilled, but there was not a lot he could do about the fact that the man was standing with his back to the security camera.

To Kat, who'd been hoping for miracles, it was deeply disappointing.

The living-room door opened, and in came Nettie. Before they could hide the photo, she'd picked it up. 'Who are these people? Why does that man have a target on his chest?'

'It's a long, sad story, and Kat finds it difficult to talk about,' Harper said in a mournful tone.

Nettie handed the photo back at once. 'Sorry, Kat, I didn't mean to be insensitive.'

Kat was embarrassed too. She stuffed the documents into her rucksack. 'It's fine, Nettie. Don't worry about it.'

'Can I make it up to you by offering you some carrot cake?'

'Thanks, Nettie, but I promised my mum and Tina I'd meet them for a walk to Durdle Door.'

'How lovely. It's one of the Jurassic Coast's most beautiful places.'

As the door shut behind her, Harper let out a breath. 'Phew! That was close. Kat, what are we going to do if a soldier or officer from the army base is involved?'

'If it involves the military, we're out of our depth,' said Kat. 'We should phone Sergeant Singh.'

This time, Harper didn't try to stop her.

19

No Mystery

'Sergeant Singh, it's Kat Wolfe. Please don't hang up.'

'Yes, Miss Wolfe,' he said with a distinct lack of enthusiasm. 'What can I do for you?'

'Sergeant Singh, this is going to sound fantastical, but you have to believe us. Me and Harper Lamb – she's on speakerphone, by the way – are ninety-nine point nine per cent certain we know the identity of the Oxford Street Phantom.'

Sergeant Singh groaned into the receiver. 'Miss Wolfe, what did I tell you about wasting police time?'

'I would never dream of wasting police time,' Kat said indignantly.

'Is that so? You may have forgotten how, only yesterday, you dragged me up the cliff path on a wild suitcase chase, but I can assure you that it's etched on my mind for all eternity. My favourite part was when you tried to persuade me that a killer had gone berserk with tomato sauce.'

'That was an honest mistake,' said Kat, annoyed. 'This is life and death. It's a matter of national security.'

He laughed. 'Does it involve Marmite?'

'Sergeant Singh, if you won't take me seriously, I'm going to dial 999 and find a proper detective who will.'

The chuckling stopped, but there was a smile in his voice. 'My humble apologies. Go ahead and spill the beans. My pen is at the ready. I can't wait to call Scotland Yard and inform them of the identity of the Oxford Street Phantom. Let me guess: it's Ramon Corazón.'

'I – How did you know? Have you heard something?'

'Indeed I have. I've heard enough about secret cover-up crews and psychos leaving messages about chopped liver to last me a lifetime. In your mystery-novel universe, Kat Wolfe, it's only a small step from there to having Ramon be whisked away by kidnappers on Oxford Street.'

'Whether you like it or not, the timeline works,' Kat said stubbornly. 'If Ramon caught the 6.20 a.m. train from Wool to London Waterloo on Thursday, it's possible for him to have been on Oxford Street at 9.39 a.m., which is when the man they're calling the Phantom collapsed outside John Lewis department store.'

'You're sure about that?' asked Sergeant Singh.

'Positive. We checked, and there were no delays that day.'

'Just because the 6.20 a.m. train from Wool reached London Waterloo on time doesn't mean Ramon was on it. In fact, I can guarantee he wasn't.'

'How?' Harper said disbelievingly.

'Because, Miss Lamb, at around 11 a.m. on Thursday, when your friend was feeding the parrot at Avalon Heights, Eric Newbolt passed Ramon on the field behind the church. So, you see, even if Ramon had wings, it's impossible for him to have been in London at 9.39 a.m. and back in Bluebell Bay, some three and a half hours distant, by 11 a.m.'

That single sentence brought all of Wolfe & Lamb's grand theories crashing down. They were crushed.

Harper recovered first. 'That was the morning the sea fog swallowed Bluebell Bay. My dad said it's one of the thickest in the history of the town. Could Mr Newbolt have mistaken Ramon for somebody else?'

'It's a fair question. The fog was a proper pea-souper. When Ramon stepped from the mist, Mr Newbolt admitted he got quite a fright. He made a quip about mad dogs and Englishmen going out in the midday mist. But he knows Ramon too well for it to be a case of mistaken identity. From a distance, they look similar – same height, same trilby, black hair with a hint of silver.

People often comment on it. I don't think either of them considers it a compliment.'

He paused to allow this to sink in.

'And another thing, you can stop stressing about Ramon. Mrs Truesdale had an email from him this morning. His business in Paraguay is going so well that he's extending his stay. His main concern seemed to be your Paws and Claws agency, Miss Wolfe. He'd heard reports that you're unreliable.'

Kat was outraged. If Ramon had concerns, why hadn't he messaged her?

'That's a big fat lie,' Harper said loyally. 'Kat takes care of my horse, and she's the best animal whisperer I've ever seen.'

'You've known her for *three* days,' said Sergeant Singh. 'Who knows what the fourth will bring.'

Harper refused to give up. 'If there's nothing suspicious going on at Avalon Heights, why was a soldier creeping about on Ramon's deck at midnight on the evening before he disappeared?'

'I'm not going to ask how you know that,' the policeman said pointedly. 'Not that it's any of your business, Miss Lamb, but Ramon hosts a birdwatching club popular with many of the soldiers. There's every chance that a couple of them were up at Avalon Heights for a last meal before he left.

'Let's be clear. There is NO mystery here. None whatsoever. Which is a pity, because now I have to inform your parents about this call.'

'There's no mystery *and* he's going to complain to your mum and my dad?' fumed Harper. 'How is that fair?'

'It isn't,' said Kat. 'But I suppose in his job he needs hard evidence. Luckily, we don't have to stick to the rulebook like real detectives do. We can go wherever the feelings in our bones lead us.'

Harper sat up. 'You're right. If there's no mystery, why would someone send Ramon a photo with a bullseye drawn on it? And why the note: "Remember this?"'

'Oh, Harper, I feel terrible. It's my fault that Ramon never received the photo. Because of me, he's on the other side of the world with no idea that somebody wants him dead. We have to try to warn him. At least we know that when he wrote to Margo this morning, he was alive.'

Harper snorted. 'Has Sergeant Singh even seen this supposed email? Maybe half the town are involved in whatever is going on, including Mr "Sour Puss" Newbolt and Edith's cleaner. What did you say her name was?'

'Maria.'

'I'm adding them all to our list of suspects. I'll put Ramon's cleaner on it too. We'll find out her name. Maybe she lied about having a family emergency. We'll call her "Maid B" and Ramon's midnight visitor "Soldier A". Every suspect is guilty until proven otherwise.'

'I agree,' said Kat. 'Until we've seen proof that Ramon's alive with our own eyes, he's still missing and still a target.'

There was steel in Harper's gaze. 'Until then, our mission stays the same. We figure out the names of the men in the photo and how they're connected. Then we find out who sent the parcel and why. We'd better move. The clock is ticking.'

20

The Exterminator

When the alarm went off, Darren Weebly, owner and proprietor of Vanquish Pest Control, bolted upright, grabbed a magnifying mirror and performed the same hopeful routine he did every morning. He ran a bear-sized paw over his scalp to check for prickles.

Miracle Sprout, which he applied liberally each night, guaranteed a full head of hair in '*100 Days or Your Money Back!*'

Three months on, Darren had yet to see a result. If it hadn't been for the product's unadvertised fringe benefits – a rich (some might say 'orange') tan and a staggering spurt in eyebrow and muscle growth – he'd have already been plotting revenge on its maker.

He hoped that wouldn't become

necessary, because Reg Chalmers, the manufacturer of Miracle Sprout Patented Baldness Cure and Miracle Veg Compost, was also Darren's golden goose. When business was slow in the pest-control world, Reg employed Darren as a bounty hunter. If customers quibbled about paying because the promised 'miracles' of hair growth or giant vegetables hadn't come to pass, Darren bullied or bashed them into parting with their cash.

A couple of years earlier, Reg had hired Darren to steal his own prize-winning pumpkin. It was an insurance scam. For a man of Darren's talents, the job was easier than falling off a ladder. He and a forklift-driver mate had loaded the great pumpkin into a van on the last night of the County Fair. The security guard in charge of the vegetable tent had snored through the whole thing.

The next day, Darren had driven the pumpkin to Sussex, where another man who grew outsized vegetables had taken it off his hands and won the Grand Jury prize at his own County Fair.

Unluckily, a bird watcher out photographing owls had witnessed the theft.

For reasons of his own, Ramon Corazón had kept quiet about it for two years. Then a week ago, he'd got wind of Reg's plan to force his mum out of her home.

The bird watcher, who was a friend of Edith's, had

hinted that unless Reg kept his greasy mitts off Kittiwake Cottage, he'd tell the insurance company and County Fair that Reg and his accomplices had defrauded them out of £100,000.

Reg had gone ballistic. He'd hired Darren again – this time to threaten Ramon Corazón with death and destruction if he ever breathed a word about Reg stealing his own pumpkin.

Irritatingly, the bird watcher had been out or asleep when Darren called. Leaving a message had not been nearly so satisfying. Now Ramon was away for a couple of weeks in darkest Peru. Or was it Panama? Darren planned to ring again. Infuriatingly, it would have to wait.

As Darren stared in the mirror, wondering if his head would forever remain as smooth as a snooker ball, his phone began playing the theme music from *Jaws*.

When Darren saw who was calling, his ulcer began to throb. He'd recently done a pest-control job at the army base. For a few days, he'd been made to feel like the most important cog in the military machine. The top brass were determined to get the base ship-shape for the Royal Tank Regiment's anniversary dinner, and Vanquish Pest Control was key to that plan.

'Can't have Prince William finding a mouse whisker in the soup,' said one soldier with a psychotic laugh.

To Darren's surprise, one of most important men at the base had gone out of his way to take care of him during his time there. He'd even suggested that Darren be given a medal for excellent service.

That was who was ringing now.

Darren was afraid to pick up the phone. Was he in trouble? Had he missed some weevils in the flour? Were a plague of moths devouring the soldiers' kit?

But the military man was positively chipper. 'Good morning, Mr Weebly, sir. I hope I haven't woken you up.'

How Darren loved being called 'sir'.

'Not at all, sir. Been up for hours, sir,' he lied.

'Excellent. Damn fine job you did for us at the base, Mr Weebly. What a pro you are. So skilful and efficient. Man, you have some nerve, doing what you do.'

It was the highest praise Darren had ever received, and he wished he was recording the call so he could play it every day for the rest of his life. 'Thanks, sir. Appreciate the feedback. All in a day's work.'

'Credit where credit is due, Mr Weebly. Now I'll get straight to the point. I have a private job that needs doing. It requires a true professional. Someone discreet, who can keep a cool head. Naturally, I thought of you.'

'Look no further,' Darren said eagerly. 'I'm your man.'

'That's what I thought. Am I correct in assuming that Vanquish Pest Control deals with large pests as well as small ones?'

'Yes, sir, we do,' Darren said proudly. 'We murder moles and rout rabbits.'

As soon as the words left his mouth, he knew he'd said the wrong thing.

A freezing silence echoed down the line.

'I've made a mistake,' the man said at last. 'You're not right for the job after all.'

That's when Darren realized that the call he'd been waiting for all his life – the one that would lead to him leaving the pest-control world behind and becoming the gangster of his dreams – had finally arrived.

'I am the right man, sir,' he almost shouted. 'I am. I will deal with anyone or anything. No questions asked. That's why my clients call me the Exterminator.'

The man gave a dry laugh. 'OK, Exterminator, the job's simple. It's a matter of neutralizing a threat. I'd do it myself, but we're working round the clock preparing for the Tank Regiment's anniversary dinner.'

Darren was shaking with excitement. 'This threat – would you like it vanquished, sir?'

'Vanquished?'

'Eliminated! Ground into the dirt! Chopped up like liver!'

'Nothing so drastic at the moment –' the soldier chuckled – 'but it's great to know there are options. At this stage, all I want you to do is have a firm word with a troublemaker who's been spreading lies around Bluebell Bay. I want you to make it clear that if they continue there will be consequences.'

'Consider it done, sir. Give me a name and an address, and I'll neutralize the threat as soon as possible.'

'Good stuff. The target should be easy to find because her mother is the town veterinary surgeon. They live next door to the clinic. This girl also has a pet-sitting business – Paws and Claws.'

Darren tried not to panic. People called women 'girls' all the time. Didn't mean they were *actual* girls.

'How old is this girl?' he asked, trying to keep the tremor from his voice. 'Teens? Twenties? Thirties?'

The soldier gave a psychopathic laugh. 'Even easier. She's twelve.'

'*Twelve?*'

Darren had never been troubled with a conscience, but he did draw the line at frightening children. That was partly because it seemed wrong to pick on someone a third of one's size, and partly because he'd had a phobia about girls ever since one had beaten him in a fight, aged ten, with a roundhouse kick. But he wasn't about to admit that to the man on the other end of the line.

'Problem, Exterminator?' asked the soldier.

Darren wiped the sweat from his forehead. 'No problem, sir. I'll message when the threat has been neutralized.'

'Can't wait. The target's name is Wolfe. Kat Wolfe.'

As soon as Darren put the phone down, he started trembling. It was something to do with the girl's name: Kat Wolfe. It gave him a feeling of foreboding. The pets, too, were a worry. Cats, in particular, had always loathed him.

Finally, he had a brainwave.

In Hollywood, there was a saying: 'Never work with children or animals.' The Exterminator wholeheartedly agreed. Children and animals had minds of their own, and a mind of one's own was a dangerous thing.

No, the best method of destroying Kat Wolfe was to do it remotely, in a way guaranteed to hurt her most.

He'd go after her mother.

21

Pleading the Fifth

'I don't understand it,' said Dr Wolfe. 'You've been a pet-sitter for three days. Not three months or years, three *days*. Two and a half, if we're being technical. How have you managed to get into so much trouble?'

Kat did her best to appear contrite while saying as little as possible. In America, Harper had told her, it was called 'Pleading the Fifth'.

'The Fifth Amendment of the US Constitution gives you the right to decline to answer questions if the answers might incriminate you,' she'd explained.

That might have worked with the Connecticut cops or in a US court of law, but it was not working well with Kat's mum. Apart from the time when the Dark Lord had tried to talk to her from the window of his limousine in London, Kat could not ever recall seeing her mother so angry.

'When Sergeant Singh first called me, I was sure it was a case of mistaken identity,' Dr Wolfe ranted. 'The Kat I know wouldn't waste police time with conspiracy theories about bloodstained T-shirts and mystery men snatching suitcases. The Kat I know wouldn't badger Sergeant Singh with ludicrous claims about Mr Corazón being the Phantom of Oxford Street. And, to top it all, I hear you've accused a birdwatching soldier of wanting to attack him.'

Kat hoped the lecture was over, but her mum was just getting warmed up.

'What's going on, Katarina? You've always been so sensible.'

Had she? Kat tried to remember. It didn't matter now. If she'd learned anything from adventure novels it was that being sensible was no use at all in a crisis.

Ramon was a grown man who, under normal circumstances, was more than capable of taking care of himself. But nothing about this situation was normal. Somebody, somewhere, wanted Ramon dead or gone. And because Kat had taken his parcel he didn't know that. He didn't have his guard up.

Which is why Kat had to be the one to save him, even if it meant keeping a secret from the mother she loved.

She bowed her head. 'I'm sorry that Sergeant Singh upset you, Mum.'

'Sergeant Singh hasn't upset me. *You've* upset me.'

'Honestly, Mum, he's exaggerating. The first time I went to Avalon Heights, it was foggy, and Ramon had left the door open. I was worried there'd been a burglary, so I reported it to Sergeant Singh. He came with me to check it out and said I'd done the right thing.'

'I suppose you did,' her mum admitted. 'But how are you going to explain away the bloodstained shirt, the Oxford Street Phantom and the soldier with the trowel?'

'The tomato sauce really did look like blood, and the trilby on the news was the same shape and colour as Ramon's. Looking back, it does seem stupid.'

Kat left out the part about the soldier. She apologized profusely twice more in the hope her mum would forgive her, but Dr Wolfe was not in a forgiving mood.

'It's all very well being sorry, Kat, but you – *we* – are now the talk of the town. Bluebell Bay Animal Clinic has barely been open two weeks. People have to feel able to trust their new vet. They're not going to do that if their vet's daughter is spreading rumours and gossiping to her friend about people's private business.'

Kat tried to speak, but her mum hadn't finished.

'Do you know who I blame for this? Harper Lamb.

I'd have expected more from a professor's daughter. Obviously, she's a terrible influence.'

Now Kat was furious. 'Harper is *not* a terrible influence. She's the kindest, smartest, most fun girl I've ever met.'

Her mum gave a disbelieving laugh. 'You've known her for *three* days!'

'Yes, and she's the best friend I've ever had,' Kat said passionately, 'apart from you.'

There was a long silence as both mum and daughter remembered that, when all was said and done, that's what they were: best friends.

Dr Wolfe counted to ten before giving Kat a hug.

'I'm sorry, darling. No mother wants to get a call from the police about her daughter. It frightened me. As if that wasn't enough, I've had Margo, the neighbours and, worst of all, a bitterly gleeful Mr Newbolt demanding to know why you'd dragged Sergeant Singh up to Avalon Heights.'

Kat realized that if she and Harper weren't careful they could jeopardize Dr Wolfe's reputation, and that would be unforgivable.

Somehow she had to walk the tightrope between protecting her mother and saving Ramon.

'I'm sorry too, Mum. I couldn't bear it if people thought badly of you because of something I did. You're the best vet in the world. I promise to stay out of Sergeant Singh's way.'

'And you'll put an end to your Paws and Claws agency?'

'What – stop pet-sitting? I can't abandon Edith and Toby. They need me. Edith's mean son keeps telling her that she'll be free as a bird if she moves out of her home and goes into one of those places where people watch TV till they die.'

Ellen Wolfe abhorred cruelty to children, animals and the elderly above all else, but she did her best to be diplomatic.

'I'm sure Edith's son loves her and only wants what's best for her, but, no, you can't possibly abandon Edith and Toby. And the parrot needs you until Ramon comes home. But that's it. No other pets.'

'What about Harper? She has two broken legs. I can't just dump her and Charming Outlaw.'

'From what I hear, the horse is more outlaw than charm,' was Dr Wolfe's wry reply. 'How's he been behaving?'

'He was just lonely. Now that he has Hero for company, he's soooo much more relaxed.'

The mention of the calico stray had exactly the effect Kat was hoping for.

'Yes, it was very kind of the Lambs to take Hero. I

suppose you can't abandon Harper and her horse – not while she's still in plaster.'

'Thanks, Mum!'

Dr Wolfe shot her a look. 'So long as we're clear that you're not taking on a single other animal – not until you've proved that you can be responsible. Then we'll see.'

'If you say so, Mum.' Kat sighed, although in truth she was relieved. Being a detective as well as a pet-sitter was a time-consuming business. She'd been wondering how she'd manage if she had an influx of new clients. Just this morning she'd turned down a hamster.

'And another thing – you're not to go near Ramon's house. There's no need, Kat, not with Bailey ruling the roost at the practice.'

Kat thought fast. Returning to Avalon Heights was her best chance of finding more clues.

'But what about the plants, Mum? I promised Ramon I'd water them. There are lettuces and herbs and flowers on the deck.'

Her mum gave her a searching stare. 'You're sure it's necessary? They'll die if you don't?'

'Lives are at stake if I don't get to Avalon Heights.'

'All right, but only if I go with you. Tomorrow afternoon would be best. Even Bluebell Bay must be quiet on a Sunday.'

22

Option Thirteen

Dr Wolfe stepped out on to the deck and spread her arms wide, as if she were on the prow of a cruise ship sailing forth across the shining ocean.

'So this is how the other half live! And a Jacuzzi too!'

Kat followed her with a dripping watering can. 'Told you it was special.'

'Yes, but now I see how spooky it must have been when you were here alone in the fog. No wonder your imagination ran away with you . . . Kat, would it speed things up if I tend to the flowerboxes while you look after the lettuce in the kitchen? Goodness, these are glorious dahlias. I wonder if they're rare. Ramon must be an enthusiast.'

Kat surrendered the watering can gratefully. She was turning to go inside when she spotted the telescope. On impulse, she put her eye to the viewfinder. It was immensely powerful. A speck on the horizon was revealed as a fishing trawler. A blurry figure leaned over the side.

Kat was about to adjust the dial when it occurred to her that if she rotated the telescope until some object or patch of landscape came into sharp focus, she might find the last thing Ramon looked at before he disappeared. If he'd been birdwatching, as he'd claimed, there'd be nothing to see, but it was possible he'd been watching something, or someone, else.

'Kat, would you stop playing with stuff that doesn't belong to you and tend to the lettuces?'

'Going, Mum.'

But Kat stayed glued to the telescope. She swung it past sea, beach, town and harbour. Only one thing popped out with crystal clarity – a red warning sign on an iron gate: MILITARY FIRING RANGE. NO ENTRY.

The coastal path that cut across the range was closed to the public on weekdays, when troops on exercise might be using live ammunition. It opened to the public at weekends, but only between 8 a.m. and 6 p.m.

Had Kat, Tina and Dr Wolfe walked to Durdle Door on Saturday afternoon as planned, they'd have crossed it. But the picnic had been cancelled because Sergeant Singh had called her mum and all hell had broken loose.

If the telescope had been trained on the firing-range gate at any time between Monday and Thursday morning, Ramon could only have been watching somebody from the army base coming or going. Who was it?

Absorbed with the telescope, Kat jumped when her mum's phone rang. She could tell by her tone it was urgent.

Dr Wolfe ended the call. 'Kat, I have to run. That was Monkey World. They have a capuchin emergency.'

'A capuchin emergency?'

'A rescue. Some fiendish family has been keeping the monkey in a bedroom for years. I need to get to the clinic ASAP. Do you want to come with me now or follow when you're done with the plants?'

Kat would have loved to be there when the capuchin came in, but she was dealing with a crisis of her own.

'Go ahead, Mum. I won't be long.'

Alone in the house, she felt tense. She'd given her mum a brief tour when they'd arrived and was satisfied that no burglars lurked, but she didn't want to linger.

She'd gather what evidence she could and get out.

She started with Ramon's study. There were no new messages on the answering machine, so she sifted through the desk drawers. They were suspiciously tidy.

The only thing of interest was a chequebook in the name of SJ Morgan. On the first day of every month, SJ Morgan made a £500 rental payment to Winterbourne Holdings, Ltd.

Two things interested Kat: 1) The rent was extremely low for such a magnificent property; and 2) Winterbourne Holdings rang a bell. She searched her memory, but couldn't think where she'd seen the name.

Downstairs, she used the control panel to water the wall of lettuces and herbs. As she struggled to rehang the owl picture, the hook came out of the wall. The photo crashed on to the counter top, landing owl down.

Miraculously, the glass was undamaged, but the plywood board on the back had come loose. Kat struggled to wedge it into its slot. Something was blocking it.

Further investigation revealed a padded white A3 envelope, stuffed with something thick, soft and heavy.

IF FOUND, POST TO
PO BOX Z1
UNITED KINGDOM

It was a peculiar address. Kat had never seen another like it.

She debated whether to put the envelope back where she'd found it or carry it home for safekeeping. Taking the last parcel had been a disaster. Potentially, she'd risked Ramon's life.

On the other hand, this envelope clearly stated that the finder should forward it to the given address. What harm would it do if she held on to it for a few days? If Ramon returned, he'd be thankful she'd looked after it. If he didn't, she could post it. Maybe the contents would help find or save him.

She put the envelope in her rucksack and propped the owl picture against the wall. Everything was done. She could leave.

Except that she didn't. She did what she'd been dying to do for days – tapped Option 13 on the control panel. The password box popped up. Kat typed in Bailey's birthdate. She held her breath and waited.

An electronic woman spoke from the control panel: '*Code Blue Response activated.*'

Kat was unnerved. Did Ramon have a private security firm linked to his alarm system? Were they going to come racing up to Avalon Heights with a truckload of guards and slavering dogs and accuse her of robbing the place? Would Sergeant

Singh be hot on their heels?

She had to get out.

But as she turned to go, she noticed a khaki-green briefcase lying on a breakfast-bar stool.

She was positive it hadn't been there earlier because she'd sat on that exact stool while sending a text to Harper. Yet it was there now.

Was it possible that it had something to do with the pressing of Option 13? There was a broad panel beneath the breakfast bar. Could it have opened and released the case?

Kat was crouching to inspect the panel when a shadow loomed in the living-room window. A soldier in combat fatigues was on the deck! He was hunched over, busy with something.

Kat did the only thing she could think of to scare him away. She dashed to the control panel and selected Option 8a: 'Maximum Heat'. A towering inferno shot from the barbecue on the deck.

As a deterrent, it worked well.

Too well.

The soldier let out an agonized yell and reeled back, clutching his forehead. He swung towards the window, his granite features scarlet with rage.

'Who's there?' he thundered, banging the glass. 'Identify yourself.'

It was Colonel Axel Cunningham. Kat had thought him scary before. Now he was murderous.

She flattened herself against the wall, pulse racing. Had he seen her? Did he have the security code for the front door, or had he climbed on to the deck using the fire escape?

She had to get away.

At the same time, she was a veterinary surgeon's daughter. All her life she'd been taught to aid those in trouble – both animal and human. Her conscience would not allow her to leave an injured man, especially when she was the cause of that injury. If he was burnt, he'd need to run tepid water over the wound for at least twenty minutes.

She pressed Option 2 and heard the cover of the hot tub slide aside. Peering out cautiously, she saw the colonel was on his knees, face in the bubbles.

There'd never be a better time to escape.

Kat grabbed the briefcase and was startled by the weight of it. She almost left it, but the thought that it might fall into the clutches of the colonel convinced her it was worth the effort.

The breakfast bar and vast sofa provided cover as she crawled to the hall. She risked one last glance through the French doors. The colonel was staggering to his feet, hair and jaw dripping.

As quietly as she could, she stole out of the house. She couldn't ever remember being so frightened. If the colonel spotted her from the deck, she might vanish like Ramon.

As she stood frozen on the doorstep, she heard a familiar miaow. A shrub rustled and out came Tiny. Kat was so astonished she let out a miaow herself.

'What – ? Why – ? How – ?'

Tiny didn't answer. When she leaned down to try to stroke him, he darted to the cliff path, paused and looked over his shoulder.

Kat didn't need to be asked twice. They rushed down the steep steps together. The whole way down, Kat kept expecting the colonel to come pounding after them. He was a powerful man, who might even be armed, but knowing that Tiny was by her side made her feel protected.

The Savannah cat led her on a twisting route to Summer Street that avoided all human contact.

As she hopped over picket fences and tiptoed through backyards, Kat couldn't stop thinking about the Code Blue Response. Had a SWAT team already descended from the sky at Avalon Heights? Had they captured Colonel Cunningham?

If he was responsible for kidnapping or killing Ramon, why had he returned to the scene of the crime?

No matter what he'd done, she felt guilty that he might be injured.

'There you are,' called her mum, emerging from the veterinary practice seconds after Kat had concealed the green briefcase under a bush at number 5. 'I was about to call you. I thought you might like to see the capuchin. Eva's been through a lot and she's sleeping now, but she's exquisite.'

Kat felt a rush of relief. Whenever life got her down, she could always count on her mother and animals to make her feel better.

She tried not to think how her mum would feel if they were run out of town because Kat had set fire to the colonel.

'Thanks, Mum. I'll be right there.'

23

Operation Cyclone

When Kat returned to her room, Tiny was draped across the window-seat like a leopard on a branch. He watched, unblinking, as she buried the white envelope and green briefcase beneath his favourite snoozing sweaters and blankets in the wardrobe. Anyone would think he'd been in the attic room all day, not taking detours to cliff-top mansions to act as Kat's own feline bodyguard.

'I'm counting on you to keep Ramon's stuff safe,' she told him. 'You have my permission to pounce on anyone who pokes their nose in where it doesn't belong.'

His green eyes narrowed, and she paused to wonder again what he'd been doing at Avalon Heights. It was hard to believe that he'd gone all that way on a hunting expedition. The only possible explanation was that he'd followed her there, and why would he do that unless, deep down, he was starting to care just a little?

Kat's phone beeped and she swooped on it. There were five missed calls and a text from Harper.

Where ARE you? Call me urgently!

Kat rang at once. 'Sorry, I've been at the practice with Bailey and my mum. What's up?'

'You first. How did it go at Avalon Heights?'

Kat's head throbbed. She hardly knew where to begin.

'Epic disaster. I think I may have accidentally-on-purpose chargrilled Colonel Axel Cunningham.'

'Is that all? I thought something really tragic had happened.'

'Harper, it's not funny. I could be in serious trouble. I also broke the owl picture, found a weird envelope and activated a Code Blue Response by mistake. Don't ask me what a Code Blue is, but it's activated. I escaped with a heavy green briefcase that looks like something an army officer would carry.'

'Slow down,' begged Harper. 'My brain is melting. I thought you were going to Avalon Heights with your mum – to water the plants.'

'We were watering the plants, but then she had a capuchin emergency—'

'What's a capuchin?'

'They're these monkeys that resemble monks in brown robes. They have huge eyebrows.'

'Right. Let's start from the beginning. You were alone at Avalon Heights and you thought you'd do a bit of barbecuing?'

'I was looking for clues. Option Thirteen was bothering me. I thought it might help if we knew what it was hiding. I cracked the passcode.'

'You did what?' Harper's tone was miffed, as if cracking passwords was supposed to be her job. 'How did you figure it out? The same one might work on Ramon's computer.'

'I'm not telling you,' said Kat. 'I'm in enough of a mess as it is.'

'At least tell me what you found in the green briefcase.'

'I haven't looked because it isn't mine.'

'Hmm.'

'Don't say "Hmm",' scolded Kat. 'If it's linked to Option Thirteen, who knows what might be in it. It could be stolen cash or even spy stuff. It doesn't matter, because I'm not going to open it.'

'If you say so,' Harper said sweetly. 'Let's hope it's not a bomb.'

'A bomb?'

'If you hear any ticking, you might want to evacuate your cottage ASAP and take your mum and cat with you. But let's not worry about that now. Where was the colonel while you were breaking into Option Thirteen?'

Kat's focus was on the wardrobe. She tiptoed over to it.

'Who?'

'The colonel you tried to incinerate.'

'He was on the deck. He'd climbed up using the fire escape. Harper, I think he's "Soldier A" on our suspect list – the one who was prowling around the night before Ramon disappeared.'

Harper was awed. 'You must have been petrified. I'd have run screaming from the house.'

'It was easier to turn on the barbecue,' confessed Kat. 'I thought that would scare him away. How was I to know that "Maximum Heat" would send up a flame that could have launched a rocket to Mars?'

'Did the colonel see you?'

'Don't think so.' Kat pressed her ear to the wardrobe. Was it her imagination, or could she hear ticking? 'Harper, what am I going to do? If I ring Sergeant Singh and accuse the base commander of breaking and entering, he'll call my mum. I'll be grounded for the rest of my life.'

As she spoke, the falcon face of the Dark Lord came into her head. Wasn't it ironic that the best person to call for advice on a rogue soldier – her Minister of Defence grandfather – was also the worst person?

'There's nothing we can do until Ramon either comes home or doesn't,' said Harper. 'Meanwhile, we have a chief suspect.'

Kat caught sight of the time. She'd promised to help Tina cook dinner. She hoped they wouldn't be blown to smithereens before they'd eaten. She was starving.

But she couldn't go until she had an answer to one burning question.

'Harper, did you discover anything more about the men in Ramon's old photo? I'm dying to know.'

'Yes, but I ended up with more questions than answers. First, I tried to find out how Evan Ross got his Purple Heart for bravery. Apparently, he was part of a Special Forces unit sent to Afghanistan in 1986. Evan and Tony were also wounded there, and Tony's twin, Mario Baranello, was killed.'

'Did the website say what went wrong on the mission?' asked Kat.

'Only that they were ambushed by Soviet troops. Jasper's going to do some investigating. He says that in the eighties the CIA had a programme code-named Operation Cyclone in Afghanistan. US Special Forces soldiers were involved in helping the *mujahideen* – they're Afghan fighters – battle the Russians.'

Kat's history wasn't good at the best of times. She could feel her tired brain shutting down. 'Not ISIS or the Taliban?'

'No, back then the Americans were battling the Russians.'

'What were the names of the other soldiers on the mission?' Kat asked. 'Could any of them be one of the unknown men in Ramon's photo?'

'Without pictures, it's hard to be sure. The other soldiers in the unit were Vaughan Carter, Trey Taylor and Scott Javier Morgan. Ramon wasn't there.'

'What did you say?'

'Ramon wasn't there.'

'No, before.'

'The other soldiers were Vaughan Carter, Trey Taylor and Scott Javier Morgan.'

The phone was clammy in Kat's hand. 'At Ramon's house, I found a chequebook. Every month, someone called SJ Morgan pays rent to Winterbourne Holdings, whatever that is—'

There was a sharp intake of breath. 'Kat, Captain Morgan is gone.'

'What do you mean? Gone how?'

'He was the only other soldier I could find any

information on. He went by Javier. It's pronounced Havier, but in Spanish it's spelled with a J. It's an unusual mix of names and probably means he's half American, half Spanish – like me. He died in a car crash just over two years ago. But that's not all.'

'It's not?'

Kat wasn't sure how much more she could cope with in one day.

'I spent ages trying to find information on your friend Ramon,' Harper went on. 'There's nothing on him in any official records in Paraguay or the US. Kat, he doesn't exist.'

Kat didn't reply because something extraordinary had happened. Tiny had sprung up on to the bed. He curled up against Kat's hip as if it was something he did every day.

Carefully at first and then with more confidence, Kat stroked his silky spotted fur. His purrs travelled up her arm and vibrated in her chest. Her imaginary kitten had come to life as a lynx-sized Savannah, and it was the most comforting thing in the world.

'Hello? Hi, Kat – are you still there?' Harper's voice echoed down the line. 'Either Ramon is a criminal who stole Javier's identity, or he is Javier Morgan and faked his own death to escape someone or something. Do you think it's possible that Colonel Cunningham discovered his secret and was blackmailing him?'

'I think we've been looking at this the wrong way round,' said Kat. 'What if it's not Ramon who needs saving. What if other people need saving from him? What if *he's* Arch Villain Number One?'

24

Double Trouble

The prime minister bit a prawn off a toothpick, swallowed it whole and said, 'Peculiar business, this Oxford Street Phantom affair, don't you think?'

Lord Hamilton-Crosse gave a non-committal murmur.

Once, he'd relished hosting these glittering parties. Now, he whiled away the hours dreaming about escaping to the Faroe Islands, where he'd spend the rest of his days photographing puffins.

'The papers are having a field day with it,' moaned the prime minister. 'Conspiracy theories galore. Mobsters. Russian hit men. Religious fanatics. Even the British government. Anyone would think we were in the habit of assassinating people in broad daylight on busy London streets . . . Uh, we didn't, did we?'

'Not this time,' said the Dark Lord.

The prime minster looked relieved.

'It occurred to me, Dirk, that with everyone distracted by the Phantom, now might be the perfect moment to announce that we're shutting the children's wing of that Manchester hospital.'

Lord Hamilton–Crosse gripped the stem of his champagne glass so tightly, it almost snapped. A red-hot fury surged through him.

If a junior clerk hadn't come to summon him to the phone, he'd have said something he regretted. As it was, he excused himself curtly and made his way out through the crowded ballroom.

He took the call in his study in the south wing of Hamilton Park, his stately home in Buckinghamshire. Beyond the bay window, the maze and landscaped gardens were bathed in moonlight. He stood so he could look out at them. He loved every blade of grass and every hair on every horse and dog on the estate where he'd been born.

For decades, he'd worshipped the trappings of wealth and class, and the privilege it came with: fast cars, expensive art, exotic holidays. Then his son was killed surfing a gigantic wave. In the midst of his pain and rage, he'd lashed out at Rufus's fiancée, Ellen Wolfe, the day after her child was born. He'd behaved unforgivably. As a consequence, he'd lost not only his boy, but also any chance of knowing his granddaughter as she grew up.

Overnight, Dirk Hamilton-Crosse had seen his glamorous world for what it was: a gilded cage. He'd been so obsessed with money and power that there'd been no room in his heart for his only son.

That same year, his wife had left him for his best friend. The Dark Lord had waved goodbye to them without a tear. Now he lived alone.

The Christmas after Rufus had died, a parcel had arrived with a south-east London postmark. He'd refused to open it. The following Christmas, a second parcel came. What it contained – childish drawings and a photo of a laughing toddler with no front teeth, covered in a heap of blond Labrador puppies – was worth more than gold. The accompanying card said simply, 'Katarina, aged two.'

From then on, that parcel had been the best and only Christmas gift he could have wished for. Kat's paintings, school essays and pictures of her beaming with an assortment of animals and books were framed or in albums around his office. Despite that, he'd never once sent a thank-you note to Ellen Wolfe. He'd been too proud to say sorry or admit he cared.

A year ago, he'd found himself near Kat's school on government business. On the spur of the moment, he'd asked his chauffeur to drive past it. By chance, the children were streaming through the gate. He'd recognized Kat at once. She was uncannily like her father. He'd been unable to resist trying to talk to her.

The look on her face when he'd told her he was her grandfather haunted him still.

So did the words of her mother, who'd come storming into his office a short while later.

The following Christmas, no parcel came. The absence of it had hit Lord Hamilton-Crosse hard. Three and a half months on, there'd been another blow. The Wolfes had moved and left no forwarding address.

If he hadn't worked in a department staffed by spies, Lord Hamilton-Crosse might never have found them again. Fortunately, he did. When V reported that they were living in Bluebell Bay, he wasn't sure whether to laugh or cry. He'd settled for being thankful he knew where they were.

Now the Dark Lord picked up the phone and said, 'Yes, V, what is it?'

As he listened to the woman he'd code-named V, a retired spy he sometimes hired as a private detective, a muscle worked in his jaw. The junior clerk, ear pressed to the door in the corridor, heard the following one-sided conversation:

'You *cannot* be serious?'

'No!'

'But *how*?'

'Please tell me this is not happening? Why this week of all weeks?'

'MI5? Great. That'll go down well with the director. Send her a gift.'

'How would I know? Maybe a hamper from Fortnum and Mason. Better make it a big one.'

'You mean there's more?'

'Oh good grief. Is the colonel going to sue?'

'Thank goodness for small mercies. Send him tickets to the Chelsea Flower Show before he changes his mind.'

'Who else knows about this?'

'Keep it that way, V.'

'Thanks, but I'll handle it personally.'

When the call ended, the Dark Lord grabbed his coat, bypassed the party and strode through the dark trees to the barn, followed by his Border collie, Flush. After giving a few treats to an old Clydesdale mare, his favourite horse, he sat on a hay bale with his head in his hands. Flush lay loyally beside him.

It was there that his assistant found him, hours later. She knew immediately that something was wrong.

'It's Kat, isn't it? She's in trouble.'

'Worse,' said the Dark Lord. 'She's the cause of it.'

25

A Bolt from the Blue

When Kat arrived to pick up Toby on Monday morning, there was a For Sale sign outside Kittiwake Cottage. Inside, Edith and her son were arguing. At least, Reg was arguing. Edith's voice was small and cracked with emotion.

'Reg, this has been my home for fifty years. Why do I have to leave? I'm managing perfectly well.'

'Today you are, but tomorrow you could break a hip or go doolally and become a burden on me and everyone else,' Reg said nastily. 'Is that what you want, Ma?'

'Nobody wants to be a burden, Reg, but can't you

221

understand how hard it is for me to let go of my cottage and library? And I will never, ever give up Toby. He's my best friend. I'd rather die.'

'Are you insane?' shouted Reg. 'He's a great hairy mutt. A fairly useless one, at that. But, don't worry, I've spoken to the RSPCA and they promised to try their hardest to find him another home.'

Kat didn't wait for Edith's response. She ran back the way she'd come and sat behind the boatshed at the harbour, where she couldn't be seen from the road. Minutes later, there was a screech of tyres. Reg's black BMW swerved around some boys on bikes and tore away.

Kat waited for a while longer, watching a windsurfer cross the bay. She felt ill as she walked to Edith's cottage.

Edith answered the door with red eyes and an extra-bright smile that didn't reach them. The first thing she did was hand over Ramon's computer, neatly packed in its padded case.

'Thanks for the loan of this, Kat. It's been a joy. For a few days, I've had a window on a world I'd almost forgotten existed.'

'Wouldn't you like to use it while I'm out with Toby? You could watch the news and give me an update on our Oxford Street Phantom case.'

Edith twisted her hands. 'Not today, love. I have a

headache. I'll just sit here quietly, if you don't mind. Toby would be delighted to join you, though. He missed his walk yesterday.'

But Toby didn't want to go anywhere. When Kat put on his lead, he dug in his paws and pressed himself to Edith's side, whining.

'I can't think what's wrong with him,' said his mistress, visibly upset. 'He's not normally so clingy. I hope he's not coming down with something.'

'Maybe it's the move,' Kat suggested gently. 'I saw the sign outside. Animals are very sensitive to moods and changes. If Toby's feeling insecure, he won't want to be away from you. It might help if you came with us.'

'I'm not sure I'm up to it, Kat.'

But Kat persisted. She was sure that it wasn't only Toby who could benefit from some sea air.

'For Toby's sake, Edith. We don't have to go far. Even walking to the harbour and back would stretch his legs.'

'For Toby's sake, then. I'll get my coat.'

'Wait for us!' called Kat, as she and Toby jogged to catch up with Edith.

It transpired that her client, so wobbly on the ground, was a speed merchant in her mobility scooter. Without a word of explanation, she'd led them up, down and around the alleys and lanes of Bluebell Bay. It wasn't until Kat found herself face to face with the warning sign she'd glimpsed through Ramon's telescope that she realized they'd reached the razor-wire fence of the army base:

MILITARY FIRING RANGE. KEEP OUT.

'We can't cross here,' she told Edith, pointing to the times on the bottom of the sign. 'It's closed to the public on weekdays.'

'I know that. I haven't lost my marbles yet, although Reg seems to think it could happen any day.'

Beside the gate was a wind-blasted hawthorn tree. Few walkers or soldiers would have glanced twice at it as they continued along the coastal path or up the tree-lined track to the army base. None would have thought to look behind the dense thicket of brambles and gorse that surrounded its twisted trunk for another path, this one cut deep into the cliff.

'Come quickly. We need to go before anyone sees us,' urged Edith, steering around a gorse bush.

Kat hesitated. The descent looked treacherous. In the unlikely event they made it to the beach in one piece, what were the chances of the scooter having the horsepower to climb back up the cliff? Kat envisioned explaining to her mum why she'd had to summon the coastguard to pluck Edith and the scooter off some crumbling precipice. What if the brakes failed?

Edith read her like a book.

'Trust me, Kat. I'm a librarian!'

Kat couldn't help laughing. Holding Toby's lead with one hand, and the basket on Edith's scooter with the other, she followed her friend down to the beach.

For much of the twisting descent, high rock walls or tunnels of vines blocked the view. When at last Kat saw the glittering ocean steaming up to wrap around white cliffs, she cried out in delight.

Toby felt the same way. Let off his lead, he raced in circles, barking at the waves. Having helped settle Edith on a boulder, Kat ran down to the water's edge and splashed her face in the freezing foam as the retriever paddled. Worn out, she collapsed beside Edith on the fine grey-blue and mauve pebbles. The sun was warm on their skin.

Edith smiled. 'Like it?'

'I love it. Do you come here often?'

'I haven't been to Starfish Cove in years. My mother first brought me when I was your age. It's a secret known to only a handful of people, and it's stayed that way for nearly a century. As a young woman, I spent whole summers here, reading and daydreaming. But when my eyes and back began to fail, it became more of a risk. I didn't dare come alone.'

Kat didn't ask if she'd ever entrusted Reg with the secret of the cove. The answer was obvious. She was touched that Edith had deemed her worthy of her special place.

'It's important to pay close attention to the forecast before venturing down here, especially if you're by yourself,' Edith was saying. 'On the Jurassic Coast, the weather can change from sunny to savage in minutes. Most deadly of all are the sea fogs.'

'I was in one last week,' Kat told her. 'I held on to the rail all the way up to Avalon Heights.'

'Then you'll understand why Dorset has more than its fair share of ghost stories. Have you heard the one about the ghost army of Purbeck? In the seventeenth century, it's said that Captain John Laurence and his brother saw some armed men marching across Creech parish in the fog. They roused the alarm. Hundreds of people came running. The army grew bigger and louder by the minute. Then those gathered noticed something odd. The army marched behind a hill, but never reappeared.'

Kat was riveted. 'The soldiers were phantoms?'

'Yes and no. Years on, science solved the mystery. There's a phenomenon called the Brocken spectre, where the sun projects the shadow of an observer on to drifting fog.'

'A bit like standing in front of a projector, when your silhouette appears on the screen?' asked Kat.

'That's right,' said Edith, raising her voice to compete with the sudden racket of a helicopter passing overhead. 'It's an optical illusion.'

Deep in thought, Kat stared unseeingly after the chopper. She pictured Mr Newbolt walking across a foggy field in his trilby and noticing his own image projected on to the wall of white. He'd called out to Ramon about mad dogs and Englishmen going out in the midday mist, but Sergeant Singh hadn't said whether or not Ramon had replied.

If Mr Newbolt had been seeing things, it meant that Wolfe & Lamb's original timeline was still in play! It made it more likely that Ramon had left Bluebell Bay by the time Kat got to Avalon Heights in the fog, and that somebody – the colonel maybe – had taken his suitcase. Or maybe they were in league together.

Timing-wise, Ramon could still be the Oxford Street Phantom, but only if his email to Margo proved to be a ruse. But Kat still found it hard to believe. She and Harper had found nothing to connect Ramon to the nameless victim on Oxford Street.

Toby came lolloping up to them and shook himself hard, showering Kat and Edith with sea spray.

'Thanks, Toby!' Kat giggled, wiping her face on her sleeve.

'I can't believe the difference you've made to my beautiful boy in a matter of days,' Edith said. 'And to me, if I'm honest. Kat, I have something to ask you. Something important. If I move . . .'

The rest of the sentence was drowned out as the army helicopter returned. But this time it didn't fly over them. It came swaying into their secret cove and landed on the beach with a deafening *thwup, thwup, thwup*.

Even before the door opened and a tall, silver-haired man ducked beneath the spinning blades and strode towards them, Kat knew it would be her grandfather. For some reason, she wasn't surprised. She jumped to her feet.

Edith was shaking with excitement. 'As I live and breathe, it's the Dark Lord!' she exclaimed. 'What in the world is he doing here?'

He came crunching across the pebbles and nodded to Kat as if nothing could be more normal than dropping out of the sky, unannounced, after a twelve-year absence. He extended a hand to Edith. 'Mrs Chalmers, I presume. I'm Dirk Hamilton-Crosse, Minister of Defence.'

Edith wasn't sure whether to be amazed or afraid. 'I know who you are.'

'But are you also aware that I'm Kat's grandfather?

I can't imagine it's the sort of thing she advertises.'

Edith nearly fell off the boulder. 'Oh, my word! Yes, I see the resemblance now. I can't think how I missed it.'

Kat was incensed. 'Because we're nothing alike. Not even slightly.'

The Dark Lord continued as if she hadn't spoken.

'Apologies for breaking up the party, ladies. I need you to come with me.'

Kat stayed where she was, arms crossed and scowling. The arrogance of the command was exactly what she would have expected from him.

'You can't tell me what to do. You're not the boss of me.'

'It was an order, Katarina, not a question. Get in the helicopter. You too, Mrs Chalmers, please.'

'Call me Edith . . . Umm, how do you know my name?'

'I'll clear that up shortly, Mrs – er, Edith. For now, I'd appreciate your cooperation and haste. Bring your retriever. We'll look after him.'

'Edith and Toby are not going anywhere, and nor am I,' cried Kat. 'Edith, don't do it! This has nothing to do with you. It's some sick power game he wants to play with my mum.'

'It has everything to do with you and Edith, and nothing at all to do with your mother,' said her grandfather. 'However, I'm happy to involve her if you'd prefer, Kat.

Is she aware that you've caused an innocent man to be arrested, and that your internet activities have attracted the attention of the US Secret Service? Thought not. Shall we proceed? We don't have all day. The soldiers are on exercise on the cliffs above. My duties might be impeded if I were to be hit by a stray bullet.'

He helped Edith up. 'Madam, allow me to assist you into the helicopter.'

Edith practically swooned. 'Don't mind if I do, my lord. Come on, Kat. Let's have an adventure.'

'That's not quite how I'd have put it myself,' said Dirk Hamilton-Crosse, lifting Edith effortlessly into his arms, 'but, yes, do come along, Kat. Let's have an adventure.'

Kat stared open-mouthed at Edith, who was resting her traitorous head on the Dark Lord's chest as if they were on the cover of a romance novel. The retriever was equally disloyal. Anyone would have thought that Dirk Hamilton-Crosse was his new best buddy.

'Still undecided?' said her grandfather. 'Do the words "Code Blue" mean anything to you, Katarina?'

Kat knew then that the game was up. Taking Toby's lead, she followed him to the helicopter.

26

Life Lessons

Hours after Lord Hamilton-Crosse had returned to the Houses of Parliament, Kat was still unable to decide whether she was in the worst trouble of her life, or had simply had a surreal conversation about spies with her estranged grandfather, followed by a scenic flight along the Jurassic Coast.

She supposed it was a bit of everything.

Before the fun part of the trip came a distinctly un-fun interrogation in a remote forest clearing.

'Easiest place to have a private conversation,' the Dark Lord said. 'No flapping ears – human or otherwise.'

While the pilot took the retriever for a walk, the Dark

Lord had what he termed a 'little chat' with Edith and his granddaughter. There was no 'Long time, no see, Kat. How's school? Having fun in Bluebell Bay?' He got straight down to business.

The shocks came thick and fast. While birds sang and flitted in the sun-dappled glade, Kat learned that in the time Ramon's laptop had been in her care, a Trojan horse had been installed on it.

US intelligence agents, who'd been tracking another Trojan horse, also linked to Ramon's computer, had spotted the virus and reported it to MI5.

Kat guessed that Harper was reponsible for the Trojan horse, but there was an added complication. It turned out that someone, somewhere at British Intelligence – the Dark Lord had refused to say who or how – had been watching the movements of Ramon's computer. Because it had spent the past two days at Kittiwake Cottage, her grandfather was convinced that Edith was guilty of installing the virus.

It didn't help that Edith had run dozens of searches for information on the Oxford Street Phantom, Mafia hit men, the SAS and foreign assassins.

With arctic politeness, the Dark Lord asked Edith the same two questions fifty different ways. Who taught her to code, and who was she working for: the Chinese or the Russians?

Edith stuck to her story. She was a retired librarian who knew almost nothing about computers. She'd done some searches because she was intrigued by the Oxford Street Phantom Mystery. Who wasn't? Some of her friends were in a knitting circle, but she didn't know any hackers.

The interview seemed to take forever. Finally the Dark Lord snapped. 'Were you one of the Bletchley Park crew? Is that it, Edith? Did you work with the code-breakers on the Enigma during the Second World War?'

'I'm not sure whether to be flattered you consider me a genius, or insulted that you think I'm showing my age,' Edith said indignantly. 'I'm ancient, but not *that* ancient.'

'Who are you calling ancient?' he quipped, and surprised even himself by bursting into laughter.

There was something rusty about his laugh, as if it didn't happen often or at all. Abruptly he ended Edith's interview and escorted her back to the helicopter.

Any hope Kat had had that he might go easy on his own granddaughter soon proved false. He was livid with her for triggering a Code Blue Response, which had alerted the British Secret Service and led to the arrest of one of the army's highest-ranking officers.

Why Avalon Heights had a Code Blue alarm system installed, and why Ramon had needed access to it, the

Dark Lord refused to say, but he did hint that a rapid-response military team had been involved. While Kat had been cooing over the capuchin at Bluebell Bay Animal Clinic, Colonel Axel Cunningham had been subjected to hours of interrogation by MI5.

'How is that my fault?' demanded Kat, as pins and needles of shame prickled her all over.

'Because I have it on reliable authority that you tampered with the house security system,' said her grandfather. 'Private passwords are private for a reason, Kat.'

'I should have known the colonel would rat on me.'

'He didn't. We found out via other means.'

'Oh!'

'And, while we're on the subject of the colonel, barbecues are not toys.'

Now Kat really did feel bad. 'Is he terribly burnt? I panicked when I saw him on the deck. It was an accident, I promise. I put on the Jacuzzi but with cool water so he could dip his face in and make it better.'

The Dark Lord tried not to smile, but didn't quite succeed. 'So I heard. His left eyebrow is now slightly shorter than the right, but otherwise he was unscathed – no thanks to you.'

Kat suddenly remembered that the reason she'd resorted to extreme measures was because Colonel

Cunningham had been up to no good on the deck at Avalon Heights.

Her chin rose. 'You might be thanking me soon, once you've found out the real reason the colonel was skulking around Ramon's deck. It wouldn't surprise me if it turns out that he's a murderer. If he's hurt Ramon, I hope he goes to jail forever.'

Her grandfather went very still. Even the birds stopped singing.

Coldly, quietly, he said, 'I've known Axel Cunningham for over ten years and he's one of the best, most decent men ever to lead the British Army. The reason he was "skulking around" this Ramon's deck, as you put it, is because they share a passion for birds and rare dahlias. The colonel decided to check that the flowers were being properly taken care of while Mr Corazón was away on business.'

'*Dahlias?*'

Kat saw then what had been obvious from the beginning: the colonel had been tending to the window boxes. In the CCTV images, he'd been holding a garden trowel – hardly the weapon of choice for an army man with access to the best revolvers and rifles around.

But she refused to believe he was entirely innocent.

'I'm not the only person who thinks Colonel Cunningham's a monster,' she said defensively. 'When he walked into the deli the other day, people were quaking in their boots. He glared at me as if I was a criminal. Maybe he does like flowers, but he's guilty of something, I'm sure.'

'If Axel is guilty of anything, it's of doing too good a job of acting tough so that the soldiers under his command don't work out that he's soft as marshmallow underneath. A few years ago, he lost his adored wife and daughter in an avalanche in the French Alps. He's never really recovered from it. If he was glaring at you in particular, it could be because you reminded him of Sylvie. She'd be your age by now. Seeing you probably made him sad.'

Kat sank down on to a log. 'Oh, the poor, poor colonel. I had no idea.'

The Dark Lord handed her his handkerchief, and it was only then she realized that her cheeks were wet with tears. He joined her on the log – albeit at the furthest end.

'Kat, I told you Axel's story not to upset you, but in the hope that you take from it a valuable lesson. You should never rush to judgement – particularly when it comes to people you don't know.'

'Nor should you.' She sniffed, thinking of her mum in the maternity ward twelve and a quarter years ago.

He nodded slowly. 'No, nor should I.'

For a microsecond, a channel opened up between them, and Kat felt connected to her grandfather in a way she'd never once felt when hearing about her long-lost father. She had an uncanny sense that they were the same.

Then the pilot and retriever came crunching through the trees. Before Kat could blink, the Dark Lord was on his feet. He glared down at her again, as if she were a field mouse, and he a falcon circling on high.

'You and Edith think you're being so cool and clever, but you're dabbling in matters that will sweep you into deadly waters faster than a riptide. Stop what you're doing before it's too late. Next time, I might not be around to save you.'

27

Square Zero

'It just slipped your mind to tell me that your granddad was Minister of Defence?'

Given a choice, Harper would have been pacing the living room. Tethered to the sofa by hulking plaster casts, she was reduced to chewing her nails.

'Like you can talk,' countered Kat. 'It slipped *your* mind to mention the Trojan horse virus you put on Ramon's computer.'

'Which I wouldn't have done if I'd had an inkling you were related to a man who hangs out with cyber-security spies,' cried Harper.

She sagged into the cushions. 'Now I'll probably end my days in a dungeon under the Tower of London.'

Kat was unsympathetic. 'I'll send a postcard.'

She glanced out of the window. The chestnut racehorse was at the paddock gate, ears pricked, waiting for her.

'Did it ever occur to you that if Ramon's computer dies because of YOUR virus, I'll be pet-sitting for the next year to buy him a new one if it turns out he really is in Paraguay on business? Oh, wait, no I won't. Because I'm already in so much trouble that Mum has threatened to make me shut down my Paws and Claws agency.'

'She hasn't! But you're the world's best animal whisperer.'

Kat refused to smile. 'How did your dad feel when Sergeant Singh called him to complain? Was he upset?'

Harper's dimples did the cute, innocent thing they did whenever she was scheming, plotting or evading questions. Kat suspected that her dimples were the reason Harper had been getting away with murder for years.

'Umm, Dad may not have got the message.'

'Harper! You're—'

'Incorrigible. I know. People tell me that all the time. Kat, you have my word of honour—'

'*Honour?*'

'Yes, honour,' Harper insisted, 'that the virus I installed is not the kind that overwrites documents or destroys things. All it did was give me route access to Ramon's computer so I could tell if anyone else was logging on to it remotely.'

'And were they?'

'Yes, but by the time I'd worked out that I was up against a master hacker that might actually be someone from British intelligence, it was too late. You'd been caught red-handed by your granddad and were on your way here.'

She took off her glasses and rubbed her eyes. She looked as if she hadn't slept. 'Are you really mad at me?'

Kat sank down beside her. 'I was a teensy bit mad for about three minutes, but I know you only did it to help our case. Besides, it's my fault too. I should have told you about my grandfather. Let's shake hands and agree never to keep secrets from each other ever again.'

'Deal.' But Harper was still anxious. 'Kat, be honest. How long do I have before MI5 come to drag me away in handcuffs?'

This time, Kat did smile. 'No one is taking you anywhere. You have Edith to thank for that. We both do. When the Dark Lord accused her of being the hacker, she guessed that you were the culprit, but she allowed him to keep thinking it was her, even when he threatened her with prison for it.'

Harper was grateful but bewildered. 'Why?

She doesn't even know me.'

'She knows you're an armchair adventurer. That was enough.'

'How did Edith feel about being accused of being a spy?' asked Harper over tea and cake.

'She said it was the best day out she'd had in twenty years, worth it for the scenic flight alone. We toured one hundred and eighty-five million years of history in twenty minutes. She also told me to tell you that she accepts the position.'

'What position?'

Kat grinned. 'Being Miss Moneypenny to our James Bond.'

'Jane Bond, you mean!'

On the sofa, Harper performed a sitting-down bow. 'From one armchair adventurer to another, tell her we'd gladly accept. Her story about the Brocken spectre was pure genius, and it's helped us correct our timeline. Were her neighbours impressed when she was delivered home by helicopter?'

'The helicopter dropped us off in a random field in the countryside, where the vicar was waiting to collect us. He didn't say a word about the Dark Lord on the way back to Bluebell Bay, just chatted non-stop about the storm forecast for the night of the army dinner. As we pulled up at Kittiwake Cottage, a choirboy turned up on Edith's mobility scooter. He'd been sent to collect it. His face was as crimson as his gown.'

Nettie came in then, so Kat didn't tell Harper that Edith's smile had faded as soon as she was reminded that there was a For Sale sign outside her home.

The vicar was staying for tea, so Kat had made her escape. Pausing on the way out to say goodbye to Toby, she'd noticed some legal documents on the shelf above the dog bed. They'd been signed by Edith. She'd given up fighting Reg and had granted her son permission to sell the cottage on her behalf. Her precious home, library and dog would soon be taken from her.

Kat had swung her rucksack and knocked the forms into Toby's bed. He'd fallen on them with glee and ripped them to bits.

It wouldn't stop the sale, but it might delay it for a few days while Reg ordered more documents and persuaded his mum to sign them again. This was Bluebell Bay. Anything could happen in a few days.

Anything at all.

'So our chief suspect is in the clear,' said Harper, crossing out the colonel's name on her yellow pad. 'So are Maids A and B. Maria is supposedly fiery but nice, and Ramon's cleaner's family emergency was real –

Nettie says the woman's daughter's been ill with malaria ever since she came home from the Zambezi.'

She paused. 'I have uncovered one thing, but you have to promise not to get judgemental on me.'

Kat eyed her distrustfully. 'What have you done now, Harper Lamb?'

'I hacked into Margo Truesdale's email account.'

'*You what?*'

'You promised!'

'But, Harper, that's so wrong.'

'I'm not the one who got an innocent colonel arrested and a senior citizen abducted in a helicopter by the Minister of Defence.'

Kat shuddered. 'Don't remind me. Did you read the email from Ramon? What did it say?'

'I thought you said it was wrong?'

'It is, but I suppose it's what proper detectives do – go through people's emails and bank statements.'

'Yes, except that proper detectives have to wait for pesky search warrants and can't just act on feelings in their bones,' said Harper with a smile. 'Anyway, I don't feel bad because I did Margo a favour. Her password was Password1. That's like laying out a welcome mat for fraudsters. I pretended to be from her bank and sent her some tips on creating an unbreakable password that even I couldn't hack. It'll keep her safer in future.'

'So you're a sort of Robin Hood hacker?' said Kat. 'You steal information, but you do something kind in return.'

Harper laughed. 'Couldn't have put it better myself. Anyway, it was only Margo's business email, not her personal one. No gossip anywhere, only a load of dreary orders for eggs and gluten-free bread and pomegranate molasses. Tons of it.'

Kat raised an eyebrow. 'Who orders tons of pomegranate molasses?'

'Chef Roley for the Tank Regiment dinner. He's probably putting it in the dessert. The only personal email was from Ramon. That made me smell a big stinking rodent. If he and Margo are so friendly that he sends her updates from Paraguay, why doesn't he have her private email address?'

Kat wondered glumly whether Wolfe & Lamb, Inc. would ever be any good at detecting. Every lead they'd followed fizzled out.

'Well, we wanted proof that Ramon was safely in Paraguay. Now we have it.'

Harper shook her head. 'That's just it. We don't. The address on the email is a generic one that can be created in two minutes using made-up contact details. Anyone could have set it up. I got into that account too. There was only one message in the sent folder and one in the inbox – Margo's reply.'

'Could Ramon himself have set it up just so he could message Margo to tell her he'd be staying longer in Paraguay? Everyone knows she likes to gossip. If he wanted to send people off on a false trail, she'd be the best person to tell. Maybe he really is running away from his debts.'

'There are hundreds of reasons he could have run away, if that's what he's done,' said Harper. 'What I'd like to know is why a bird watcher rented a house with a Code Blue alarm?'

'Maybe he's a spy and thought he'd need rescuing.'

Harper looked thoughtful. 'That would explain why US intelligence agents were tracking his computer, but it could also mean he's a criminal. Did your grandfather hint at which it could be?'

Kat had a flashback to the moment when she'd accused the flower-loving colonel of murdering Ramon.

'He didn't seem to know much about him. As far as he's concerned, Ramon's just some random bird watcher who had the misfortune of hiring the world's worst pet-sitter.'

'So, basically, four days after you found the half-packed suitcase, we have no suspects and no answers,' said Harper. 'Square Zero, that's us.'

A frustrated whinny carried across the orchard. The

Pocket Rocket had grown tired of waiting for Kat and was tearing up the paddock. He bucked so high that his silver shoes flashed in the sunlight.

Kat grabbed her riding helmet. 'I'd better go before Charming Outlaw takes off over the garden hedge.'

As she walked through the cherry blossoms, she took her grandfather's pale blue handkerchief from her pocket. Their morning encounter had been so otherworldly that if it weren't for Edith and that square of pale-blue silk she'd have had difficulty believing it happened.

Over and over, his warning went through her head.

Stop what you're doing before it's too late. Next time, I might not be around to save you.

28

Monkey Business

'Don't wait up for me,' said Dr Wolfe over pineapple fritters on Wednesday evening. 'I'm going to do some filing at the clinic while I monitor the bull terrier who had the dental op. If he hasn't improved, I'll put him on a drip.'

'Would you like some help?' asked Tina.

'After you've spent ages preparing this fabulous meal? Not a chance. Besides, you've been on call for the last two nights. You need sleep. Kat, please bear that in mind when you're up in your attic. Give the Elephant Yoga a break.'

Tina looked across at Kat. 'Is that what you were doing when you were crashing about the other night – Elephant Yoga? I thought it might be Rhino Ballet.'

Kat laughed, but made a mental note to practise her mongoose moves more quietly in future.

'Elephant Yoga is just Mum's way of telling me to keep the noise down,' she told Tina. 'I hope I didn't keep you awake. I was trying something I saw on YouTube.'

'I love dancing too,' said Tina, putting two and two together and making five. 'You don't have to be quiet on my account.'

After dinner, Dr Wolfe went over to the animal clinic. The bull terrier was not recovering as well as she'd hoped. She put him on fluids to boost his hydration levels.

There were two other dogs in the kennels, both restless and barking. The spoodle was convinced there was a bogeyman lurking in the dark.

'It'll be a fox,' the vet told her. 'I'm reliably informed that there are no burglars in Bluebell Bay.'

When the dogs had settled down, Dr Wolfe lugged three boxes of dusty files from the storeroom to her office. She tipped them on to the desk. Scanning them was a boring job, and she was swallowing a great yawn when the spoodle began to bark again.

Sighing, Dr Wolfe returned to the kennels. She opened the back door and shone a torch at the bushes and trees that grew thickly on the slope behind the practice. A night bird flapped from a branch above her head. Quickly she slammed the door.

Concerned that the spoodle and mongrel were getting stressed too soon after major operations, Dr Wolfe gave them both sedatives. They dozed off immediately.

The baying dogs had upset the other animals. Dr Wolfe went into the aviary, where Bailey was kept at night, and soothed him with the aid of some Brazil nuts.

'Tell Kat! Tell Kat! Tell Kat!' screeched the parrot.

She stroked his green feathers. 'What would you like to tell Kat?'

'*Deuce testy it. DEUCE TESTY IT.*'

Dr Wolfe stared at him in surprise. '"As God is my witness"? What have you witnessed, Bailey dear?'

The parrot was nibbling a nut and said no more, but his words had got Dr Wolfe's attention. It was so unlike Kat to tell an untruth that ever since Sergeant Singh's call she'd wondered where the truth lay. After seeing Avalon Heights for herself, she'd put the episode down to Kat being nervous in the fog. Now she wondered if her daughter's suspicions had been justified.

Was it possible that Ramon really had been abducted? Were rogues operating in idyllic Bluebell Bay?

There was no time to mull it over further because the capuchin needed attention too. When the Monkey World staff had brought her in, Eva had been in a desperate state. Years of living on the wrong food in a flat in Poole had left her with diabetes. But her progress since Sunday had been remarkable. Capuchins were among the smartest animals on the planet, and Eva was no exception. She'd stolen the hearts of everyone at the practice.

Dr Wolfe cuddled her on the cattery sofa. It was warm in the room, and the vet rested her eyes while she summoned the energy for more filing. She was soon asleep. The capuchin prodded her to get her to play, but she didn't stir.

Eva decided to entertain herself. She scampered along the passage and into the dark reception. That was fun for a while, because there were pens to scatter, brochures to rip, balls to juggle, and some catnip bananas to destroy. But, once that was done, it was boring again.

The light was on in Dr Wolfe's office. Eva climbed on to the chair and set it swinging. She tugged open a drawer. Thrillingly, it held a bag of dried mango. She popped a strip into her mouth and closed her eyes in bliss. As she reached for another, her ears caught a creak.

Someone was coming.

19

Pistols and Piranhas

Before breaking into Bluebell Bay Veterinary Surgery on Wednesday night, Darren Weebly crunched up some stale peanuts he'd found at the bottom of his bag. He'd missed dinner and could have eaten an ichthyosaurus if one had been passing.

The first two nights of the Kat Wolfe assignment had been a cold, rainy, miserable waste of time. Bluebell Bay Veterinary Surgery advertised a twenty-four-hour emergency service, but, sadly, there'd been no hurt hamsters or pups with poorly paws in need of 3 a.m. care.

That evening, Darren had been mightily relieved when the

vet had emerged from her cottage at around 10 p.m. and made her way to the practice next-door. Not long afterwards, a lamp came on in her office.

Darren's plan of breaking into the kennels was foiled when the dogs barked their heads off. He'd had to wait ages for them to stop yammering. Now Darren stood and pulled a balaclava over his head. He was ready to neutralize the threat.

He'd brought his lock-picking kit, but it wasn't required. The front door of the practice was unlocked. Darren simply stepped in.

A triangle of yellow light spilt from Dr Wolfe's office, lending an eerie glow to the reception area. Darren was surprised at the state of the place. Shredded brochures, pet toys and pens were strewn from one end of the floor to the other. As he picked his way through the debris, he heard a faint scuffle. Good. The vet was still at work.

Darren had always prided himself on his nifty footwork. He was in her office and sitting in the visitor's chair before Dr Wolfe had time to move.

Disconcertingly, her desk was piled high with files. All he could see were her eyebrows. They were quite astonishingly thick and furry – almost as bushy as his own. He didn't remember them from her website photos, but then she'd mostly been obscured by various animals. Was she a fan of Miracle Sprout too?

The eyebrows made an excellent target. He aimed his revolver right at them. It was a starting pistol, not a real gun, but it looked real, which was the main thing.

'Do what I say and you'll live to see tomorrow, Doc,' he barked. 'Try to get smart and your next breath will be your last.'

Dr Wolfe's eyebrows hopped up and down like caterpillars with fleas. She gibbered with terror. Darren was pleased. It showed that the decision to target the mother rather than the daughter was the right one.

'They call me the Exterminator, Doc. Maybe you've heard of me. Anyone who crosses me gets vanquished. Now, I've got bad news for you. Your daughter has been poking her nose in business that doesn't concern her. If you value Kat's life, listen carefully. Tell her that if she doesn't cease and desist asking questions about Mr Corazón, she won't just be mincemeat – she'll be soup.'

Darren paused to allow the vet time to absorb the full horror of this threat. Slurping sounds emanated from behind the files. The vet was a blubbering wreck.

He'd saved his best threat for last. 'Put it this way, Doc: if your sprog doesn't zip her trap and stick to bunny-hugging for the rest of her natural life, I'll hunt her down and feed her and her pets to my piranhas.'

Not that he had any piranhas, but she couldn't know that.

Throughout Darren's tirade, Eva had reclined, unbothered, in Dr Wolfe's chair, munching her way through the mango. For many years, she'd had to endure the angry bleatings and deafening television habits of the family who'd imprisoned her in the flat. She'd learned to tune them out.

But as Darren rose from his chair, he glimpsed the packet of mango between the files. Famished, he seized it and turned to go.

This final outrage was one too many for Eva.

Using the ergonomic chair as a springboard, the capuchin flew at him and sank her teeth into his ear. Disorientated in the dark reception area, Darren whirled around in agony. Eva bit down harder. Only when he fired his starting pistol into the air did she let go.

Darren burst out of the practice and lumbered into the trees. He expected lights to go on and sirens to come wailing up the street, but nothing happened. It seemed he'd terrified Dr Wolfe into silence. Even the dogs were quiet. Perhaps they'd barked themselves hoarse.

As he swallowed two painkillers with a can of soda, Darren's mood darkened. The vet had done nothing to save him when that unhinged creature – a cat probably – had leaped out of the darkness and tried to rip off his left ear. He could have rabies! Thankfully, he'd brought his first-aid kit. Inexpertly, he stemmed the bleeding and wound a bandage round his head.

He glared up at the dormer window of 5 Summer Street. In his fury, he forgot his resolution about never harming those who were only a third of his size. He decided to shake Kat awake and be her worst nightmare come to life.

This time, his lock-picking kit did come in handy. With a wicked smile, Darren let himself into the Wolfes' kitchen.

Upstairs, Tina was on a video call to her mother in Singapore. She had headphones on and was speaking softly so she didn't wake Kat in her attic room.

'You'd love Bluebell Bay, Mama. It's so beautiful and safe. In ten years, they've had one crime here – a stolen pumpkin. That's right: a pumpkin!'

The conversation was interrupted by the arrival on the screen of some Malaysian relatives with a new baby. They crowded around her mum's laptop to show off the child.

In the attic above, Kat had fallen asleep with her headphones on, listening to music.

Both were oblivious to the carnage unfolding in the kitchen.

As Darren padded across the tiles, starting pistol in hand, Tiny ambushed him from the top of the kitchen cupboard, crash-landing on his shoulder and sinking his claws and teeth into Darren's neck. For the second time that evening, Darren found himself being savaged by an enraged animal.

This one, however, was infinitely more lethal. It seemed intent on going for his jugular. He caught glimpses of it during their struggle, and it looked like a small leopard.

Just when a disembowelling seemed imminent, Darren managed to fend Tiny off with a chair. He slammed the door on the beast and staggered up the stairs.

The bang penetrated Tina's noise-cancelling headphones.

'Hold on a sec, Mama. I heard an odd noise.'

The nurse bounced off the bed, tripped over her power cable and fell heavily against the door, banging her knee.

Out on the landing, Darren was leaning dizzily against the banister. A scratch had rendered one of his eyes useless. The other was swollen from a bite he'd incurred at the animal clinic.

Half blind, he didn't see the door swing open until it collided with his forehead. He did a backflip over the railing and was unconscious before he hit the ground.

Tina, seeing nothing, returned to her bed to rub her sore knee. She started chatting to her mum again. Pretty soon, the bang she'd heard earlier went out of her mind altogether.

When Dr Wolfe entered the kitchen shortly after 2 a.m., she found an upturned chair, a broken mug, a fistful of fur and a seething Tiny. It had been a night of wreckage. The capuchin too had left a trail of destruction at the practice.

Dr Wolfe was unruffled. The antics of the many creatures that crossed her path rarely bothered her. Animals and children had minds of their own, and a mind of one's own was a beautiful thing.

'How did you end up stuck in the kitchen, Tiny?' she asked. 'Did you knock the door shut fighting with some other cat, or was it the wind?'

The Savannah streaked past her and up the stairs to his mistress.

Not wanting to wake anyone, Dr Wolfe made her way to bed in the dark. She missed treading on Darren's unconscious form by millimetres.

30

The Owl Service

The Exterminator was still lying comatose on the floor two storeys below when Kat surfaced from a dream. She found Tiny sleeping on her chest. He was purring so loudly that it took her a while to register that her phone was vibrating too. Freeing an arm with difficulty, she answered the call.

'It's 3 a.m., Harper,' she croaked. 'Can't you sleep?'

'No, and when I tell you what Jasper's found, you won't be able to either. The soldiers in Afghanistan were betrayed by a double agent. One of their comrades was a US spy who was also working for the Russians.'

Kat struggled out from underneath her cat and sat up. 'What soldiers?'

'The soldiers in Ramon's photo. In 1986, they were part of a top-secret CIA mission to destroy a Soviet bomb-making factory. But someone leaked the plans, and the Russians ambushed their unit. Mario was killed, and the other five soldiers were wounded.'

Kat turned on her bedside lamp. 'Remind me of their names again.'

'There was Mario's twin, Tony, then Evan Ross, Trey Taylor, Vaughan Carter and Javier Morgan, who we think might be Ramon.'

'Who discovered that the mole was a double agent?'

'There was an official investigation. The soldiers themselves were under suspicion for a while, but they'd been friends for years and were fiercely loyal to each other. All five left the army after that. Apparently, they were convinced that the mole was someone inside the CIA. Turned out they were right. The officer who planned the mission had a cardiac arrest a few months later. CIA investigators found documents in his home proving that he was a Russian spy.'

Kat put an arm round Tiny. 'I feel as if I'm dreaming. Are you sure you're not making this up, Harper? It's sounds a bit fanciful.'

'Fact is always more fanciful than fiction,' asserted Harper. 'The only fanciful thing is that the Russian mole conveniently died.'

Kat was startled. 'You don't believe he had a heart attack? Do you think he was murdered?'

'Maybe. Dead men can't answer questions,' Harper said darkly.

'Imagine how it would feel if someone on your own side knowingly led you and your friends into the line of fire,' said Kat. 'Tony's brother died because of that monster. Tony must have been devastated. You can't blame him and his friends for leaving the army.'

'I'm sure they were broken-hearted, but they were also Green Berets,' Harper reminded her.

'What's a Green Beret?'

'In the US, our Special Forces are known as the Green Berets. They're the best of the best. The fittest, the fastest, the toughest, the most skilled. What if Tony and the others quit the Special Forces not because they were broken men, but because they wanted to avenge Mario's death?'

'Why would they do that if the CIA officer who betrayed them was already dead?'

'That's what we have to find out,' said Harper. 'Urgently.'

Kat caught sight of the clock and yawned. 'Why urgently? The Afghanistan ambush was more than thirty years ago. Why do we have to investigate it now? What does it have to do with us anyway?'

Tiny agreed. He yawned too.

'Because while Jasper was trying to find something

on our soldiers, he came across a post by a military blogger called Argonaut,' said Harper. 'After Tony died of a supposed cardiac arrest, Evan got in touch with the blogger. He claimed that Tony and Vaughan had been killed using an undetectable poison.'

'If it was undetectable, what made Evan think they were poisoned?'

'Because right before they died they were sent photos of themselves with a target over their heart.'

'No!'

'Yes,' said Harper. 'Evan told Argonaut that he was sure someone was picking off members of the Owl Service one by one.'

Kat was incredulous. '*The Owl Service*? As in the children's fantasy novel?'

'The very one.'

'What does a children's book set in Wales have to do with ex-Special Forces soldiers in the USA?'

'Argonaut doesn't say. He just describes them as a "legendary task force". Jasper's going to try to find out more for us. But get this. Evan told Argonaut, "We always believed that some ties go deeper than blood. I'm beginning to wonder if that's true." Kat, those were the words Ramon used in that podcast I heard.'

'Remember that anonymous message we found in Vaughan's local paper?' Kat said. '"*All for One. One for*

All. RIP brother." Maybe the soldiers made a pact to be there for one another no matter what. Did Evan say anything else?'

'He said, "Once we hunted ghost owls. Now we're the hunted." Kat, within weeks of that blog being posted, Evan died of a supposed stroke. Whoever or whatever these ghost owls are, it sounds as if they hunted him down.'

Kat thought of the ghost owl picture in Ramon's kitchen, and a chill shuddered through her. 'Did Argonaut contact the police or the US Secret Service?'

'They wouldn't have paid any attention to him. Jasper said he was notorious for badgering the authorities with conspiracy theories. But it looks as if a ghost owl – a *death* owl – got to Argonaut too. The Owl Service story was his last ever post.'

'Seriously?'

''Fraid so,' said Harper. 'He'd been blogging for years, but he shut down his site the next week. Jasper found mentions of it on other blogs and websites.'

Kat's head swam. It was hard to take in.

By contrast, Harper's neurons seemed to be sparking like firecrackers. 'Still think it's a coincidence that Ramon has a ghost owl in his kitchen and an owl icon on his computer?'

'He's a bird watcher. White barn owls could be his

speciality . . . No, wait. I've just thought of something. Ramon talked about owls in the note he left me.'

Kat took it from her bedside drawer.

See the framed photo of Tyto alba? *That's ornithologist for 'white owl', though some call it the ghost, silver or death owl. I've spent half my life in pursuit of this silent hunter. Wrapped up in this one picture is my whole history.*

Harper said, 'He's practically telling you that his life story is in the white envelope you found hidden in the back of the photo. Kat, you have to open it.'

'Why don't we hold on to it for another few days? If he doesn't turn up, I'll post it to the strange address. It could be that whatever is in the envelope was an insurance policy in case something happened to him.'

'Something *has* happened to him,' insisted Harper. 'He's been gone for a week. Someone sent him a picture with a bullseye over his heart. His supposed email from Paraguay was a red herring. If he's not already dead, he's a marked man.'

'OK, OK – but if it goes horribly wrong, YOU'RE taking responsibility.'

Kat put her phone on the bed and turned on the speakerphone. 'Here goes.'

'Hurry, hurry,' urged Harper from amid the folds of her duvet.

'Keep your voice down,' whispered Kat. 'I don't want to wake up Mum or Tina.'

The envelope contained a thick sheaf of documents. Each set was about a particular type of owl. There were pages and pages of scientific notes about the habits and migration patterns of the silent hunters.

Kat picked up her phone and relayed the news to Harper.

'They're in code,' said her friend. 'Have to be.'

Kat wasn't sure. 'They seem fairly ordinary to me. I'll post them to the address on the envelope. If they really are about owls, maybe they'll help another bird watcher with their research. If Ramon is in danger, someone, somewhere, might know how to help him.'

'But what if you were right and it's Ramon who's the danger?' demanded Harper. 'Criminals and spies often fake their own deaths in crashes. If he really is Javier Morgan, then posting the envelope might help him pass on nuclear secrets or something. Why don't you ask your granddad to look at Ramon's papers? He probably knows a dozen code-breakers.'

Kat's pulse spiked at the thought of another grilling by the Dark Lord. 'Are you nuts? N.O.! Anyway, I doubt I'll ever see him again.'

'Didn't he give you his business card?'

'Yes, but all he said was, "Stay out of trouble." He didn't invite me to tea at Hamilton Park, or say, "Ring if you need any documents decoded or advice on undetectable poisons."'

Kat fished out the Dark Lord's card from its hiding place – a removable slat in her futon. She'd shoved it in there without glancing at it. She'd been too busy worrying about whether or not to tell her mother about her helicopter ride. In the end, she'd said nothing. For the first time in years, her mum was truly happy. Kat was not going to be the one to rain on her parade – not if she could help it.

The card was charcoal grey. Dirk Hamilton-Crosse's contact details were etched into it in bold lettering.

Kat flipped it over. Beneath the family crest were the words 'Winterbourne Holdings, Limited'.

'So what do you say?' Harper was asking. 'Will you call your granddad or not?'

'I don't think that's a good idea. I have his card in my hand. Want to know the name of Ramon's landlord?'

'Don't tell me the Dark Lord is renting Avalon Heights to our missing man?'

'Looks that way. Or at least his company is.'

Kat was reeling. She'd thought the Dark Lord was angry with her for hanging out with a hacker and getting the colonel wrongly arrested. Now she wondered whether he'd been more concerned that she'd drawn attention to Avalon Heights when she triggered the Code Blue. He'd talked about Ramon as though he were a stranger. Obviously he knew more than he'd let on.

'I don't think it's a good idea to say any more on the phone,' Harper said. 'Yours could be bugged. Dad's at a conference till late tomorrow night. Any chance you could come for a sleepover?'

'I'll check with my mum. Harper, if Ramon is Javier Morgan who was in the Owl Service in the US, why do you think he chose to rent a house in Bluebell Bay?'

'The thing we keep coming back to is the army,' said Harper. 'That's the thread that connects the ambush in Afghanistan, the dead soldiers in the US, Ramon and even your granddad – the UK Minister of Defence. The key to this whole mystery must be on the army base on the edge of town.'

'Let's say that Ramon, like you, is on the side of the angels,' said Kat. 'If he came here to hunt a ghost owl down, it could mean that the person responsible for killing at least four American soldiers is living on the base where Prince William is due be guest of honour tomorrow night.'

Harper gasped. 'Ohmigod, you don't think . . . ?'

'I think that if the future King of England sits down

269

to dinner with an assassin who likes to kill people with undetectable poisons, it's not going to end well. But who's going to believe us if we try to warn them?'

'Not a soul. So what do we do?'

'We need proof,' said Kat. 'Ramon gave me his computer for a reason, and it wasn't about Move 58. He wanted me to keep it safe in case anything happened to him. Harper, is there any way you can try to hack into the password on the owl icon on his desktop? The clue to the identity of the ghost owl could be hidden behind it.'

'I'll give it everything I've got.'

When Darren regained consciousness on the Wolfes' hallway floor at daybreak, the leopard cat was crouched on a shelf above him, as if deciding which bit to devour first.

If there was a world record for escaping from seaside cottages, Darren would have broken it.

After many hours in A&E (a pest-control job gone bad, he told the doctor), he emerged raging from the hospital.

So far that morning, the military man had sent him nine messages of increasing menace, demanding proof that the 'pest' had been neutralized.

'Job done, sir!' Darren had replied in his most confident tone, hoping the soldier would be satisfied.

No such luck. He wanted to hear the grisly details in person.

Thankfully Darren had had another brainwave. He could put off the military man and ensure Kat's silence by threatening her best friend – an American girl who'd broken both legs. No fear of a roundhouse kick from her!

For added insurance, he'd take a gun – a real one this time.

He messaged the soldier a lie:

Turns out that the threat has opened her big mouth to another small pest. Want that one neutralized too?

The reply was instantaneous:

Not neutralized, Exterminator. Vanquished. Chopped up like liver.

Overjoyed to have both a reprieve and a meaty new assignment, Darren momentarily forgot the pain of his cracked ribs, torn ear, black eye and fifty-seven scratches.

Roger that, sir. Consider it done.

31

Agent Orange

Sergeant Singh put his foot on the accelerator, crawled forward two metres and ground to a halt again.

This time, he turned off the engine. A tractor and trailer had overturned on one of the narrow lanes leading to Bluebell Bay. Combined with Friday evening commuter traffic, road closures, the rain and the volume of vehicles bound for the Royal Tank Regiment's anniversary dinner, it had caused gridlock in every direction.

When the notice about the dinner had landed in his inbox, Sergeant Singh automatically assumed he'd be involved in policing the event. The army base was on the edge of Bluebell Bay, after all. But his superintendent in Wareham had been quick to set him straight.

'This is not a village-bobby affair, Singh. Prince William will be attending. A job like this needs officers with experience of policing high-profile, high-security events. We'll be bringing them in from London. Stick to helping the good citizens of Bluebell Bay sleep soundly and keep their pumpkins secure at night. It's what you're best at, Sergeant. Except for the pumpkin part.'

Laughing at his own joke, he'd ended the call.

A policeman's lot was a thankless one, and for the most part Sergeant Singh tried not to take it personally. But the super's words were a bitter pill to swallow.

Days later, Kat Wolfe said something similar: *You spend years sweating over a stupid stolen pumpkin, then when a real mystery lands in your lap you can't be bothered.*

Sergeant Singh loved his work and took real pride in it. He hadn't realized how much he'd hungered for a proper mystery until Kat had asked him to go with her to Avalon Heights. As he'd searched the house, truncheon in hand, he'd felt as if he were a real detective. Adrenalin had raced through his veins.

But it had all amounted to nothing. Once again, the joke was on him.

As he restarted the engine, his police radio crackled to life. Prince William was unwell and wouldn't be attending the dinner after all. Sergeant Singh almost cheered. Not because His Royal Highness was ill, but because it meant the superintendent's plans had been thrown into disarray. A replacement celebrity would have to be found at short notice.

Now Sergeant Singh really *was* glad to be in his plain clothes, heading home for a rare Friday night with his family.

Drumming his fingers on the steering wheel as the traffic halted again, he noticed the sign for an industrial estate up ahead. Miracle Enterprises, the headquarters of Reg Chalmers's company, was top of the list of businesses.

For weeks now, the policeman's wife had been asking him to buy her some Miracle Veg Compost. Their neighbours used it to grow enormous vegetables in their backyard, and Asha wanted to do the same.

Sergeant Singh had kept putting her off because Miracle Veg was sold by Reg, whom he detested. Dealing with him at the height of the Missing Pumpkin Crisis had been a wretched experience. At every opportunity, Reg had poked fun at his detecting skills. Sergeant Singh was quite certain that Reg was responsible for the theft of his own pumpkin, but in the absence of proof he'd had to stand idly by while the man pocketed £100,000 in compensation.

Much as he hated to enrich Reg further, he knew that sooner or later he'd have to buy the Miracle Veg for his wife. Since he was going nowhere fast in the traffic, it might as well be now. Indicating left, he turned into the industrial estate.

Reg's BMW was in the director's parking space

outside Miracle Enterprises, but the office was empty. A new delivery had been dumped in reception.

Sergeant Singh examined the pile of boxes plastered with skulls and crossbones. Though they'd been shipped from the Far East, the list of ingredients was in English. So was the warning at the bottom: NOT FIT FOR HUMAN CONSUMPTION. The policeman was interested to note that a separate delivery contained tubs of vanilla and chocolate flavouring.

Sergeant Singh looked at the poster on the wall. It featured photos of orange-tinged, muscle-bound athletes running, cycling and rowing while drinking Miracle Sprout smoothies. Reg himself was a pale shade of orange, and he too had bulging biceps. The cogs in the policeman's brain began to turn.

A security guard ducked in out of the rain. 'Looking for Reg? Try Vanquish Pest Control.'

He gestured towards a portable office at the end of the row of warehouses, its outline fuzzy in the deluge. 'Reg is always over there, talking to Darren Weebly. Thick as thieves, they are.'

Vanquish Pest Control was shut. Sergeant Singh peered through the window, rain dripping down his collar. The guard's comment replayed in his head. *Thick as thieves . . . Thick as thieves.*

Weebly's desk was neat and tidy. Fluorescent lighting

made a nightmare of the stacks of brochures promising to murder or maim anything that crawled, hopped or squeaked. There was a notepad beside the phone. On it was written 'Paradise House – HARPER'.

Alarm bells rang in Sergeant Singh's head. If Weebly was doing a pest–control job at Paradise House, it would make sense for him to jot down the name of either Professor Lamb or the housekeeper. That it was Harper's name made the sergeant deeply uneasy.

As he turned to go, his trainer dislodged something shiny in the gravel. Sergeant Singh bent to pick it up. It was a bullet.

Weebly was exactly the sort of thug who'd enjoy blasting away at fluffy bunnies, but this was not a shotgun slug. It was a revolver bullet.

Sergeant Singh had told Kat that policemen couldn't go around acting on feelings in their bones, but it wasn't entirely true. Instinct is a powerful tool in policing, and every cell in Sergeant Singh's body was telling him that something was terribly wrong.

Circling the portable office in search of more clues, he spotted Reg. The Miracle Sprout director was leaning on a forklift at the cement warehouse opposite, talking to the driver.

In that instant, the pieces fell into place for Sergeant Singh: he saw how Reg and Darren Weebly, might have conspired to steal the pumpkin, with the aid of the forklift driver, and share the insurance money between them.

As he considered his next move, a sound penetrated his consciousness: S*tamp, stamp, stamp, ping*. The cement bags were being bagged and sealed.

In an instant, he was back at Avalon Heights listening to Kat Wolfe insist that she could prove the threatening message was real because she'd heard a '*stamp, stamp, stamp, ping*' in the background. And here was that exact noise, close to the office of Darren Weebly, a man who killed for a living and had Harper Lamb's name on his notepad.

If Kat had been telling the truth about the message and vanished suitcase, she and Harper could be right, or partly right, about everything else. What if some sinister character with a revolver had got word of their detective efforts?

The rain was coming down in sheets now. Sergeant Singh tried calling Professor Lamb, but the landline was engaged, and his mobile went straight to voicemail.

Paradise House was five kilometres away, on the other side of Bluebell Bay. Driving there through the traffic could take an hour.

Leaning into the storm, Sergeant Singh began to run.

32

Operation Ghost Stories

'I've tried every trick I know,' said Harper, looking up from Ramon's computer. 'Nothing works. Unless we can find his original password, it's unbreakable.'

Kat stood at the window, watching rain pelt the panes. It was 6.45 p.m. on Friday, though it felt much later. Between thunderbolts, lightning shivered across the violet sky, lending the clouds a silver lining. Kat kept hoping for a real one. In little over an hour, the Royal Tank Regiment would be sitting down to their anniversary dinner, and she and Harper were no closer to identifying the ghost owl.

The only good news was that the future King of England was

no longer the guest of honour and, therefore, quite safe.

'Tummy troubles, they say,' reported Nettie, shortly before she'd hurried off to collect Professor Lamb from Wool station. His London meeting had finished early, and he was on the train home.

'I shouldn't be more than an hour, girls. If you think you might be scared with this electrical storm raging, I can get my friend Sue to check on you.'

'We're not scared,' chimed Harper and Kat.

Now they were all alone.

Well, almost alone.

'Keep the change, ya filthy animal!' ordered Bailey from his perch atop the piano.

Harper giggled. 'That's hilarious. Isn't that a line from *Home Alone*?'

'Mr Newbolt didn't find it funny when Bailey told him he was a filthy animal this morning,' said Kat. 'Mum can't have her patients' owners being called names – even when they deserve it – so I had no choice except to bring him here. No parrot would last a day in our cottage, not with Tiny around.'

'Is that all I am to you – a repository for unwanted pets?' Harper asked mildly.

'What's a repository?'

'It's what Paradise House will be once you've finished turning it into your own personal animal shelter.'

Kat lifted the parrot on to her shoulder. 'You said

Charming Outlaw is a changed horse since Hero moved in.'

'He is,' admitted Harper. 'And, I suppose, it will be fun having someone besides Nettie to talk to while Dad's off sifting the Jurassic Coast for the fifth rib of *Pliosaurus funkei*. Bailey and I can watch action movies and speak Spanish together.'

'You'll have a great time,' Kat enthused. 'Only –'

Harper threw her a suspicious glance. 'Only what?'

'Don't be alarmed if he starts shooting.'

'*Don't be alarmed if the parrot starts shooting?* One of these days I'm going to record you, Kat Wolfe, and you'll see that your conversations about animals are not normal.'

'Normal is overrated,' Kat told her. 'Anyhow, Bailey might only be with you for a few days. If we're wrong about Ramon, and he's been painting bellbirds in Paraguay, he'll be home in a week.'

'I hope we're wrong,' Harper said fervently. 'For Ramon's sake, and for Bailey's.'

Her laptop pinged. 'That's Jasper. Let's see what he's found.'

Hey, Geek, she typed.

Hey, Ace. Ever heard of Operation Ghost Stories?

Be serious.

I am. Whatever you're mixed up in is heavy stuff. It goes back to the Cold War, when the Russian Foreign Intelligence Service (SVR) set up a network of spies in the US. They were sleeper agents known as Illegals. The idea was that they'd spend decades pretending to be regular American citizens in cities and suburbs, making friends, being good neighbours, having children. Then the Russians would 'wake them up' and set these Illegals to work wherever they needed them. These sleeper spies were so skilled at blending into offices and neighborhoods, at being invisible, that the FBI investigation to catch them was called Operation Ghost Stories.

Kat squeezed up beside Harper so she could watch the words blink up on the screen. 'Ask him what this has to do with Ramon or the Owl Service.'

According to my source, the Owl Service was a task force of ex-Special Forces soldiers who worked with US intelligence agencies to track down the Russian mastermind behind the network of Illegals, code-named Ghost Owl. The officer who betrayed them in Afghanistan was a suspected Russian Illegal, so your soldiers might have seen it as their chance to avenge Mario's death.

Harper's fingers flew across the keys:
How many of them were in the Owl Service?

Javier (Ramon), Evan, Vaughan, Tony and Trey. The guys from your photo. I've confirmed them all now. We still don't know who was behind the camera. Best guess says it's Brad Emery, who owned the boat they were on. I found him through a boat registry. He was Tony and Mario's neighbour and the only one who wasn't a soldier.

'So, in all the years of hunting, this task force never caught the Ghost Owl?' asked Kat. Harper relayed the question.

They got close a couple of times, but
then the trail went cold. Next, Owl
Service members started dying. Tony
and Vaughan from cardiac arrests, Evan
from a stroke, Trey from pneumonia,
and Javier in a car crash. I think your
hunch about Ramon moving to Bluebell
Bay because he learned that the Ghost
Owl might be hiding on the local army
base is spot on. That's why this ends here.
Harper, you and Kat need to stop this
Nancy Drew stuff before you disappear
too.

Harper and Kat looked at each other.

'But what about the Tank Regiment dinner tonight?'
protested Kat. 'What if the Ghost Owl has some
diabolical plan?'

Harper nodded furiously. She begged Jasper to keep
digging, but he flatly refused.

Ace, the men and women on the base
are professional warriors. They can take
care of themselves. I promised Professor
Lamb I'd keep you safe online, not get you
tangled up with some Russian ghost spy

**haunting Bluebell Bay. Promise me you'll
stop playing detective, Harper? Harper,
are you still there? Nuts, I've gotta run to
a lecture. Harper Lamb, BEHAVE!**

The screen went blank.

'He has a point,' Kat said.

Harper pulled a face. 'About us stopping being
detectives?'

'No, about the soldiers at the dinner being professional
warriors. They have more chance of surviving a Ghost
Owl attack than we do.'

'The men in the Owl Service were ex-Green Berets,
and even they weren't safe from the Ghost Owl.'

A spear of lightning sizzled across the sky.

Kat's brain lit up at the same time. 'What if the traitor
was someone so close to the soldiers that he was never,
ever suspected? A member of the Owl Service, say.'

'That's it!' cried Harper. 'It has to be. We know that
these sleeper agents—'

'Illegals.'

'Yes, Illegals are trained to act as if they're everyone's
favourite colleague or friend.'

'And,' said Kat, 'we also know that the men in the
Owl Service had their own code of honour: "*All for One.
One for All*." That might have made them blind to the

idea that one of their friends could be a traitor.'

'It must be Ramon,' said Harper. 'He was the last man standing. You met him. Did he seem the type to betray or kill his best mates?'

Kat had a sudden memory of Ramon's kind but haunted face. 'No, he seemed like someone who'd lost his friends. How about Brad? Could he be the traitor?'

'Who's Brad?'

'The neighbour who owned the boat: Brad Emery. The one who we think took the photo. *He* might be the last man standing. We haven't managed to discover whether he's dead or alive. It's like he's invisible.'

'But he wouldn't have been invisible to Ramon,' Harper pointed out. 'If Brad had moved to Bluebell Bay, sooner or later Ramon would have spotted him. Plus, he couldn't have worked on the base because he wasn't a soldier.'

They collapsed into the sofa again, stumped.

'We're running out of time,' Kat fretted. 'It's terrifying to think that at this very minute the Ghost Owl might be getting ready for the Tank Regiment dinner. He could be putting on an officer's uniform or getting ready to wait tables.'

Harper checked the time. 'Fifty-two minutes until the dinner begins, and we don't have a clue who we're looking for. It's like trying to find a ghost in a fog.'

'Or a Russian bullet on an army base.'

33

Amazon Warrior

'Kat, is that you? You won't believe it, but I've cracked the Oxford Street Phantom Mystery. I've deduced how they did it.'

Kat had answered her phone without looking at it, assuming it would be her mum. Now she was regretting it.

'That's great, Edith. Can we talk about it when I come to walk Toby tomorrow? I'm at Harper's now, and we're in the middle of something.'

'It's an emergency, love. I suspect Harper would like to hear about it too, as would the Minister of Defence. You asked me if I had any information on undetectable poisons in my library. Well, I've found something.'

Kat mouthed, 'Harper, Edith has turned up something that might help with our Ghost Owl case. I'll put her on speakerphone.'

'Good evening, Edith,' Harper said cheerfully, as if she had all the time in the world and wasn't trying to solve an international murder mystery in fifty-one minutes. 'What have you discovered?'

'There are an awful lot of lethal chemicals in the world, so I decided to start with the ones used in high-profile assassinations.'

'Excellent thinking,' said Harper.

'Back in 1978, a Bulgarian writer by the name of Georgi Markov was stabbed with a poison umbrella on London's Waterloo Bridge. The pathologist found a ricin pellet in his thigh. KGB agents were suspected, but never caught.

'Then in 2006, Alexander Litvinenko, a former Russian agent, had radioactive polonium-210 slipped into his tea here in the UK.'

'Grim,' said Harper.

'Quite. Of course, those poisons were detected so, for the Oxford Street Phantom, I knew we were looking for something more advanced. That's when I remembered the heart-attack gun.'

Kat blanched. 'The *heart-attack* gun?'

'Sounds like a conspiracy theory, but it's as real as steel. The CIA developed it in the mid-seventies and spent years perfecting it. Some claim it's been used in numerous assassinations.'

'Why's it called the heart-attack gun?' Harper wanted to know.

'Because the miniature dart it fires is made from ice and tipped with an undetectable poison – most likely from shellfish. It's sharp enough to penetrate clothing and skin, and brings on an instant heart attack or stroke. When the ice dart melts, it leaves no trace. Victims simply crumple and breathe their last breath.'

Kat and Harper exchanged horrified glances. At least three of the Owl Service members had died that way.

'Edith, you're a better Moneypenny than Miss Moneypenny,' said the American girl. 'Thanks. That's really helpful.'

'Kat, I'd be grateful if you'd pass this information on to your grandfather as a matter of urgency?' broke in Edith. 'As Minister of Defence, I'm sure he'd want to know if foreign hit men are targeting innocent civilians on the streets of the capital!'

Kat tried to find a diplomatic way to say that she wouldn't ring the Dark Lord if they were the only two survivors of a meteor strike.

'I will if I can, Edith, but it'll probably be tomorrow. Right now, we have an owl emergency on our hands.'

Kat switched off her phone before Edith had finished

saying goodbye, and tucked her phone into her pocket. She scowled. 'Why does everyone think I have a hotline to the Minister of Def—'

Harper cut her off with a scream that could have shattered a mirror. Wordlessly, she pointed. A hideous pirate, his face clawed and puffy, was peering through the rain-streaked window. A bloody bandage was wrapped round his head, and sagging in the rain.

Kat screamed too, frightening Bailey off her shoulder. He flapped wildly around the room, emitting ear-splitting screeches, before coming to rest on the skull of the model dinosaur. From there, he delivered volley after volley of automatic rifle fire.

When Kat plucked up the courage to look again, the face had gone. She flew to shut the curtains. On the sofa, Harper was covering her ears. Neither heard Sergeant Singh until he burst into the room.

'Freeze!' he yelled. 'Drop your weapon and put your hands in the air.'

A stunned silence met this command.

From atop the dinosaur, Bailey gave a subdued *cheep*.

Sergeant Singh's mouth opened and closed several times. His lungs were still pumping from his marathon run through the storm. Kat had never seen anyone more drenched. He was a human rain cloud, leaking on to the rug.

'Is that . . . ? That's not . . .' He gestured weakly at Bailey.

'Ramon's Amazon parrot,' Kat finished. 'Sorry, he's watched too many action films.'

'I've never been so happy to see a policeman in my life, Sergeant Singh,' interrupted Harper, 'but while you and Kat chat, a real intruder is getting away. He leered through the window like Frankenstein's monster. He's scratched to pieces and has a filthy bandage round his head.'

'Don't worry about him' said the policeman. 'Your parrot scared him off. I saw him running for his life. I know who he is, and I'll arrest him in the morning.'

Harper eyed the spreading pool of water beneath Sergeant Singh's trainers. 'You look as if you've been swimming in your clothes, Sergeant Singh. What are you doing out with no coat? Kat, would you mind getting the sergeant some of Dad's dry things before he catches pneumonia? There's laundry on the rack beside the Aga. Put the kettle on too.'

Sergeant Singh dripped after Kat. 'You're kind, but there's no need to bother.'

In the kitchen, Kat pulled a flannel shirt, socks and jeans from the pile of ironing. 'Why aren't you on duty at the Tank Regiment dinner?'

'They didn't have any use for a village bobby.'

'Well, *we* did,' Kat said firmly. 'You just saved our lives. Anyway, the dinner won't be half so much fun without Prince William.'

He smiled. 'I can take or leave Prince William, but I am sorry to miss the Minister of Defence, who replaced him. The Dark Lord, as they call him, is not everyone's cup of tea, but I confess he intrigues me . . . Uh, are you quite well, Miss Wolfe? You've gone as white as a—'

'Sergeant Singh!' yelled Harper from the living room. 'Kat! Get in here.'

The policeman tore to her rescue, with Kat in hot pursuit, clutching a rolling pin. Braced for Frankenstein's monster, they were startled to see Harper on the sofa where they'd left her, bent over Ramon's computer. The parrot was on her shoulder.

'Tell Kat. Tell Kat,' Bailey said in a pleased tone. 'September-Nile-Otto-Quarter. Deuce Testy It.'

'It's Latin!' cried Harper. 'Kat, he's speaking Latin. *Ut Deus mihi testis est*: For God is my witness. *Septemdecim nihil octoginta quattuor* – those are numbers: seventeen, zero, eighty-four.'

Kat was incredulous. 'Ramon's password is in Latin?'

'Uh-huh. He *did* give you the computer for a reason.'

'I feel as if I've blundered into a madhouse,' said Sergeant Singh. 'Gun-toting parrots, Frankenstein's monster, secret codes. Whatever next?'

'That's what we're about to find out.'

Harper entered the code, and the owl icon flapped twice. Up came a list of contents. Number one was a video link. It was surreal watching a former CIA agent describe the making of the heart-attack gun, a double-barrelled revolver.

'What *is* this?' demanded Sergeant Singh. 'And why do you have Ramon's computer? Am I going to have to arrest you both?'

But he didn't stop them. Instead, he perched on the arm of the sofa and watched in growing amazement as Harper navigated from link to link, bringing up a plan of the army base and a guest list for the Tank Regiment dinner.

'Imagine how much time we would have saved if you'd understood Latin that first day at Avalon Heights,' Harper said to Kat.

Kat didn't answer, but Harper didn't notice because she was engrossed in a story on undetectable poisons. It was a while before she glanced up again. 'Where's Kat?'

Sergeant Singh tore his gaze from the screen. 'In the bathroom maybe? I hope she's all right. I'm worried that the face at the window might have traumatized her. When I told her about the Minister of Defence replacing Prince William as the army's guest of honour, I thought she might faint.'

Harper gazed at him in panic. 'Oh, no. Oh, good gosh. You shouldn't have told her about the minister.'

The policeman was bewildered. 'Lord Hamilton-Crosse is a politician, not a royal or rock star. Why should it matter to Kat whether he lives or dies?'

'Because he's her granddad,' said Harper, 'and whether they like each other or not, the same blood runs in their veins.'

34

The Pocket Rocket

Not until Charming Outlaw stepped out of the shelter of the field on to the open moor did Kat feel the full ferocity of the storm. It almost blasted her from the saddle. Beneath her, the little racehorse rocked on his hoofs.

She worried that he might refuse to go any further. The horses at her London riding school had been experts at digging in their heels. If they were tired or fed up, an earthquake couldn't have shifted them. Even on their best days, the most energetic of them moved as if they had lead in their legs.

But the Pocket Rocket didn't hesitate. He jogged forward as if he were on springs. Though his ears were flat against his head and he snorted at the rain, he felt as light as air, unconstrained by mere gravity.

Kat was a bundle of nerves. She'd planned to spend a couple of leisurely weeks getting to know Charming

Outlaw before attempting to ride him. She hadn't envisaged test-riding the thoroughbred in a storm.

As if that wasn't enough, she was afraid that Sergeant Singh might come sprinting out of the gloom and grab the bridle. For a moment, she almost hoped he would. But Charming Outlaw trotted faster, and the house rapidly receded.

With every stride, the insanity of what she was attempting became more apparent. She had no plan beyond getting to the army base to warn her grandfather that a Russian assassin was on the loose. She'd tried calling, but his phone had gone straight to voicemail. Whether or not he'd believe her was doubtful, but she knew she had to try.

If the future King of England sits down to dinner with an assassin who likes to kill people with undetectable poisons, it's not going to end well, she'd told Harper.

But killing the Minister of Defence would be almost as great a prize.

Getting to the base by road would take too long because she'd need to take a roundabout route to avoid being spotted. To have any chance of reaching her grandfather before the dinner began, Kat had no option but to take a short cut across the firing range. On Friday nights, it was closed to the public. If the soldiers were out playing war games in the rain, she'd have no option but to turn back.

Her other challenge was managing Charming Outlaw. Her best friend had tried it and had two broken legs to show for it. He'd spooked at a rabbit on a cloudless day. Kat was about to ask him to cross a shooting range in a thunderstorm.

Under different circumstances, she'd have loved riding him. The London horses had needed constant nudging, squeezing and pleading. Charming Outlaw was self-propelling. He was cantering now, tossing his head and snatching at the bit. The razor-wire fence came into view before she was ready for it. Beyond it were the cliffs and oil-black sweep of sea. It crashed and sucked at the rocks far below.

The warning sign reared up red in the rain: **MILITARY FIRING RANGE. KEEP OUT.**

Somehow it made everything more real. No tanks or camouflaged warriors were visible, but that didn't mean they weren't there. The soldiers could be concealed in the undergrowth, readying themselves for an ambush.

Before tackling them, she had to get past the locked gate. Up close, it was enormous. Kat had only once jumped anything near as high, and that was because a horse had bolted and she'd had no choice. It was an experience she'd hoped never to repeat, especially since she'd fallen off and nearly broken an arm. And yet here she was, sizing up the iron equivalent of the

Grand National's Becher's Brook.

On a dry, sunny day, Charming Outlaw could have jumped it with little difficulty. During his short, chequered career, he'd been a National Hunt racehorse. He'd leaped similar heights every day. But how he'd approach a metal gate in a storm, ridden by a girl he barely knew, was anyone's guess.

With effort, she steadied him to a walk. She wanted him to take a good look at the gate, but not too good. He might decide it was a suicide mission. So might she.

Kat guided him past it and nudged him into a trot. She'd loop him round so he had a proper run at it. As the lights of Bluebell Bay came into view, emotion clamped her chest. She thought of her mum, out at the cinema with Tina, with no concept that her daughter was planning a night ride across a firing range.

She was torn between doing the right thing as her mum would see it (returning to Paradise House while she and Charming Outlaw were still in one piece), and doing what she intuitively knew she had to do – risking her life and that of Harper's horse to warn a man who'd never shown her one day of affection that he might be in danger.

As she hesitated, Charming Outlaw swerved away from some unseen terror. The choice was snatched from her. So was any hope of approaching the jump in a collected canter. Charming Outlaw accelerated at warp speed.

In the driving rain, the silver poles were nearly invisible. Kat wished with every cell in her body that she'd stayed at Paradise House and begged Sergeant Singh to race to the base instead. But it was too late now. She was careering, out of control, towards a gate that grew higher with every step.

Charming Outlaw took flight sooner than she thought he would. Kat had to fling herself forward to stay on. Mid-leap, the edge of the cliff caught her eye. For an instant, she thought they were going over it. Then Charming Outlaw splashed down. Kat was nearly catapulted over his head. With superhuman effort, she managed to pull him up and wriggle back into the saddle.

As he swished his tail and picked up speed again, she felt a rush of euphoria. So far, luck was on their side.

He settled into a fast canter. Despite the weather, he seemed to be enjoying his night-time adventure. They made rapid progress across the open moor. Kat's confidence returned. She mentally told off the British Army for having such lax security. Why wasn't the place crawling with guards with automatic weapons? Why hadn't she been picked up on CCTV?

No sooner had she thought it than a harsh beam swept the ground, bathing them in light. A warning shot cracked. A shrub exploded almost at their feet.

The Pocket Rocket exploded with it.

Had Kat not grabbed a fistful of mane, and had her wet breeches not been glued to the saddle, she'd have been flung into the mud. Somehow she stayed on as he bolted. Now she knew how the Pocket Rocket had got his nickname. It was, as Harper said, like being strapped to a comet.

Riding blind in the dark and rain, Kat had the sensation of being whirled through a galaxy. The wind roared in her ears as the little racehorse blasted up the track through the pines. Kat had to put her faith in Charming Outlaw. One false move, one slip, and it would be over.

She'd lost all track of time. It could have been five minutes or an hour since she'd sneaked out of Paradise House. Finally she glimpsed lights and heard the faint brass strains of a military band. They were nearing the base.

Snorting with nerves and exhaustion, Charming Outlaw slowed to a ragged trot. His neck was a bubble bath of sweat.

Beyond the trees lay a fortress of walls, razor wire and CCTV cameras. As they burst from the relative safety of the wood, Kat felt sick. What had she been thinking? What if Charming Outlaw was gunned down or attacked by guard dogs? They had to turn back.

But, as she tried to rein him in, three soldiers in black rain gear rushed from the guardhouse, rifles in hand. 'STOP OR WE'LL SHOOT!'

Charming Outlaw shied violently, throwing Kat. She landed on her feet, still clutching the reins, but the wild ride had turned her legs to jelly. She sat down hard in the mud.

Shoving back her rain hood, she pleaded, 'Please don't come any closer. You'll only frighten my horse even more.'

'My God, it's a kid. A drowned rat of a kid. Are you hurt?'

She saw the soldier's nametag – Lieutenant Winterman – and had a sudden memory of him getting out of an army vehicle as she strolled down the high street asking her mum if she could start a pet-sitting agency. Nine days later, she was staring down the barrel of his rifle.

A baby-faced soldier leaned over her. 'I recognize you from the deli. You're that pet-sitter girl. What the heck are you doing out here? Are you lost? You could have been killed.'

He hauled Kat to her feet. She wrenched away and turned to Charming Outlaw. His flanks heaved and his nostrils were scarlet, but she felt him calm beneath her touch. When she looked round, three guns were trained on her.

'I need to speak to the Minister of Defence. It's an emergency.'

The soldiers laughed.

'Oh, you do, do you?' said the officer in charge. 'I think you'll find you need an appointment for that. Next time, write him an email.'

'My name's Kat Wolfe. I'm his granddaughter.'

'Do you have any ID?'

'No, I—'

'How about a photo on your phone of the two of you at some family gathering?'

Kat felt chilled and shaky. 'I – I – No.'

'What's so urgent that you'd risk your life getting here?' Lieutenant Winterman asked more kindly. 'If Lord Hamilton-Crosse is your granddad, can't you just call him? What's really going on here? Have you run away from home?'

The officer checked his watch. 'Lads, I need to go. The dinner starts in ten minutes. Judd, you know about horses, don't you? Take the beast down to the stables and see that he's looked after. Winterman, find someone to babysit the girl ASAP. Try the nurse. I'll deal with the situation when the dinner is over.'

He glared at Kat. 'We've been planning our regiment's anniversary dinner for over a year. We have high-ranking generals and officials in attendance. I'm not having our special night ruined by a hysterical girl, especially not one in your state. Wait until your mother hears about this.'

Ignoring her pleas, he marched away. Judd prised Charming Outlaw's reins from her hands, and she was left with Lieutenant Winterman. He marched her to the guardhouse. After giving her a towel to dry her hair and mop up the worst of the dirt, he presented her with an XXL Royal Tank Regiment sweatshirt.

'Lieutenant Winterman, you have to believe me,' begged Kat as they went in search of the nurse. 'I need to speak to my grandfather *before* the dinner, not after it.'

'Sorry, Kat, the security for this event is intense. Bomb detectors, sniffer dogs, background checks – you name it, we've done it. We can't make exceptions for anyone, least of all a girl with no ID who shows up on a horse. Lord Hamilton-Crosse is our guest of honour this evening. Unless you can tell me what you want to see him about, there's nothing I can do.'

'I can't,' she said miserably. 'It's top secret. I can only tell my grandfather.'

They'd reached the nurse's office. The lights were off, and her door was locked.

The soldier threw up his hands. 'Now what?'

'Problem, Lieutenant?'

It was Chef Roley George, ruddy from his hot kitchen.

He smiled down at Kat. 'I remember you. You're the vet's girl. The pet-sitter. Is everything all right? Can I help?'

'Thank you, sir, but I don't think so,' said Lieutenant Winterman. 'There's been a bit of an incident, and Kat here needs speak to one of our dinner guests. That won't be possible until it's over, so I was hoping the nurse would take care of her. I have to get back to the guardhouse.'

'Relax, Lieutenant. I think I saw the nurse in our catering tent, having a bite on her break. I'd be delighted to take Kat to her.'

'Are you sure, sir?'

'No problem at all. Go back to the guardhouse. She's in safe hands.'

'What can I do to make things better?' the chef asked when Lieutenant Winterman had gone. 'Looks as though you've had a rough evening. Is that mud in your hair?'

'I've had a terrible evening,' said Kat. 'And if I can't speak to the Minister of Defence in the next five minutes, it's about to get a lot worse. No one will believe he's my grandfather or that it's a matter of national security. It's life and death. Will *you* help me, Chef Roley?'

He put a hand on her shoulder. 'A matter of life, death and national security? Kat Wolfe, it would be my pleasure.'

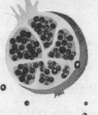
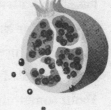

35

Recipe for Disaster

'I don't know what else I can do,' said Sergeant Singh. 'The Tank Regiment's phones are just ringing and ringing. I've left three messages, but I doubt they'll check them till the morning. I did get hold of one of the coppers guarding the road that leads to the base. If they see a girl on a horse, they'll hold her there and alert me. Do you have Dr Wolfe's number?'

'Sergeant Singh, take a look at this,' called Harper. 'From what I can make out, it's the man Ramon suspected of being the Ghost Owl.'

He rushed to her side. On her screen was an out-of-focus photo of a smiling man with thick black hair. Beside it Ramon had written: *Kazimir Gorev?*

'Must be a case of mistaken identity,' said Sergeant Singh. 'That's Roley George, the army chef. Top cook. The soldiers love him over at the base. He's a friend to everyone. Harper, what's wrong?'

'Sergeant Singh, Kat had this theory that the Ghost Owl might use the Royal Tank Regiment anniversary dinner to assassinate Prince William. But what if it's about something even worse?'

'Worse than assassinating the future King of England?'

'You've seen the guest list for the anniversary dinner. There are aristocrats and five-star generals. And the guest of honour is the Minister of Defence. Imagine the catastrophe if the chef slipped poison into their food!'

Sergeant Singh began pacing the room. 'Say you're right, and I feel in my bones that you may be, the dinner starts in minutes. I don't have my car. I can try to ring my superintendent again, but he's not going to halt the dinner on a hunch.'

Harper clicked on the dinner menu. 'The starter is asparagus with balsamic vinegar, but there probably won't be too much of that. If I were Roley George, I'd doctor the main course or dessert.'

'Margo Truesdale gave Chef Roley her famous lasagne recipe,' said the policeman. 'It could be in the sauce.'

'The pomegranate molasses,' cried Harper. 'Chef Roley ordered an industrial quantity of it. That must be the secret ingredient. If the dinner begins at 8 p.m., it'll be twenty or thirty minutes before the guests get to the main course. Sergeant Singh, how fast can you run?'

36

Move 58

'Where are we going?' asked Kat as the chef steered her through a poorly lit section of outbuildings. 'I thought the dinner was in that big tent back there. The one beyond the trees.'

'If we go directly there, we'll be stopped by security.' Chef Roley smiled. 'I'm taking you to a place where you can wait while I call your grandfather. But first I have to pick up an item from the cold room. It'll only take a minute.'

He took the keys off his belt and approached a humming trailer. When he opened the door, a cloud of meaty mist billowed out. Rows of beef and pork carcasses hung from hooks.

'Come take a closer look,' said the chef. 'An army

marches on its stomach, you know. This is how we feed our fighters.'

Nerves buzzed in Kat's stomach. 'No, thanks. I'm a vegan.'

She tried to move away, but his bulky frame blocked her. 'Just take a peek. It'll be educational.'

'Chef Roley, is everything all right?'

A sous chef came hurrying up with an empty basket. 'If you needed anything from the cold room, you could have asked me. I was on my way to get the ice cream and raspberries anyway . . .'

He stared at Kat in surprise.

'This is the granddaughter of our guest of honour,' explained the chef. 'I was giving her a quick tour of our kitchen and facilities between courses. Get what you need, Jerome. I'll lock up.'

Kat wanted desperately to ask Jerome to take her back to the guardhouse, but something about Roley George's stance, and the fixed smile he turned on her, caused the words to dry up in her throat.

After the sous chef had gone, Roley George steered Kat into the cold room and dug a slim black case from the bottom of a cabinet of yellow chickens. Even before he removed the heart-attack gun, Kat knew she'd made an error she was going to pay for with her life.

The Ghost Owl gestured with the gun. 'Let's go,

before we're interrupted again. Move. I don't have all night.'

'Why are you doing this?' Kat spoke between chattering teeth as he forced her along a dark walkway behind a long building. 'You don't even know me. Why would you want to hurt me?'

'Because you wouldn't stop nosing around, asking questions about the bird watcher,' said Chef Roley. 'I had to email Margo, pretending to be Ramon in Paraguay, because she started gossiping too. Then your little hacker friend got half the spies in Britain and America sniffing around my Trojan horse. That's OK. She'll get what's coming to her. I sent an assassin to shut her up for good.'

It was on the tip of Kat's tongue to say that if he was talking about the clawed and bandaged pirate, a parrot and Sergeant Singh had prevented him from doing any such thing. But she managed to stop herself. The less he knew, the greater her chance of survival.

He paused at a fire exit, entered a code and shoved her in. They were in a split-level gymnasium. The lights were off, but the flickering glow of the torches that lined the path to the dinner shone through the windows, pooling like gold on the floor.

'Up the stairs. Go.'

'You'll never get away with this,' said Kat.

He chuckled. 'I've been getting away with it for years.

If you think you're going to jeopardize my final mission by telling tales to the Minister of Defence, I'm happy to inform you you're too late.'

Kat stopped in shock. 'What do you mean? What have you done? If you've hurt my grandfather, I'll do everything in my power to have you locked up for the rest of your life.'

'You and whose army, kid?'

'Not all battles are about who's strongest,' Kat said fiercely. 'The world is changing. Some day a girl who can code will be able to take on an army and win.'

He laughed. 'Unless that happens in the next hour, it'll be over for your grandfather and the others.'

'What others?'

'The doomed dinner guests. The Minister of Defence will make an excellent scalp, but why stop there? One might as well be hung for a sheep as for a lamb, as they say. Within the hour, Colonel Cunningham and some of the more famous lords, ladies and army generals will be extinct. It will be headline news around the world.'

In the half-light, his pupils blazed like fires.

Kat's only hope was to keep him talking and pray that help would arrive. 'You're planning to start shooting people in front of a tent full of soldiers?'

He chuckled. 'Who said anything about shooting? I have twenty-five waiters dishing up death as I speak.

I've also added a secret ingredient of my own to Margo's special lasagne recipe.'

Two guards marched past the window, boots drumming the concrete. The chef clamped his palm over Kat's mouth. Despair engulfed her as the soldiers moved off in the direction of the tent.

The chef removed his hand, but shook a finger in warning. 'If you scream, you're dead.'

Kat pictured her grandfather and the other guests chatting and smiling as the jazz band played, not knowing it was their last supper. She had to do something. A dumb-bell shone dully beneath a workout bench. Kat sneaked out a foot and set it rolling. The chef lunged for it, but snatched air. The twenty kilogramme weight hurtled off the stage, smashing on to the wood floor of the cardio studio below.

The chef grabbed Kat by the throat. 'I'd throttle you now if I had the time, but the gun will be more efficient. Turn around.'

Kat did as he ordered. It seemed bizarre that she was going to die in an army gym, looking out at the treadmills and bikes.

Tears burned her eyes. Around about now, the mum she worshipped would be sharing a box of popcorn at the cinema with Tina, blissfully unaware that her daughter was moments away from dying at the hands of a Russian

311

spy pretending to be a British Army chef, using a heart-attack gun invented by the Americans.

She almost wept when she thought about Tiny, whose nightly purring made her feel so safe and loved. Who would understand him if she wasn't around?

If she had the last week to do over, she'd tell Harper she was the best friend anyone could wish for. She'd thank Sergeant Singh, and give a whole packet of almonds to clever Bailey, and make sure that Edith and cuddly Toby knew how smart and amazing they were too. She'd tell them that libraries and homes were like adventures – worth fighting for.

As for Charming Outlaw, who'd carried her so bravely through the storm, she'd take him to the beach and let him race the waves and be free.

Because of one evil man, she would not now get to do or say any of those things. It filled her with rage. 'You're going to shoot a girl in the back? What kind of coward are you? Is that what you did to Ramon?'

'That fool. He got what he deserved. One kiss of the ice bullet and it was all over.'

The cold gun pressed against her back, level with her heart. 'Don't worry. They tell me it's quick. Say your prayers, Kat Wolfe—'

'I'd rather you said yours, Kazimir Gorev.'

The Dark Lord stepped from the shadows. He was in

a tuxedo, his Glock pistol rock-steady in his hand.

'Put your weapon down and step away from the girl. We have the place surrounded. This madness ends here, tonight.'

'Lord Hamilton-Crosse, how good of you to come,' said the Ghost Owl. 'You've saved me from trying to get a gun past security at dinner. I can kill you and be gone before dessert. Put *your* weapon down, and I'll consider sparing your granddaughter. If you love her, you'll give up now.'

'Grandfather, don't listen to him,' said Kat. 'It's a trick. He has a heart-attack gun with a deadly ice bullet. Save yourself and the other guests. He's put poison in the lasagne.'

The Dark Lord didn't take his eyes from the Russian. 'Gorev, she's a child. No one but a psychopath would use that abomination of a gun on a girl with her whole life ahead of her.'

'If you care so much, save her,' jeered the chef. 'Put down your weapon and kick it away from you.'

The pistol clattered across the floor. Though she couldn't see it, Kat knew that the ice dart was now aimed at her grandfather. For some unfathomable reason, he'd volunteered to take a bullet for her.

The chef clamped an arm round her throat. 'Put your hands behind your head. One squeak and you'll be joining Granddad in the next world.'

As Kat raised her arms, weak with terror, Ramon's words came back to her: *I'd recommend Move 58. All are excellent, but in a life-or-death situation Mongoose masters consider that to be the most effective. They call it the 'Get out of Jail Free Card'.*

Kat calculated that she was around a metre from the edge of the stage. There was no banister, only a low, decorative rope.

A commotion erupted outside. Soldiers ran past the gym windows and into the trees.

'Say your prayers, Minister,' said the Ghost Owl. He cocked the heart-attack gun, ready to fire.

And, with that, Kat pulled Move 58.

As a plan of action, it worked spectacularly well. A short, sharp tug on his chef's jacket, a lunge and a twist, and Chef Roley soared out over the gymnasium. He crash-landed on the studio floor below and was out cold.

Weak with relief, Kat turned to her grandfather. It was only then she realized that in her desperation to keep the Russian from firing, she hadn't thought of what might happen if his finger was on the trigger at the time. The Dark Lord lay motionless.

Kat raced to his side and fell to her knees with a sob. 'Grandfather, you can't die yet – you just can't. Not before I've had a chance to get to know you.'

Soldiers burst through the entrance at the far end of the gym. 'Lord Hamilton-Crosse! Kat!' yelled Colonel Cunningham.

'Help!' screamed Kat. 'Call an ambulance.'

The Dark Lord's eyes blinked open. Wincing, he struggled upright.

Kat stammered: 'I d–d–don't understand. He shot you. How are you alive?'

Her grandfather patted the chest of his tuxedo. 'Bulletproof vest. Wouldn't be without it. But my collapse was a little too theatrical and I banged my head on the floor. Was I dreaming or did you just perform Mongoose Move 58?'

Kat grinned. 'Wouldn't be without it.'

37

Families and Other Animals

On one of those dazzling seaside days when water, sky and beach look freshly laundered, a curious procession made its way along the coastal path.

The army firing range was closed on Sundays, so the guard in the watchtower merely looked on with amusement as the party ambled, rolled and pranced in the direction of Durdle Door.

Leading the charge were two mobility scooters, one driven by Edith and the other, borrowed one, by Harper.

Kat wouldn't have put it past them to start racing.

Next came Kat herself, sitting high on the bouncy, but so far charming, Outlaw. Nettie and the retriever dawdled behind them.

Bringing up the rear were Professor Theo Lamb and Tina Chung, engrossed in a conversation about Malaysia's carnivorous 'fish-eating' dinosaurs.

Eleven days after answering his desperate call at Bluebell Bay Veterinary Surgery, Kat had finally met the professor. She'd imagined him with grey Einstein hair and a coffee-stained corduroy blazer, but he wore a flat tweed cap tugged over brown curls, faded jeans and a Grateful Dead T-shirt.

Dr Wolfe was following by road. She'd stopped off at the farm adjoining Paradise House to check on a patient. A bull had cut his nose tossing a prowler out of his field on the night of the thunderstorm. On Saturday, when she'd first gone to see him, she'd arrived to find Sergeant Singh handcuffing Darren Weebly.

'He was covered in the most horrendous bites and claw marks,' Dr Wolfe told Kat, 'which he claimed were inflicted during a pest-control job. He'd also been kicked by the bull. Incredibly, he was smiling from ear to torn ear. He explained to Sergeant Singh that it was because he'd regained consciousness to find a fresh growth of hair on his head.'

On the coastal path, Harper gave a shout. 'There they are!'

Kat nudged Charming Outlaw into a trot, easing up at the point where the path sloped down towards Durdle Door. The Jurassic Coast's famous limestone arch stood proud in a turquoise sea. Beyond it, a pale gold beach tapered into the haze.

The Singh family were laying out colourful rugs on an emerald patch of grass overlooking the bay. As Kat unsaddled Charming Outlaw, Sergeant Singh introduced everyone to his wife, Asha, and ten-year-old son, Prem.

Everyone had contributed to the picnic. The Singhs had brought vegetable pakoras and filled a flask with mango lassi, and there were rice-paper rolls from Tina, and a salad and chocolate cake from Nettie. Edith had brought freshly baked scones, jam and coconut cream, and Dr Wolfe was stopping en route to pick up chips, dips and ginger beer.

Kat had remembered to bring carrots for Charming Outlaw. She fed him a couple as she tethered him to Edith's mobility scooter. Shading her eyes, she squinted into the empty sky.

When she turned, she found Sergeant Singh leaning against the scooter. 'If he said he'll be here, he will.'

Kat shrugged. 'I don't care whether he shows up or doesn't.'

'If you say so,' said the policeman, hiding a smile. 'Kat, I wanted to apologize for doubting you. Thanks to you and Harper, I've solved two mysteries in one weekend. It's exceedingly strange how Darren Weebly, the pest-control salesman I found lurking about outside Paradise House during the storm, held the key to the Case of the Missing Pumpkin. However, the moment I arrested him, he confessed everything!

'Better still, he spilled the beans on Miracle Sprout, a banned baldness cure Reg was manufacturing. That and Miracle Veg, another of his products, are so packed with chemicals they're practically radioactive. Darren and Reg are unlikely to go to jail, but they will be doing hundreds of hours of community service. Picking up litter, cleaning toilets and so on.'

He glanced over at Edith. 'I thought Reg's mum would be devastated to find out that her son's a petty criminal, but she took it very well. Says a spell of charity work will be character-building for him.'

Kat had a feeling that it would take more than a spell of good deeds to alter Reg's ways, but it was definitely a start.

'I'm sorry I doubted you, too, Sergeant Singh. About twenty Tank Regiment dinner guests owe their lives to you. So do me and Harper. I can't believe you ran almost nine kilometres to save me and Harper and raise the alert at the base. My grandfather says the army are going to give you a medal for bravery.'

He grinned. 'The best part will be seeing the look on the super's face when he has to present it to me.'

'One thing still puzzles me,' said Kat. 'How did you know me that Harper and I needed rescuing?'

'I felt it in my bones.'

A black dot appeared in the sky. Moments later, a shiny blue helicopter buzzed overhead and landed in the nearby car park. Kat was worried that Charming Outlaw might panic, but he was too busy snatching up grass.

The Dark Lord came striding up the path carrying a Fortnum & Mason's hamper. He wore grey silk trousers and an open-necked white shirt, which, Kat guessed, was as close as he ever got to casual. After the introductions, he unpacked a china tea set, two flasks of boiling water and canisters of Earl Grey tea and Ethiopian coffee.

Kat could tell it wasn't easy for him, relaxing and being normal. But it meant a lot that he'd made the effort to come.

'This is the most magnificent feast I've ever seen,' said Edith. 'I hardly know where to begin.'

'I always find that the middle is as good a place as any,' the Dark Lord remarked. 'Take a deep breath and dive in.'

Edith was putting on a brave front, but Kat could tell that the joy of being involved in a proper spy caper was offset by fears for her future. Reg's arrest meant she would have to sell her cottage to cover his legal bills. She'd have no choice but to move to Glebe Gardens Home for Seniors, and they'd never allow her to take her beloved retriever.

Kat was in possession of news that might make Edith feel better, but she'd been sworn to secrecy until it was confirmed.

Dr Wolfe was next to arrive. When she saw her nemesis, her smile faded and she hesitated, as if she might sprint away.

The Dark Lord stepped forward with a smile and put out his hand. 'Dr Wolfe, it's a pleasure to see you. May I offer you a cup of Earl Grey tea?'

Kat saw her mum's shoulders relax.

'Do you know, Lord Hamilton-Crosse, I can't think of anything I'd like more.'

'Call me Dirk.'

'Call me Ellen . . .'

Picnicking where dinosaurs had roamed 140 million years ago was one of the best experiences of Kat's life. It wasn't only the feast, delicious though that was. It was the infinite blue of the coast, the chestnut racehorse looking out over it, and the company. The Wolfes had been in Bluebell Bay for only two weeks, but somehow Kat felt that everyone present was family.

Even her grandfather.

When the tea and treats were gone, and the rest of the adults were snoozing or exploring, he had a private word with Kat and Harper.

The Ghost Owl's story was classified, which meant that most of those involved in it were told bits of it only on a need-to-know basis.

For example, Sergeant Singh, whose heroic run had saved Colonel Cunningham and other dignitaries from eating lethal lasagne, would never learn who Kazimir Gorev was, or what had driven him to attempt such a heinous crime.

Kat and Harper, whose efforts had stopped one of the deadliest Russian spies of all time and saved the Minister of Defence, were entitled to know more.

'Who was the Ghost Owl?' Harper asked Lord Hamilton-Crosse. 'I'll die of curiosity if you can't say. Was Chef Roley actually Brad, the boat owner from San Antonio, in disguise? Or was he a member of the Owl Service?'

'You came close to the truth when you suspected the neighbour. The real story is a tragedy all round. Brad Emery was best friends with Mario Baranello. He grew up believing he was an all-American boy and that his parents were a loving couple from Texas. Not until he was sixteen did he learn that he'd been adopted by Russian Illegals. They'd lived undercover for years, doing ordinary work, being ordinary citizens. When the Ghost Owl "woke them up" and put them to work, their duty was to train their adopted son to be a Russian agent. They told him that if he refused he'd spend the rest of his life breaking rocks in Siberia.

'Once his friends joined the US Army, Brad was ordered to plant bugs in their homes and in their military kit bags and sleeping bags and spy on them. That's how the Russians learned of their mission to blow up a Soviet bomb factory in Afghanistan in 1986. When Brad learned that he'd indirectly caused Mario's death, he was devastated. The other soldiers assumed, rightly, that he was in mourning for his best friend. They wanted him to know he would always be part of their circle, so they swore an oath of allegiance.'

'*All for One. One for All,*' finished Harper. 'But what about the CIA officer who planned the mission and was found dead with papers proving he was KGB?'

'It's possible that he was an innocent man, killed by an actual double agent,' said the Dark Lord.

'It's hard to keep up with everything,' said Kat. 'So did Brad actually kill his friends with the heart-attack gun?'

'From what we've learned from the coded documents you posted to us, he did not. But he was forced to give information on their movements and missions to a

Russian agent code-named the Ghost Owl. His name was Kazimir Gorev, aka Roley George. Kazimir was an Illegal who'd spent years working as a chef in the British Army. He used an imaginary aunt as a cover for trips to Moscow or the US.'

'Do you mean he organized the assassinations of Evan, Trey, Tony and Vaughan from Bluebell Bay?'

'Evan, Trey and Tony were the victims of the Ghost Owl's hitmen,' said the Dark Lord. 'It looks as if Tony had an actual cardiac arrest. By the time he died, Javier had become convinced that the Owl Service members were being targeted by the Ghost Owl. He knew he'd be next. To keep himself safe while he redoubled his efforts to track the Russian down, he faked his own death in a car crash. In the US, the Ghost Owl's trail had gone cold. Javier was close to giving up when he had a breakthrough. Tragically, Brad passed away in a climbing accident, but in his will, he left Javier a beautiful photo of a white barn owl.'

'The one in the kitchen at Avalon Heights!' said Kat.

'Exactly. In an envelope hidden at the back of it were Brad's secret files on everything he'd discovered about the Ghost Owl. It was his way of making amends for what he'd done. Javier turned them into code.'

'The owl notes in the white envelope I found?' Kat wondered if this was the right moment to mention the green briefcase she'd taken from Avalon Heights. There was nothing in it. She'd looked. Just pens, pencils and some old sunglasses. But the Dark Lord was still talking and it went from her mind.

'Brad revealed that, far from living in America, the Ghost Owl operated his network from the army base near Bluebell Bay. So Javier Morgan reinvented himself as Ramon, a Paraguayan bird artist, and moved here immediately. Once in the UK, he contacted me through a mutual friend and told me his history and everything he knew. Of course, I wanted the Ghost Owl found as much as he did. I gave him the use of Avalon Heights for free, but he insisted on paying rent. British Intelligence set him up with everything he needed, security-wise.'

'Option Thirteen?' said Kat.

He gave her a reproachful look. 'Yes, Option Thirteen. For two years, we worked with him to track down the Ghost Owl. But Ramon grew frustrated with our slow progress. He wasn't a particularly good bird watcher, or artist, and he was afraid his cover would be blown. Nine days ago, he took matters into his own hands. He'd identified Chef Roley as the potential Ghost Owl and decided to lure him to an address in London with a note only he would understand:

I know what happened to Evan and Vaughan.

'That's where you come in, Kat. He needed to find someone to pet-sit his parrot. He didn't know the chef already had his suspicions that Ramon was Javier Morgan, the supposedly dead former Owl Service-member, and had sent him the package containing the photo of the soldiers. Unfortunately, the delivery was delayed and in the meantime the chef received Ramon's note. He knew immediately that his suspicions were correct.

'At dawn that Thursday, Ramon was looking through his telescope when, by chance, he saw Chef Roley coming through the firing-range gate and making his way to the station. Ramon didn't hesitate. He grabbed his wallet, abandoned his suitcase and ran. He boarded the same train but travelled in a separate carriage. The chef led him to a very crowded Oxford Street. Ramon didn't realise that it was a trap. As you know, it was almost the death of him.'

Harper gasped. 'So Ramon *was* the Oxford Street Phantom after all?'

'I'm afraid so. Our Waterloo station camera picked him up by sheer chance and we sent a tail. Our agent saw him collapse on Oxford Street, but not who shot him. We had a Secret Service ambulance on the scene in minutes. Annoyingly, someone noticed the false plates. The whole thing has turned into a conspiracy-theory circus. We'll wait a while longer, then feed a couple of tame reporters a story about the victim living happily in a national park in Paraguay, recovering from a rare illness.'

'If Ramon was shot with the heart-attack gun,

how did he survive?' asked Harper.

'Bulletproof vest,' said the Dark Lord, patting his chest.

'Never be without it,' piped up Kat, and they both laughed.

Harper looked from one to the other and shook her head. 'So it *was* the British Secret Service that took the suitcase from Avalon Heights after Kat had been to feed Bailey in the fog?'

'It was. They didn't want the cleaner finding it and asking questions. They left a fake travel itinerary there too. They didn't know that Ramon had organized a pet-sitter, nor that she and her best friend were budding detectives with a formidable skill set and array of animal warriors, village bobbies and ex-librarians to provide back-up.'

Kat grinned. 'Is Ramon ever coming home to Bluebell Bay?'

'He's alive somewhere in the world. That's all you'll ever know.'

'Wherever he is, try to let him know that Bailey, his parrot, has found a forever home with Harper and Professor Lamb,' said Kat. 'He's going to have the best life. They speak the same languages.'

He smiled. 'And that's important?'

'Yes, because parrots never lie . . . Grandfather,' Kat said nervously, 'how much did you say to my mum about what happened? Am I going to be banned from pet-sitting for life?'

'I didn't go into details. I told both your dad, Harper, and your mum, Kat, that because you refused to accept Ramon's disappearance without question, you've done a tremendous service to national security and saved many lives. I said they should be proud. *I* am.'

Kat looked up shyly. 'Are you?'

'Yes. However, I don't ever want you risking your life to rescue me again. As Minister of Defence, I'm the one who should be saving you, not the other way around. And Harper, I'm going to recommend that you take some coding lessons from one of our cyber-security experts. You skirted dangerously close to crossing lines that could get you arrested. I'd rather we nurture and guide your talents and keep you safe. Some day in the future, we might like to work with you.'

'Anything is possible,' said Harper.

He smiled. 'Yes, it is. Now, girls, are you sure you don't want to change your minds about the Ghost Owl reward money? Half a million pounds is a lot. I could put it into a college trust fund for the two of you.'

'Absolutely not,' said Harper.

Kat agreed. 'We've made up our minds.'

'Very well,' said the Dark Lord. 'I'll see that your instructions are carried out.'

In the car park, the helicopter roared to life. The Dark Lord grimaced. 'Duty calls.'

He looked back at the picnic rugs, where Tina, Asha and Dr Wolfe were leaning together, laughing. A wistful expression flitted across his face. Kat had a vision of him returning to his stately home and wandering the empty rooms all alone.

'I suppose this is goodbye,' said her grandfather. He put out a hand, and Kat shook it formally.

'Oh, don't be so British,' cried Harper. 'Give each other a hug.'

They laughed and embraced.

'Stay out of trouble,' instructed the Dark Lord.

'Define trouble,' Kat said innocently.

'For starters, you can avoid leaping over iron gates on out-of-control racehorses during electrical storms. If I were you, I'd give snipers, barbecues, pest-control salesmen, Russian spies and the army base a wide berth too. Oh, and don't open any mysterious packages from dodgy couriers either. They might just be from an assassin.'

The blades of the helicopter spun into a blur. His mouth tugged into a smile.

'See you when I see you, Kat Wolfe.'

'Not if I see you first,' she said softly, but he was already walking away.

38

The Armchair Adventurers' Club

'You cut it,' said Kat.

'No, you cut it,' countered Harper.

'Oh, for goodness' sake, why don't you both cut it?' said Edith. 'It's a wonder the two of you managed to solve a whole mystery together when it takes you this long to tackle a ribbon.'

'We had help,' Harper told her.

'A lot,' Kat agreed.

Edith put an arm round each of them. 'And, in my case, you've repaid that help about half a million times.'

About ten minutes after the Dark Lord had left the picnic at Durdle Door, Edith's phone had rung. When she'd hung up, she'd been in tears. 'That was the estate agent. Kittiwake Cottage has been sold.'

'Oh, Edith, I'm so sorry,' said Sergeant Singh.

'No, it's good news – the best I've ever had. I feel as if I've won the lottery.'

'You do?'

'Yes,' Edith said joyously. 'A gentleman who wishes to remain anonymous has just offered a stupendous sum for my cottage. He wants to turn it into a library and gift it to Bluebell Bay for all eternity.

'And that's not all,' she'd continued as the picnickers crowded round to congratulate her.

'It's not?'

'He's asked me to stay on in the cottage as librarian for as long as I'd like the job – forever, if that's what I want. He's offered quite a generous salary too. And a laptop. I'm going to have my very own computer!'

'What an extraordinary man,' said Dr Wolfe.

'Yes, he is.' Edith smiled. 'But I suspect he has had some rather extraordinary assistance. Kat and Harper, I don't suppose the two of you know anything about this?'

'Us?' Kat said innocently. 'Not a thing.'

'Clueless, that's us,' seconded Harper.

'Perhaps it shall forever remain a mystery,' murmured Edith.

'I must say that Bluebell Bay has certainly livened up since the Wolfes and Lambs moved to town,' remarked Sergeant Singh. 'I do hope that you're going to be continuing with your Paws and Claws pet-sitting agency, Kat. You're really rather good at it.'

'Yes, she is,' chorused Edith and Nettie, and Toby barked his approval. Even Tiny, stretched out on a nearby wall, looked up as if he wanted to hear her answer.

'It's up to my mum,' Kat said. 'If she says I can, I'd love to.'

Her mum laughed. 'Looks as though you have the unanimous support of your fans. Who am I to stand in your way?'

'Thanks, Mum.'

'However, I may have to lay down a few ground rules.'

'Such as?'

'Such as not risking life and limb. Mr Newbolt is adamant that he saw the Pocket Rocket racing across the firing range in the storm on Friday night.'

'Mr Newbolt has a reputation for seeing things,' said Kat.

Charming Outlaw chose that moment to whinny furiously. He'd enjoyed his afternoon out, but now he was bored.

'What about taking him for a run on the beach?' suggested Dr Wolfe.

Kat said eagerly: 'Would that be OK?'

Her mum smiled. 'Yes, darling, it would. It is your dream after all.'

'Perfect beach for it too,' said Edith. 'That's Man o' War Bay. Man o' War was one of the greatest racehorses of all time. Won the 1920 Belmont Stakes in New York by twenty lengths. He was a chestnut too.'

'Don't give her any ideas,' said Dr Wolfe, but she'd been smiling as she helped her daughter into the saddle.

And that was how Kat Wolfe found herself galloping a chestnut racehorse along the edge of the shimmering waves, on a coast where dinosaurs once walked.

Outside Kittiwake Cottage, the mayor of Bluebell Bay cleared his throat. 'Have you decided which of you is going to cut the ribbon?' he asked.

'We both are!' said Kat and Harper.

As they snipped the purple ribbon, a banner unfurled across the front of the cottage: '**THE ARMCHAIR ADVENTURERS' CLUB**'.

'It's an unusual name for a library,' commented the mayor.

'But entirely appropriate,' Edith assured him as the gathered crowd applauded. 'And could I just say that Kat and Harper, who inspired it, will be honorary lifetime members.'

Beyond the Armchair Adventurers' Club, the bay was a dazzling blue. Between the kayaks and sailing boats, dolphins flashed silver. Summer was coming, Kat could almost taste it.

'See you tomorrow?' Harper asked her friend hopefully. 'Same time, same place?'

Kat laughed. 'I wouldn't miss it.'

Author's Note

If the idea of sleeper spies living undetected for decades in Dorset or Texas seems far-fetched to you, think again.

The novel in your hands might be fiction but the story behind it is real. I know that because one of the highest-ranking spies ever to defect to the United States told me so himself.

How did I end up chatting to Lt. General Ion Mihai Pacepa, who as head of Romania's foreign intelligence agency, spent many years working with Russian illegal spies? Long story short, as Kat would say: I was doing an investigation for a newspaper.

First, though, some background.

Until I was thirteen, my dream was to become a veterinary surgeon (though I'd have settled for becoming an Olympic eventer). I wanted to be a vet so badly that by the time I was ten, I'd read every one of James

Herriot's hilarious books on life as a vet in the Yorkshire Dales. I also had a 'vet kit' – a wooden trunk packed with bandages, dressings, wound spray and antiseptic.

The reason it was so well-equipped, is that whenever the local vet visited our farm and game reserve in Zimbabwe, Africa, I'd plead with him to donate anything he could spare – the last scrap of a tube of antibiotic ointment or, thrillingly, a brand-new bandage – to add to my collection.

My farmer father gave me bits and pieces too. We lived a long way from the nearest town, so dealt with most veterinary emergencies ourselves. Every chance I got, I helped out. If there was a lamb or calf to deliver, or a wild animal with a wound to patch up, I was there. One of my proudest childhood moments was saving a racehorse called HeMite from colic, using tips I'd read in an Enid Blyton novel. Maybe something you read in this story will help *you* one day!

Aged 17, I flew to England alone, hoping to become a pop singer! I'm relieved to tell you that didn't work out, though I did briefly sing in a band. Instead, my best friend, Merina, and I spent an enjoyable year working as veterinary nurses. Within weeks of starting we were working as anaesthetists on operations, giving intravenous drips and injections, and coping with all kinds of emergencies.

But on a return visit to Africa, I was offered a chance to study journalism. Being a writer meant that I could help animals – and humans – in other ways. I could expose cruelty or injustice, or try to inspire people to care. It also meant that I could work towards a seemingly impossible dream: becoming a novelist.

Readers often ask authors where their ideas come from. Well, the detective part of *Kat Wolfe Investigates* is easy. Growing up, I was crazy about mystery novels. I read every one I could get my hands on, from the Famous Five and Nancy Drew to Sherlock Holmes and Agatha Christie.

I was obsessed with martial arts too, and have tried many over the years. I'm still learning, but I've done enough to know that in jiu-jitsu, Wing Chun, Krav Maga and my own (possibly fictional!) Way of the Mongoose, there are locks, throws and other techniques which, if practised regularly and correctly, can help a girl like Kat overcome a person many times their size.

Mongoose 'Move 58' was inspired by a technique I was taught many years ago. It's quite amazing what a tug, a twist and a dropped knee can achieve! When the burly *sensei* demonstrated it, I flew over his head like an aircraft taking off. Moments later, I did the same to him! And one of my favourite jiu-jitsu moves is the one used in the Way of the Mongoose video Kat watches. Correctly applied, there is almost no way to guard against it.

The animal-training techniques used by Kat are genuine too. A lot of horses love playing with balls – both soccer balls and large gym balls. Horse 'football' relieves stress, helps combat boredom and improves communication between horse and rider. I learned 'Join-up,' a bonding method created by Monty Roberts, on a horse-whispering course with Kelly Marks, who runs Intelligent Horsemanship in the UK.

Kat's cat, Tiny, was inspired by Felix, a part-African wildcat stray I adopted from Mozambique as a kitten. I had him for seventeen years and loved him more than I can possibly say. Like Tiny, he was so wild, big and strong, that his bad moods were slightly terrifying – sometimes even his playful moods. If my friends or relatives came to stay, his favourite game was ambushing them on the stairs. Some still bear the scars.

Yet as strange as it might seem, Felix's good qualities were so wonderful that everyone adored him, me most of all. It helped that I grew up surrounded by wild animals – warthogs, monkeys and even a pet giraffe. Wild, or even partly wild creatures can't help but express their wildness – that's what makes them special. To attempt to crush their beautiful spirit would be a crime. Far better to cherish it, as Kat does, and accept that the occasional scratch is a small price to pay for sharing your life with a loving, intelligent, fiercely loyal cat.

Unfortunately, exotic cats such as Savannahs and Bengals, and wolf-like dogs such as huskies, have become very fashionable. Unscrupulous breeders charge huge prices and don't always care who pays. Some import serval cats and other wild animal parents illegally to use in breeding, failing to inform those who buy their kittens that F1 Savannahs require a wild animal license. Not everyone understands these animals' unique but challenging personalities. Consequently, rescue shelters are crammed with them.

My own Bengal, Max, is a rescue cat. The shelter where I found him had 56 other unwanted Bengals. I've had him for nine years and he's my best friend, but then I wanted a challenging, highly athletic cat. Don't get one unless you do. And always, always, consider adopting.

This is all very well, I can hear you thinking, but what does this have to do with ghost owl spies?

Well, back when I was a full-time journalist, there were few things I enjoyed more than investigations. It made me feel like a detective. A single paragraph in a second-hand book began a quest that led me first to Transylvania, to the home of a Count, only recently returned from exile. But I only really cracked the case when I started corresponding with Lt. General Pacepa, who until 1978 had headed up Romania's espionage service, the DIE *(Departamentul de Informatii Externe)* of the Romanian Securitate.

It was he who told me about the recruitment and training of Soviet illegal spies in Romania, which he was authorised to oversee by the KGB chief. This training took up to eight years and was conducted in 150 safe houses around Romania. Western identities were created for each spy, but once they were embedded in the UK, Europe or the US they were on their own. They would spend years living as apparently ordinary neighbours and becoming good citizens. When they were truly trusted and accepted as locals, they'd use that trust to penetrate important government or industrial targets.

Lt. General Pacepa defected to the US in July 1978, helped by the American CIA. The information he provided destroyed the intelligence network of Romania. Decades later, the FBI uncovered a network of more than ten Russian illegals in the US.

One illegal couple, Vladimir and Lidia Guryev, who called themselves Richard and Cynthia Murphy, had daughters aged nine and eleven. Another couple had teenage sons who believed themselves to be Americans. They were stunned and heartbroken to discover that their parents were Russian agents.

It would be nice to believe that when those arrests were made in 2010, that that was the end of the era of sleeper spies. That the Russians were no longer spying on the Americans or anyone else, and that the rest of the world was no longer spying on them.

However, in 2013 the US diplomat Ryan Christopher Fogle was arrested in Moscow by Russian intelligence officers and accused of being an American spy. They had good reason to be suspicious. He had in his bag, two bad wigs, three pairs of sunglasses, a knife, a microphone, a map of Moscow and thousands of dollars in cash. He also had a letter from the US government offering $1m a year to a Russian agent he was hoping to persuade to spy for them.

There have been other arrests too. In December 2017, a Russian accused of spying for the US was charged with high treason by a Moscow court. Days later, a Russian who'd visited the British prime minister, Theresa May, was arrested in the Ukraine on suspicion of spying for Moscow.

In other words, the spies that feature in *Kat Wolfe Investigates* are not just operating in Bluebell Bay. They could be in your neighbourhood too!

Recently, I re-read my interview with Lt. General Pacepa. I'd asked him if any other country used illegals in quite the same way Russia does. His reply sent chills through me:

'The concept of the illegal officer was and still is

unique to Russian intelligence. It is Russia's most secret weapon of the future.'

Whether you're interested in spies, cats, horses, martial arts or mysteries or, like me, all five, I hope you enjoy reading *Kat Wolfe Investigates* as much as I've loved writing it.

Lauren St John
London 2018

HELP KAT & HARPER SAVE OUR SEAS

Kat Wolfe and Harper Lamb are lucky enough to live in an idyllic seaside town in Dorset, England. Kat loves racing Charming Outlaw along golden beaches or swimming in the waves, and Harper and her paleontologist father adore the nature and history of the Jurassic Coast.

If you're as passionate as they are about dolphins, whales, turtles and other marine life, please help us stop the plastic tide from destroying our oceans. There are 1.8 trillion bits of plastic in the Pacific Garbage Patch alone. Be the change you want to see in the seas. Here are Kat's top 10 tips for making a difference:

1. **Say no to plastic straws** *before* you order milkshakes or sodas at restaurant or cafés. In the US alone, 500 million plastic straws are used every day. Ask for paper straws or none at all.
2. **Say no to plastic bottles.** A single bottle can take 450 years to decompose. Take a flask or reusable water bottle everywhere you go and fill it with tap water

3. **Say no to plastic bags**. They take up to 1,000 years to decompose! During that millennium they'll be choking whales and strangling turtles. A bull shark in India had 20 kilos of plastic removed from his stomach. Use tote bags or biodegradable bags

4. **Say no to the cotton buds** that kill marine life. Use cotton buds made with sustainable wood and other eco products.

5. **Say no to glitter.** It's fun, pretty, sparkly and completely innocent, right? Wrong. Glitter is a microplastic and as harmful to oceans as any other plastic.

6. **Say no to coffee cups.** Think they're easy to recycle? Think again. Carry a flask or reusable coffee cup if you're commuting or travelling.

7. **Say no to plastic forks, knives and spoons**. Ask your school, café or bookshop to consider using biodegradable cutlery.

8. **Say yes to picking up plastic litter** on beaches or near rivers! If you're fortunate enough to live near the water or go on holiday to the sea, consider taking time to organise a beach or river clean.

9. **Say yes to sustainable fish.** Check that your fish and chips or smoked salmon comes from a renewable source. Avoid tuna. Bluefin tuna are heading for extinction and Yellowfin tuna are near-threatened. Eating them harms dolphins, sharks and other marine species and takes food from the communities that depend on it.

10. **Don't buy a ticket to a dolphin show.** Dolphins and orcas are highly intelligent creatures with rich, complex and loving families. They suffer horribly when they're captured and condemned to a lifetime in a concrete pool, eating frozen fish while turning cartwheels for human entertainment. Show them you love them by helping keep them where they belong: in the wild.

BE THE CHANGE YOU WANT TO SEE IN THE SEA
For more information, visit: www.Authors4Oceans.org